4-99

D0559869

# tender as hellfire

# tender as
# hellfire

## joe meno

St. Martin's Press ✖ New York

*Design by Jane Adele Regina*

Library of Congress Cataloging-in-Publication Data

Meno, Joe.
    Tender as hellfire / Joe Meno.—1st ed.
      p.   cm.
    ISBN 0-312-20051-X
    I. Title.
    PS3563.E53 T46 1999
    813'.54—dc21                                                          98-37687
                                                                              CIP


First Edition: April 1999

10   9   8   7   6   5   4   3   2   1

for my old man

# acknowledgments

Thanks to Koren, who makes everything possible, Cheeb, Dana Albarella, C. Michael Curtis, Randy, Don, my friends and family, and the Columbia College Fiction Department.

# tenderloin

They split us up at the end of summer.

Now most people will call you a liar if you tell them a truth they don't want to hear, but I know me and I know my brother and looking back before our bare-legged Val left town all covered in dull blue bruises or Shilo got shot in the neck or the Deputy just damn disappeared, before my brother lit a perfect match to the Devil's hot-toothed hatred before any of that, they decided to split us up, and I guess that was where all the trouble really began.

"This place is Hell. This place is shit."

My brother, Pill, shook his head, agreeing with himself, I guess, as he lit the match. There was that sharp striking sound of the match-head against the thin strip of flint, snappppp, then the big red blossom of fire that crinkled down along the black match's spine. He held the flame to the end of his cool smokin' Marlboro and inhaled, taking a long drag that crept out of the side of his mouth in a quick spurt.

We spent that first lousy morning before the first day of school in a lousy new town, smoking in the dirt, taking deep drags on my older brother's stolen unfiltered cigarettes. We sat right behind our lousy new mobile home in the square shadow of our dirty gray trailer, the one that shone dull with old aluminum siding and refused to sit level on its concrete blocks. Pill tapped another square out of the pack and handed it to me, then struck the flame from the match-cover and lit the cigarette that jutted from the end of my lip.

"This place sucks," I grunted, coughing up some smoke

through my nose. I was ten back then, Pill-Bug had just turned thirteen, and as I remember it, there wasn't anything better than sitting in the dusty gray gravel of Hell's sweet mobile home, sharing a cool smokin' square with my older brother, not because he was especially talkative or insightful or anything like that, but he was always good for some stolen cigarettes or a new dirty word or two. He had on his blue stocking cap, half pulled down over his eyes, down to the long red-and-black scab that ran where one eyebrow should have been, a wound he got by lighting our neighbor's hedge on fire the day before we moved out of Duluth. Pill had his legs spread out in front of him as he laid back against the concrete base of the trailer, staring at his dirty brown shoes. I finished buttoning up my brand-new school shirt, my brother's old red-and-black flannel that was long enough for me to half-tuck in my underwear. Nothing in those stolen cigarettes or dirty old clothes gave us a portent that we might both be doomed, doomed past any of our years, or any of the barely felonious things our poor dirty hands had already done.

"Do you know what a girl's tittie smells like?" Pill asked, staring up into the cool blue sky, taking a long drag that turned the length of his cigarette gray.

I kind of shrugged my shoulders.

"Well, yes or no?" He squinted, leaning forward.

"No. Guess not," I mumbled.

"It smells like sweat. It smells the same as the rest of her sweet naked body parts."

This made me suck my teeth in reply.

"Get to school!!!!" my mother shouted, shaking her poor white fist, hollering from inside the godawful silver trailer. A goddamn trailer. Back in Duluth, we had had a whole damn house to ourselves. Pill and I had had our own beds. Now in this lousy dump we had to share a crummy brown and blue bunk bed. My older brother got the top bunk after a short skirmish that ended up with him sitting on my neck. The damn toilet in the trailer kept backing up until a drowned rat finally floated up. There were hard-bellied silverfish crawling all over the goddamn floor. The nearest comic book and baseball card shop was forty-three miles away in a town called Aubrey. Nothing in this lousy place was any damn good. My mother's goddamn boyfriend, French, had gotten a supervisor's position at the meat-packing plant in this horrible town of Tenderloin and my mother packaged us all up to move hundreds of miles into a lousy goddamn trailer and now we were all going to be in Hell, unhappy as spit altogether.

"You better be going!!" my mother shouted again, knocking the gray screen door open. My brother hoisted his bookbag over his shoulders and I followed, kicking up dirt at each other as we headed toward the two new lousy schools.

There in Tenderloin they sure split me and my brother up good. Pill and me had been going to the same school ever since I'd been attending, but here they sent me to the Tenderloin Elementary, and him to Tenderloin High School, even though he had never graduated eighth grade back in Duluth. He would have graduated, but he was always on some sort of probation from all the fistfights he was always getting into, and finally his homeroom teacher, Mrs. Henckel, this ghastly ol' hag, who I'd say had it out for ol' Pill-Bug, found near a dozen porno magazines and a single box of cool smokin' Marlboro cigarettes in his locker. They threw him out just a week before graduation, no matter how much my mother pleaded, glad as hell, I bet.

Three days, though. That's all it took before Pill tried to light one of those damn farm-grown, meat-eating bastards on fire. To be honest, I didn't think he'd last that long. Back in Duluth, he used to get in a fight almost every day with some dumb fool or another. My brother, Pill, he liked to get in fistfights, don't ask me why, but here in Tenderloin, he waited three days before starting any trouble.

It all began at lunchtime. I guess the Tenderloin High School was small enough so everyone had to eat all at once in this big cafeteria that was all painted red and white, the damn school colors. The walls were decorated with this big painting of a side of beef with little arms and legs, right with the school logo, "Fightin' Meat Packers." All these dumb farm kids must have been going to school together since they were born, heck, all of them were prob-

ably cousins or half-sisters or whatever. They all had the same
dumb square-looking faces and grunted the same kind of dumb animal drone anyway. All the big ugly football players had their own
lunchtable, and the cheerleaders had their own, too, the snotty
student council kids, and big red-haired, red-lipped slutty girls
each had their own nice big rectangle table, then in the corner was
this round table with a broken leg where all the losers and faggots
were sent to sit. Pill was no faggot, I'll attest to that, he might have
been so crazy about girls that he would have masturbated every
hour on the hour if he could, but he was the new kid in school, so
the only spot he could find was at the table in the corner there.
There was this huge, flabby fat white girl, Candy, her name was
Candy, I'm not lying, she filled up half one side of the table, her big
white gelatinous blob of a body kind of undulated and wavered
above her three trays of food, mostly snack items and ungodly
helpings of sloppy joes that left deep orange stains all over her fat
digits and round, formless chin. Then there was Kenny, who rode
the short bus to school; he had grabbed a kite string off an electri-
cal wire and fried his brain good. He had to ride around in an elec-
tric wheelchair and wear a big white protective helmet. Kenny was
a real bastard, though. People didn't like him because he used to
try to run you down in the hall between classes, or sometimes, I
guess, during football games, he'd ride around the track and no
one would try to stop him because they all thought he was damn
near retarded anyway. There was some flitty kids and some real
brainiac types who didn't even bother eating lunch because they
were so worried about studying and getting good grades and getting the hell out of Tenderloin. Then there was my brother, Pill,
who didn't fit anywhere there at all. He was short and dirty and
mostly mean-looking. He still had only one eyebrow and a huge
red scab in the other eyebrow's place. He wore his dirty black
drawers and a gray flannel jacket and his godawful blue stocking
cap that no one could convince him to take off, because his hair
was still growing back from the fire and there was still a bald spot
big as a fist right on the crown of his head.

   "Faggot," one of these big, real square-faced meat-fed farm

boys mumbled, standing over ol' Pill. My brother didn't even look up. He just shoveled another helping of greasy black meatloaf over his lips and swallowed, staring across the table. A few more of these big football-types with their red-and-white varsity jackets and big dumb grins gathered around, grunting and smiling to themselves. Poor fat Candy squealed and folded in on herself like some sort of flesh-filled jellyfish. Kenny and the other losers at the table just got all quiet and pretended to be finishing their lunches.

"I called you a faggot," this big square-faced one, Rudy, I guess his name was, all embroidered there in white on his lettermen's jacket, grunted again. "Faggot!!!"

My brother kept eating, cleaning his plate, shaking his head to himself a little. Then he stood and stared right in this bastard's face without saying a word. Rudy grabbed him by the front of his flannel shirt and shook him.

"Tell me you're a faggot and I'll leave you alone. Go ahead. Tell me."

Now that was one thing ol' Pill-Bug couldn't stand, quiet and crazy as he was, he didn't like anyone touching him or his stuff. He snarled his dirty pink lips and clenched his fists, kind of staring at this big dumb farm-boy's jugular vein, gripping a dull plastic fork in his trembling hand. A teacher or lunch room monitor stared over at them both, eyeballing them hard, Rudy holding Pill there, my poor brother almost foaming at the damn mouth, and shouted something.

"Break it up over there," the glassy-eyed lunch monitor mumbled in a lazy tone. Rudy smiled and nodded then pulled my brother close.

"Faggot," Rudy repeated, letting my brother go. He shoved Pill just once and swiped the blue stocking cap from his still-bald head.

Jesus.

My poor brother just froze with shock and horror. His blue eyes went wide and shallow as he glanced around the lunch room. Everyone was looking at the huge blot of red skin where his curly black hair hadn't grown back. All these goddamn cheerleaders and sluts and student council kids and football players were mumbling and giggling and pointing right at him.

"You will all die!!!!!!!!!!" he shouted. Then he let out a howl and ran out through the lunch room doors, screaming like a madman, down the hall, knocking over a garbage can, tearing a Homecoming poster off the wall. He ran right into the boy's bathroom, he hissed and swung his fist through the first mirror he could see and then jumped out the window into some hedges and ran across the football field toward the trailer park, still screaming and tearing anything up that fell in his path. That was his first day at school. Jesus.

My first day was just as lousy.

My teacher was this real sexy type, Ms. Nelson, boy, her legs were longer than me, the whole damn class all I could think about was her long white legs, she just kept smiling and laughing and sitting on the corner of her desk and talking about getting good grades or not being late or any of it, just sitting there being nothing but beautiful. Her hair was all straight and black and long down her back. Her eyes were so blue and covered by these nice glasses. She wore this short flowered dress that hung just over her knees, man, I was in heaven, heaven, until she took out the fifth-grade roster and started calling out names for attendance in her sweet honey-coated voice. I kind of slunk in my chair, shaking my head, trying to disappear. Ms. Nelson worked her way through the alphabet. There was damn near half-a-dozen Jo-Jos and Jimmys and Mary Lous in my class, then she passed the Is and then the Js and then the Ks and then her perfect pink mouth opened like a rose when she said my name.

"Dough?"

My heart snapped in my chest. Her crystal-lit eyes scanned the room, over the sweaty-dirty rounded heads of ten-year-olds, through the virtual forest of pigtails and sprouting pony-tails, right to me. Her pink, pink lips parted a smile as she called my name again.

"Dough Lunt? Is your name Dough?"

Everyone in the damn class turned around and stared right at me, all these Jimmy-Joes and Suzy Qs and Huckleberry Hounds, all of them, dumb and round-headed and glazed from all the damn meat their mothers must have fed them for breakfast. I kind of raised my head just enough to nod and then slumped back down to the desk.

"Please say 'Present' if you're here, Dough."

Her eyes suddenly seemed meaner and blacker. Her one eyebrow cocked over her glass frames as she stared down at me. This was bad. There was no way she'd be mine this way.

"Present," I murmured, and dropped my head between my arms, feeling my heart shriveling up in my chest.

"You're new here in town aren't you?" she asked.

Jesus. It wasn't bad enough all these damn meat-breeders knew my name, now she was going to introduce me. I nodded slowly and stared at Ms. Nelson's smooth white face for some sort of reprieve.

"Why don't we welcome Dough to Tenderloin Elementary by giving him a nice 'Hello'?"

The whole class let out a sigh and the palest, weakest chorus of voices rose from the room.

"Hello, Dough."

The dumb, three pig-tailed girl next to me squinted and stared at me.

"What type of name is that?"

I shrugged my shoulders. My old man had been some sort of madman to insist on such a name for his kin. I wasn't named after some famous relative, neither was my poor brother, we were the victims of my old man's all-seeing plan for our life-long portentous humiliation. Me and my brother had been in some uncountable number of fistfights because of our lousy names. They were like two huge magnets that hung around our necks, attracting all kinds of trouble, I guess.

"That ain't a Christian name," this girl frowned.

I turned and stared her hard in the eyes. Her eyes were brown and kind of crossed. Her hair was blond and pulled so tightly in those three rubber bands that her forehead looked stretched. She smelled mostly like urine and dirt.

"I bet you live in the trailer park, don't ya?" she whispered.

I tried to ignore her.

"No. Just be quiet."

"You like living in the trailer park? My father says there's nothing but trash living out there."

I shook my head slowly. What was wrong with these people? They were all some sort of a string of lunatics. Ms. Nelson finished off the class roster and began writing something on the board. Her thin white slip showed between her legs as she moved, reaching up on her toes. I sighed to myself.

"Did you come from Nevada? My father says everyone's crazy out there."

"Do you ever shut up? Do you?!!"

Ms. Nelson turned around, staring right through the rows of sleeping faces, right to me. She glanced down at the roster and nodded.

"Dough, do you have something to share with the rest of the class?"

"This girl here won't shut up!"

"Lottie, is that true?"

Lottie, this goddamn piss-girl with three blond pig-tails, just smiled and shrugged her shoulders, staring at me like I was crazy.

"Both of you will be quiet from now on, understood?"

I nodded. This was no way to win the heart of a woman like that.


The nice thing about living in the trailer park was not having to mow the lawn. Mowing the lawn was a real damn pain. But here there was nothing but gravel and dirt. My mother had laid out some orange pots of flowers all around the front of our trailer, but she wasn't fooling anyone. The trailer park was ugly in all our hearts, and no number of flower pots could change that.

I came home from my first day of school, dragging my bookbag in the dirt. My mother's boyfriend, French, was working on the big black 1972 Impala he had on cement blocks in front of our trailer. The car itself was a real beauty, but it was all gutted out, its poor metal innards were strewn all about the dusty gray front of our trailer, disconnected and hopeless as hell. The engine had never even turned over. Hopeless. Really hopeless. Poor French had bought it from some slimeball back in Duluth who promised to help him rebuild it, but then the dirtbag split town as soon as French paid the car off. Now old French had to walk to work. The plant was only a mile or so away, and most days he could get a ride with someone if he stood out on the road and hitched. My mother had her own car, a nice blue Corolla hatchback with rusted-out wheel wells and a dangling muffler that she drove to her job at the beauty parlor. My mother's car was in a poor state. My old man probably turned over in his grave every time that muffler dragged. He had been a real man with the tools. He had been too proud to let the damn muffler drag on his bride's old car.

"Hey there, Dough, feel like giving me a hand? Hold the flashlight for me?"

French was all bent over the hood of the car. His face was all greased up and sweaty. He held the yellow flashlight in one hand and an open can of beer in the other. This man was the damn reason for all my troubles. He was a square guy, really, the least dangerous of all my mother's boyfriends, but there was no way I was about to offer any of my help to the same person who was solely responsible for taking away my own damn bedroom.

"I got homework, French."

"All right, chief, that's what I like to see. Smart man like you hitting the books. Your mother will be proud."

"Sure."

My mother had a real swell dinner cooked for us, on account of our first day being at new schools and all that. She had made some blackish meatloaf with a raw egg cooked right in the middle and a horrible gray spinach salad or something hellacious like that, but both me and my brother passed and just went to our new room, lying on our lousy new beds, half the size of our old beds, neither of us uttering a goddamn word.

"You boys alright in there? Not hungry tonight?" my mother shouted through her caked-on red lipstick and the thin wood door.

"Ate at school," Pill-Bug lied, shaking his head.

"I got homework," I grunted, turning on my belly.

There were loud, silver-toothed crickets scraping their files outside our tiny square window, breathing heavily in any direction, just as sad and hopeless as us, staring up into the darkness. Me, I fell asleep in my school clothes, watching a thin daddy longlegs crossing the ceiling on its tiptoes. My old pillow didn't even smell the same.

The next day, heck, the next day, Pill and me ate some dough-nuts for breakfast and walked to school without saying a word until we got to the intersection where he had to walk three blocks to the high school and me another block to the elementary school.

"This place sure sucks," I kind of mumbled.

Pill nodded. "This town is full of assholes."

Just then I noticed he had a red stocking cap on instead of his trusty old blue hat. His blue hat. He always wore his blue hat.

"Hey, where's your blue hat?"

"I lost it."

"Lost it? But . . . "

"I said I lost it, okay?" He heaved his bookbag over his shoulder and turned down the block toward his high school. That's when I knew there was going to be some sort of trouble. His eyes had that faraway look in them like he was thinking. Like he was looking ahead to something that was about to unfold at the end of his dirty fingertips.

Pill just wandered through his classes until lunch, he bought a plate of mashed potatoes and some french fries, then took a seat at the reject table right in the corner. Harlo Mullet, one of those fat, round-headed freckled kids who had probably been picked on since he was born, kind of giggled to himself as Pill sat down. Harlo Mullet got picked on not only because he was fat and round-headed but because he had chronic nosebleeds and used to draw blood and sweat all over his poor, poor self on a daily basis. Pill-Bug didn't pay the fat sweaty kid any mind. About midway through the lunch hour, the same big dumb football player, Rudy, came right up to the loser table, this time waving my brother's blue hat right in his damn face. Pill kind of ignored him for a while, then he began snarling and growling like a sick dog, snatching at the cap as the Rudy-guy kind of jerked it away. It was awful. Everyone in the damn cafeteria was watching and grinning, maybe even some of the lunch monitors, they just sat there and giggled, even Harlo Mullet and all of the reject kids, because for once, no one was picking on them. Pill leapt to his feet, digging his hands around this kid's throat, who just happened to be twice his damn size. The guy, Rudy, shoved my brother's head right down into his plate of brown gravy and mashed potatoes without too much effort at all.

Damn. "You will die, you bastard!"

My brother picked his face up and ran out through the doors again, howling and screaming, tearing posters and announcements down. My poor brother, Pill. He ran out the front school doors this time and disappeared somewhere down the street, still shouting.

My own second day was not much better. There was some sort of math quiz everyone seemed to know about, and all I could do was try to stare up Ms. Nelson's dress, so I just drew a real sweet picture of a tank fighting an airplane right on the quiz paper and handed that to her instead. Ms. Nelson just shook her head, marking a big red "F" at the top of the page with a frown, and then I knew this whole thing between us was going to be pretty hopeless. The damn pig-tailed Lottie talked my whole head off that day, saying something about how her father's chickens were all dying off one by one, waking up with their necks wrung, then she told me about her older sister, Susie, who was pregnant and wouldn't tell anyone who the father was so her own old man wouldn't go out and kill the poor fool. I fell asleep somewhere between her chattering and missed some crucial information about world geography, which I was sure to need to know for another upcoming quiz. Walking home from school, none of these dumb kids had comic books or porno magazines or cigarettes or anything, so I walked on one side of the street by myself then down to this drainage ditch by the trailer park so I could just be alone and think about important things like Ms. Nelson's legs and spitting.

There was no one else around the ditch. I laid on my back and put my books under my head and practiced spitting a good gob of spit up in the air and catching it, then spitting it again. The grass was soft and kind of wet, it still smelled like summer, green and warm, there was some old wet newspaper sunk in the water and an old tire that floated past me. This was a place of some death. There was an old dead gray sheep that looked like it strayed off from somewhere and had laid down right beside a gray metal irrigation pipe. Its eyes were cold and black and its big ivory sharp teeth were spread apart over its red, red gums. There were tiny purple insects creeping all over it. The sheep's gray wool was full of brambles and dried leaves and there caught in one of its teeth was a bright yellow flower that sat still in its dried breath like a prize. Its head was barely hanging on its body. Then under the gray pipe, right along the surface of the water there were some dead birds, tiny yellow sparrow-birds and big thick black birds, dozens of them, maybe almost twenty, all with their wings spread open and drowned and piled beside one another. Their eyes were black and hard and their fat white and gray bellies were bloated with the dirt and water and sewage. They looked like they were all trying to somehow keep warm. They all looked comfortable as hell. They all somehow sank into the soft gray surface of my eyes, their hearts and wings fluttering as they circled in my head. They burned in a place of my heart I couldn't understand. Then they were all swallowed up by something cold and dark, impenetrable like deep water, but lit on fire, a shape, a face, a black form that whispered in my mind. An old ghost, a demon of my own sorts. I turned away from the dead birds and wiped the sweat from my face. I tried to put them all out of my head. I walked along that ditch for about a mile, staring into the dark gray water, then turned back home. I didn't want to go on back to the trailer and have to talk to my mom or her boyfriend, French, about school, so I waited down by the ditch until it was dark, crawled in through the sliding metal window to our bedroom, and let my mom think I had come home from school and just fallen asleep so she'd just pat me on my head and let me be.

My brother wasn't home. I laid there all alone until my mother came in. Her lips were warm when she kissed me goodnight and made me think everything might work out. Those kinds of things I don't like to mention too often because they always make you look just plain silly when someone else finds out, being kissed good-night by your mom and all, but it struck me as a nice quiet moment, laying there, pretending to be asleep, having your mom kiss you goodnight, things like that always give you some kind of nice feeling you can dream a nice dream to.

The day after that, Pill and me walked to school together. He was still wearing that red hat and not his blue one and by then I was too worried about Ms. Nelson and fifth grade and having to listen to this girl, Lottie, ramble to me all day that I wasn't paying much attention to my brother's problems. But then I noticed he was carrying a goddamn black plastic bag, all shiny and full and heavy and stiff with something, just holding it there by his side. The bag was dripping fluid in tiny gray droplets that smacked the ground and turned dark, disappearing into the dirt. I stared at my older brother there as we stood at our intersection, eyeing each other hard.

"What the hell's in the bag?" I grunted.

He just kept staring at me then muttered, "Don't let these bastards push you around, Dough. You understand? Don't let anyone push you around."

I kind of nodded and walked down the block a little. Then I turned around to see him, but he had already walked off and it was too late for me to do anything about my brother now because I could hear the first bell already ringing.

He didn't go right off to school.

He stood in front of this nice white A-frame house, smoking feverishly. Gray smoke trailed out between his tight white lips and ran around the end of the square jammed between his two fingers. He stood under a nice wilting maple tree, turning the soft book of matches over and over again in his pocket. The black plastic bag sat at his feet. He squinted a little, smoking hard. Pill had gotten into a fistfight with nearly every kid I knew back home in Duluth. He had plenty of teeth knocked out, his nose broken, clumps of his hair torn out; Diffy Morrison once sicced his dog on Pill and my brother had to get fifty-two stitches in his leg from it. He had been smacked by my mother's old boyfriend, Joe Brown, at least half a dozen times, hit by the school bus once, not to mention getting his hair and eyebrows burned off from the fire he started the day before we left for Tenderloin. He was a tough kid and no one knew it better than me, but this was different, he wasn't in Duluth and he wasn't fistfighting just one bully in the dirt. He hated the whole goddamn town, and when the fat girls and retards at the only stupid round table in the cafeteria laugh at you, too, it gives you a certain feeling that just makes you want to stare at things by yourself and smoke a cool unfiltered Marlboro for a while. He had something awful to do and he knew it. My brother wasn't a moron; he wasn't a monster, either; maybe people like to think when you know you've got something awful to do, you just don't think about it first, but that wasn't true. He had something horrible he was about to do and he knew it and that made it all the worse. He had been made a damn fool of and now he had no choice but to make it right.

He stared at the nice silver mailbox, turning the soft book of matches over in his palm. LaDell, the mailbox read. Their driveway was empty. No one was home. Their green grass glimmered with the morning light. Pill stood there a long while just thinking and smoking. Thinking and smoking. The gray smoke hung around his face. The matches were soft with his sweat. He lit another cigarette and took a long drag. He stared at their shiny green grass, seeing how each blade moved like a whisper, like a single sigh, like a curse word spoken over and over again. My brother flicked the cigarette into the grass, picked up the black plastic bag, slammed the red metal flag down on the mailbox and walked up to the nice white porch.

Snap.

Snapppppp.

Snappppppppppppp.

There it was.

The lunch bell clanged. It was already lunch time.

Pill nodded to himself and walked inside the goddamn high school cafeteria. He held his hands inside his pockets as he marched down the rows and rows of brown tables and chairs, kind of sweating a little along his forehead. His eyes were shiny and black like he was about to cry, but he wasn't; his red cap was nearly pulled down over his eyebrow and hard red scab. He pushed through the line of meat-hungry farm kids in their dull flannel school clothes, the big-thick-necked boys in blue jeans and floppy-yellow-haired girls in denim overalls who giggled and pulled on each other's sweaters. He walked past them all, right up to the back table, rectangular and filled with the ugliest, dumbest-looking football players, all with big blond heads and tiny black eyes. They all sat there eating, shoving bits of meatloaf and mashed potatoes in their hard red mouths, not even blinking, these kids, maybe without souls, all clean-cut and without a single damn thought in their own heads. Ol' Pill-Bug squinted, stepping up to the biggest one of them all, Rudy LaDell. His face was big and square, his eyes deep and dumb and blue, his hair was blond and cut short in a buzz that showed his big sloping forehead. The big ugly kid just shoved another fork full of beef stew in between his huge white teeth and stopped midsentence when he caught sight of my brother's dirty, scab-covered face. Maybe the whole table went quiet, maybe the whole damn lunch cafeteria hushed and held its breath. My brother licked his lips and stared the big-square-jawed boy in his eyes and stepped right up to him.

"You took my hat. I want it back."

Rudy cracked a big, white-toothed smile.

"Too bad, faggot."

Rudy gulped down another mouthful of food.

My brother shook his head with a grin.

"No, I want it back. And you oughta apologize for it, too."

Rudy shook his head, dumbfounded, dropping the fork beside the heavy paper plate. He sucked in a breath and stood, smiling, towering over ol' Pill, who didn't falter under this big white-faced kid's dark black shadow.

No one said a goddamn word. No one moved.

"You better take a walk, faggot, before I snap off your goddamn neck."

His big hand clamped down on my brother's shoulder.

My brother didn't move. Maybe some of these dumb kids confused that with being stupid, too, but he just stood there, staring into
that bastard's eyes. It was this look my brother had, like a wild goddamn animal if you've ever caught one and tried to make a damn pet
of it, he just held his teeth set against each other and stared hard
into Rudy's big square face. All the dumb football players kind of
cowered away from the table. They sat there gape-mouthed and
stunned. No one moved. The lunch ladies stopped serving lunch.
These bastards stared out over the mounds and mounds of mashed
potatoes and applesauce, french fries, and dull green Jell-O, as my
brother, Pill, looked up onto Rudy's clean white skull.

"You're about the dumbest kid I know," Rudy mumbled, shaking my brother a little. "Looks like I'm gonna have to break your
damn nose."

"Looks like you will." My brother smiled, then closed his eyes
tight.

Big Rudy LaDell curled his huge white fingers into a fist and
clobbered my brother hard in the jaw, still gripping the front of my
brother's sweatshirt. Crack . . . The big kid swung again, this time
lamming Pill right in the bridge of his thin white nose. Crack . . . A
thick red dollop of blood skirted around Pill's nostril as his dark
black eyes rolled into the back of his head. Some of my brother's
blood splattered on Rudy's big round cheek.

"Had enough?" Rudy asked, still holding up my brother.

"I don't know." My brother smiled through a mouth full of
blood and spit.

"Damn . . . you sure are dumb." Rudy swung again, cracking
my brother right in the corner of his eye. Pill's head went heavy as
he fell on his back, splayed out like he was dead, bleeding from his
nose and mouth as all the parts of his face began to swell with
pain.

"Now are you done?" Rudy shouted, leaning over my brother's

ugly face. Finally a lunch room monitor, Mr. Gunderhal, a big bald, gray-faced biology teacher who had served in the Navy, stepped between Rudy and my brother. Ol' Pill laid on the ground in a pool of his own blood, broken and bent. "You done yet?" Rudy shouted.

My brother, Pill, just cracked a smile. His teeth were sore with blood and pain, his bottom lip had been split, his nose was all swollen and gruesome and red. His one eye had begun to darken blue-black and puff up and swell, his red cap had nearly slipped off his head, showing where the red scabs of his burns lay beneath. But he just pulled himself up a little, lying on his side, grinning like a madman, and dug his fist inside his coat pocket. He pulled something out, something dark, he held something in the hollow of his palm tightly. He lifted his hand near Rudy's big dumb face and unfolded his tiny white fingers.

Three dark black matches.

There were three burnt matches resting in my brother's palm.

"What the hell is that?" Rudy grunted, staring down at my brother's hand. Pill just smiled through his sore white teeth and closed his hand. The fire in Pill's eyes was deep red and wild and ready to burn off that poor bastard's face. Rudy shook his head. The dark unimaginable confusion of all that dumb kid's blood on his hands. His hands were sore from that kid's blood. "What the hell were those?" Rudy muttered again. He could feel the sweat run along both of his palms.

One. Snapppp.

Two. Snapppppppp.

Three. Snappppppppppp.

They couldn't hear. They couldn't see. The lunch room was all up for grabs now, all those lousy meat-swilling kids were shouting and screaming, pushing each other and poking each other's ribs, and poor ol' Pill just laid there still and bleeding, grinning with his split lip and swollen nose, staring hard as Rudy backed away. Rudy's big head suddenly felt empty. Mr. Gunderhal shouted something, but Rudy was gone, he just shook his head and ran into the hallway. His eyes were burning. His face was all full of sweat. He felt like he was lost. He needed to go. He needed to go home. Something was wrong. He could feel it now in his chest. He leaned against the wall and stumbled toward his locker.

There was a hush all over his dumb face. Someone had forced open his locker.

"No . . . no way," he mumbled, and ran right toward it, shaking his head.

His mouth dropped open. He felt his stomach fall straight through his spine. He ran down the hall and stared at his red metal locker which bustled with thin gray smoke. There were tiny bits of gray dust that hung in the air. There was smoke that filtered between the metal grates of his locker door there.

"No . . . ," Rudy muttered, shaking his head. "No way."

He squinted a little and tore the door open, spilling the charred contents all over the floor.

There were six or seven tiny black birds left dead inside.

They were shrunken with lighter fluid. The stench of burnt feathers and flesh and fabric rose through the air. The odor made all the spit run from Rudy's gaping mouth. He felt ready to gag. The weight of something hung in his throat.

"My god," Rudy mumbled, shaking his head. Their bodies were small and twisted and torn. Their tiny black eyes shone as they dropped to the floor, dark and black and burned and covered in ash. "What in the hell?" Rudy mumbled. His things were ruined. His nicely pressed football jersey was blackened and torn. His tiny bag of pot was burned and covered in ash. His cleats, his towels, all his gym clothes were black and singed from the fire. His bottom lip was trembling. His eyes were shivering with tears.

He leaned his head against the locker, mumbling to himself. The tiny dead birds fluttered a little with smoke and fire. They wore tiny sweaters of ash and dirt. His jaw was left open. He needed to get away. He needed to go home. He backed away and ran down the hall, past the cafeteria and outside through the shiny glass doors. He stumbled across the shiny black-paved parking lot to his car, fumbling through his varsity jacket for his car keys. There it sat. His hopeless pride. The red clad jewel of all the lousy muscle-cars in this town. He slid the keys into the driver's side lock. He lifted his head.

"No," he coughed. "No way."

His shiny red Camaro was on fire, too. His bright red car's interior was covered in ash. Smoke trailed out from under the hood through the vents. His nice vinyl dash was buried in dirt. He pulled open the driver's side door and gave a scream.

"No! Not my goddamn car!!"

More and more smoke poured and emptied out through the open door. The same rotting stench of burnt fabric and smoke rose through the air. There was a fire. There was a tiny fire burning in the backseat. There was something lying there, too. Something that was badly burned. All the smoke rose from its thin gray form. He dug his face inside, squinting his thin black eyes. No. No. He couldn't make it out. He coughed, trying not to breathe. There . . . there it was. No. No way. A sheep's severed head. A dead goddamn sheep's head. Its thin skin and musty wool crackled with lighter fluid. Its round fleshy eye was all puffed up black, bloated with fire. It seemed to be moving in its severed skull. There were its thin gray teeth. They were wrapped in some hideous mortal grin over its pink and ashen lips. There was something carved into the dashboard. "FAGGOT," it said in scrambled letters.

"Call the fire department," Rudy muttered to himself, as the fire spread along the backseat. "Someone call a fireman!!!" Rudy's nice varsity jacket and clean-cut face and hair went over with sweat as he stared at his nice red T-top Camaro rolling with smoke. He held his own face tight. There was something on his lips he couldn't figure how to say. There was something in his eyes that couldn't describe the hate. He held his face tight and shook his head. He couldn't move. He couldn't even shout. He could feel his eyes squinting to keep from crying. This was too far. This was way too much.

There were clangs from a siren that rang from down the street. Rudy nodded to himself and smiled, his eyes blistering with tears.

"Okay, it's all right," he mumbled, still shaking his head. The fire trucks approached, clanging down the main street. Rudy nodded feverishly, rubbing the side of his wide white face. It wasn't too late. Not too goddamn late. His car could be saved. He stared down the street as the shimmering red fire trucks approached then stopped and began to turn. Rudy shook his head, mumbling to himself.

"What in the hell?!!"

His big bottom lip seemed to grow with panic as the big red firetruck Number Five turned and swerved, speeding down another street, disappearing down the block.

"What the hell?" he muttered. "What the . . . "

He looked over the tops of the nice white and blue houses, staring hard as a dark black cloud of smoke rose from only a few blocks away.

"No," he whispered, his eyes swollen with tears. "That would never be."

The dark black cloud rose swollen and heavy in the sky.

"Rudy, no, no . . . " he mumbled to himself. "No."

Then he was already gone, running down the block and heading over to Erlapeck Street. There was fire blooming right in the distance, turning the bright blue sky dark and black with smoke. There were two firetrucks split across the road, shining bright red as the fire grew and grew.

The boy stopped running and stared down the street. His face was covered in sweat. His eyes were shaking with tears. "Not my house, not my house, not my house," he mumbled over his big white lips. Then he was a block away and he could see the place where the firetrucks had stopped and the smoke and flame had grew and the dark black space where his nice white porch was supposed to have been. His big dumb eyes dropped still in his head. His hands unclenched at his side. His neighbors gathered around him. Mr. Filinard in his dull white tee-shirt held Rudy back, gripping the boy by his shoulder. The boy wanted to shout, he wanted to scream, but his big red tongue had somehow been burned. He knew who it had been, he knew who it was, but his whole big mouth had somehow been burnt closed.

Then, there in the cafeteria, my brother just closed his fist and placed the matches back in his coat. My brother just laid on the cafeteria floor and smiled. He turned and smiled at them all; their clean white faces shook yellow with disgust and fear, they all winced and cowered behind their clumpy brown gravy and brown lunch bags, unable to even whisper in their own stupid monosyllabic drone. No one said a word. Not one big, dumb-mouthed, square-headed soul. They knew who it had been. They knew my brother was the one. But no one was dumb enough to whisper it, no one was brave enough to let anyone know. Rudy was at his neighbor's house, shaking, mumbling to himself in the Filinards' poor white guest bed. He wouldn't say a word. He couldn't say the word. He had been left dead birds. Goddamn dead birds. No police came and knocked on our trailer door. No insurance lawyers laid claim over the telephone. No, the whole town was still and silent and pure as the nice white porch had been before it had burned right on down. There was a kind of dark red fear in all their faces that made them too afraid to talk. They had been touched by the tiny white flame of our sorely roaring anger, left too cold and dumb in their own hearts to mumble and stir. This sweaty rage was something new they thought they felt. This fear and hatred was something they pushed from their poor red hearts and minds for fear of it all being talked about or understood.

Two big, sweaty-foreheaded teachers in brown suits had grabbed my brother by each of his shoulders and had dragged him down to the principal's office. They took away the goddamn switchblade he had hidden in his pocket and gave him three days' suspension for starting the fight, three days' suspension, that was it, because he was new at the school and they didn't know what to make of him, I guess. Pill didn't give a damn about the suspension anyway. He hadn't ever aimed to be a model student, but the school administrators called my mother at her new job at the beauty salon and her pulling Pill home by his ear was something awful, too. But I wished I could have seen all of that town's dumb white looks, even just for a second, one lousy second, when they stared at the dark black and orange and red flames that burned from my brother's sore red and bloody face. I know it's not a nice thing to think, but it was true, and if it's one thing, I ain't a damn liar, no matter what anyone might say.

"Did you light that fire?" I asked my older brother that night as we were lying in our new dull blue beds. "Was that you?"

I had heard about the whole damn fire after school. That was all any of those stupid dirty-lipped kids would talk about as I walked behind them home. I could see their faces dumbfounded and burning bright red with all kinds of fear and excitement as they described the whole thing over and over, making that awful fire seem like a goddamn mystery, like a thing they couldn't have ever conceived all on their own. "Did you do that or not?" I repeated as my brother turned in the bunk above mine. His breath was short and shallow as he cleared his throat.

"No," he whispered. "No, that wasn't me at all."

No, my god, I wanted to believe him. More than anything in that dirty little world, I wanted to pretend he had told me the truth. He was my only brother and he had never lied to me about anything important in my whole life. He had always been the one person to tell me things everyone else was afraid to say or thought I shouldn't ever know, like how my old man had died or how to French-kiss or to make it with a girl or how to stand up for myself no matter what lines my mother or a teacher gave, but this was all something different, this was a new sort of lousy dark place, and so him lying to me right then was something new and terrible I thought I ought to forgive right away. Maybe he had lit the fire to get back at the whole goddamn town. Maybe it was only meant for that big square-faced boy. But the longer that fire burned, the worse off the both of us were for certain.

He rolled over and pulled the covers up over his head.

But that's what I meant by what I said.

Them splitting us up is where all the trouble really began.

# le kiss of soft gravel

**D**o you know, if there is a heaven, it is somewhere within the bathwater of my old babysitter, Val. Val . . . her legs were the cool white reflection of beauty. Her whole naked form could drive any young mop-headed bastard to any random act of trailer park violence. You see, my attraction for older women always led me into trouble. Didn't you ever love someone you knew you couldn't have? People might call you stupid or silly but there's nothing you can do to help it. My whole prepubescent life was filled with all kinds of stupid lust. My lust for Ms. Nelson, my fifth grade teacher, would go on for another few weeks until she had scolded me and shot me enough dirty looks to make me cringe and shrink in my poor wooden seat. There was enough unrequited love there to finally urge me to draw a picture of Ms. Nelson being bombarded by a melee of WWII fighters on my geography exam.

But Val. Her dull blue eyes would make me want to melt or light the whole damn world on fire.

My mother and her boyfriend, French, were swingers and needed somewhere to send me and my brother every other Friday night. My brother, Pill, was thirteen and old enough not to need a babysitter, but I was only ten at the time, and both of us were always prone to theft and arson and other acts of puberty. Between me and my brother lighting stuff on fire and shouting and running all around and my mother screaming at us all night and French walking around in his underwear most of the time, we weren't appreciated there in that gravel-laid trailer cesspool. No, no one came right out and said anything, but a dumb, listless stare can tell you a lot of things ignorant people are afraid to ever say. So my mother and French paid this young truckstop waitress at the other end of the trailer park to keep us in her spare boudoir every other Friday night and make sure we didn't burn or steal anything we couldn't afford to repay ourselves.

Val . . . spring couldn't have whispered me a sweeter name.

Do you want to know the truth? Maybe the only woman I'll ever really love is Val. My prom date, Bunny, who shimmered in a strapless blue evening gown, the girl who left the goddamn dance with another guy, or even the only lady I ever lived with, Teresa, who changed the locks on my door and took off with my poor dog, these ladies hold no candle to the fire that still burns in my heart for my old babysitter.

Every other Friday, my mother would give me and Pill a brown grocery bag of our clothes and toothbrushes and send us down the gravel road to Val's big silver trailer that was round and looked like a kind of silver space capsule. My brother was never happy about going. He still hated Tenderloin and being cooped up inside on a Friday night when he could be out knocking mailboxes over or pissing someone off must have burned up him pretty bad. He'd kind of sulk behind me with his hands in his pockets as I'd cross the court to her trailer. I'd wipe my nose clean with the back of my hand and then knock on her screen door. Val's trailer was always lit up with a string of white Christmas lights around the door. I don't know if she put them up for Christmas or not, but she sure never took them down.

Her bare white legs would appear at the door. I don't know what it was about her legs; she was tall, really tall, taller than my mother's boyfriend, French, her legs were just so long that I'd kind of whistle to myself every time I'd see them, not like I'd know what to do with them if I had the chance, but there was something inside my chest that would light up like a match whenever she'd answer the door. Her bare white thighs have been permanently burned in my mind. Before I even think about her name, I see her great bare thighs hung open on the end of her red velvet sofa. Her voice was a honey-coated radiator, husky with sweet tones that would drip off her tongue the way her thick waxy makeup would begin to melt late at night. Her hair was blond and cut short, she'd usually be in her work uniform, which was a yellow dress with a white apron, her hair all done up with a white paper tiara, she'd lead us inside and pat my head and lick her finger and stick it in Pill's ear. He liked her, too, he really did, but most of the time we were there he was in a mean mood anyway. Her trailer always smelled the way I thought a woman should, like cigarettes and sweat and baby powder. Her mouth was a sweat-wrinkled pink hole that hardly ever closed. Her breath was always hot and musty, moving over some wad of pink bubble gum and would leave bright red lipstick marks on the spotted white glasses she drank gin from. There was nothing I wanted more than to kiss her mouth and have her kiss my forehead and fall asleep in her bed without anyone but me and her, alone sleeping in her golden arms all night. Maybe after we got there, she'd pour us some RC Cola in some giveaway glasses that she'd gotten at a fast-food joint or maybe she'd light a cigarette as she got undressed, but every Friday night we were there, she would strip down to her smooth white skin behind this dark black Oriental screen, decorated with a slick yellow tiger, and tie her red Oriental robe around her middle, tucking the edges between her breasts. Man, that would make my teeth hum in my head.

Then she'd take a bath. Honest to God, she'd take a bath right while we were there. She'd close this small wooden door and slip into her pink bathtub and take a goddamn bath. Don't think she was a pervert or anything, she always announced for us not to look, but what the hell, we were boys, we were in the heated vernal season of puberty, it was as though we didn't have a choice at all. Pill always got first look, then me. Our greasy white faces would smear against the silver keyhole, breathing shalllow so she wouldn't hear, unable to breathe as her cool naked shoulders appeared in my eyes.

My God . . . my sweet God, have mercy on my poor soul.

My face would get all red and hot and once I think I nearly passed out when she suddenly stood and stepped out of the tub and I gazed upon her wondrous naked form, her smooth white belly, her wide hips that slipped down to form the most perfect V I thought I'd ever see. I very nearly blacked out right there, but Pill grabbed me by the back of the shirt and held me up by my collar. His face wouldn't get all red or anything, he'd just get kind of quiet and mad, heck, I knew why, he was three whole years older than me and he was thinking he should be out necking with a stupid farm girl named Suzy-Q and making it in her barn or whatever, but since I knew the closest I was about to get to any of that was that steamed-up keyhole, I didn't complain.

Her bare white legs would appear from behind the bathroom door, clouded by steam, still a little wet with singularly perfect beads of bathwater. She'd have her hair wrapped up in a pink towel on the top of her head and be wearing that crazy Chinese robe, all black and red and white and flowery; she'd tuck her legs beneath her and take a seat on her red sofa. Maybe she'd turn on the radio or something. Maybe she'd put on a nice record and stare out the screen windows into the dull blue night. By then, Pill would be getting all kinds of anxious. He was a boy with sex on the brain, and maybe Val would send him out to pick up dinner. That was fine with me, just me and Val in the trailer alone was fine. She'd unwrap her hair and let it fall all above her white shoulders, or maybe blow dry it a little, then go behind that black screen and pull a tight gray tee-shirt on and some overalls. Anything looked good on her, I swear. We'd sit on her red sofa and watch the night come up, the clouded blue sky giving way to pleasant blackness, me leaning in close to smell the shampoo and soap just evaporating off her body; sweet and heavy like perfume it would just hang in the air. I'd nearly drown on it all. Then she'd ask me something nice like, "How many girlfriends do you have now?" or "How come you're such a heart-breaker?" and just when I was ready to burst with unadulterated passion, Pill-Bug would return with some fried chicken or hamburgers or something from down the road and we'd all eat, laughing and giggling and throwing food and having the best times of our lives. Well maybe not Pill. Or Val. But being with them both felt all right to me.

Anyway, later, we'd go out on Val's porch. She'd pour herself another drink and keep patting me on the head and giving me wet kisses on the cheek. We'd watch the last of the damn fireflies burn themselves into the tall brown grass and listen across the trailer park courtyard to our own trailer sweeping with laughter and booze and sex mostly, I guess. We'd all lie down on her porch and drink gin and water, which isn't such a strong drink I guess, but enough to make your head swim if you're lying next to the beauty of your life.

"My men," she'd laugh, hugging us both. Pill would just keep drinking the booze and kind of frowning, but when a nice lady like that puts her finger wet with spit in your ear, you can't help but feel a certain way. "My two men, that's all I need."

My face would feel warm against her belly where my head lay just below her breasts.

"Val, will you marry me when I'm older?" I'd ask.

"Sure thing, darling."

Then right there, I knew there wasn't anything better in the world. Maybe Val would give us some firecrackers to light off or maybe we'd go for a walk down the road and watch the fat-bellied brown toads scurrying from one side to the other, by then it would be dark and late. Val would make us brush our teeth and wash our faces and let us fall asleep on her velvet sofa, listening to some old records or watching her tiny television. Then she'd help us into her big white bed in the spare room, the bed that always smelled like the soft, wrinkled part of her neck where there would always be a greasy dab of perfume. Her head would hang over us as her robe would drop open a little, snowing the smooth white plain that she would only share with truck drivers and cowboys who drove pick-ups. Her mouth would swell as she'd smile and wink us a good-night, and then I'd reach up and kiss her on the soft side of her red, red mouth. That moment, right there, is still what I think about when I think about love. The soft side of someone's mouth. That's it, right there.

My brother, Pill, he would lie on his belly, burying his face in her wide white pillows. I would lie on my back and then we would hold our breath and listen, because there would always be some lust-filled cowboy coming over to fuck her, because even as young as I was, I knew that's all they wanted with her anyway. Pill would flip and flop around, frustrated, I guess. He'd grit his teeth all night and shake his head and then we'd hear a pickup or big block engine Chevy die outside, then the boots, scrape-scrape-scraping over the gravel, his bare-knuckled knock on the door, the screen door would slide open, they would both be whispering and giggling, maybe there would be the sharp and clean kiss of glasses striking together, then it would stop, then it would be so quiet that I could hear my brother's nasally congested chest rising and falling with each shallow breath. Maybe there would be the sonorous squeak of furniture, of wood against tile, or metal against metal spring. Then I'd slip out of bed and stare out the tiny gold keyhole, out in the dimly lit darkness. Then from only a few bare feet away, my whole world would burn apart.

My Val's long white legs might be straddled around this cowboy's middle, his shirt unbuttoned and her mouth moving over and between, maybe she'd be on her back or bent over the same velvet sofa, but they would be fucking, not gently, not like a sweet whisper or kiss, they would fucking hard and tearing at each other's clothes and scratching and pulling and rubbing their desperate white bodies together in a way that made me hate her and him and everything about them both. Maybe I'd try to go back to sleep, maybe I'd curl my head under some of her blankets and listen to them fucking all night. These men, these truckers and cow-men had some sort of endurance I couldn't even imagine. All their dumb hard ignorance must have made them insensitive to any of her. The cold black glimmer in all of her men's eyes was always the same. These men didn't ever make faces or moan or growl, they all gripped her like they hated her with their cold blank eyes and black-hair-covered chests that showed more expression than anything else about them. They were full of anger and frustration and want to bury it somewhere inside Val's breasts with the flat part of their thumbs, pressing hard to make her hurt, too. Maybe they were just like Pill and me, but older, full of the same hate and rage and needed to let it go somehow, through someone's soft body.

These men I hated more than anything in my life.

These men would appear every Friday night as soon as we had been tucked on, every Friday night, another cowboy or trucker would have a time with my sweet Val. Only one time did she get herself in a bind.

This one night a big blond-haired, sweet-faced cowboy in tight jeans came knocking on Val's thin screen door. He was the one with the sandy-colored cowboy hat and silver-toed boots, with his blue Western shirt half-buttoned down to his navel to show off the thin trail of hair that led down to his wanton nether region. He was drunk as hell and stunk like a pig and my poor Val refused to let him in, not on any account of him being drunk, but she was expecting some other visitor that night in tight drawers, stinking of whiskey or his wife.

"Just let me in for a second, Val, honey. Just for a second." The cowboy's voice was sweet and cool, his eyes were nearly all red and crossed with sincerity.

"Not tonight, baby." Val smiled, pulling her robe tight around her waist. "Go on home."

"Just a second," he groaned. "Please, honey, just fer a single kiss." He clawed at the thin screen like a trapped vermin, kneeling in front of the door.

"Don't make a fool outta yourself. Go on home, baby. You're drunk and ornery. I'm not in the mood for any of that."

The cowboy pulled his sand-colored hat down over his eyes. He yanked himself to his feet, leaning against the door, and tore a big bone-handled knife from the side of his boot.

"Looks like I'm coming in anyway."

He dug the big silver blade into the screen, yanking the knife down and across in a big L-shape. Val let out a scream and I shot up in bed, rustling my brother awake. Val backed away from the front door slowly.

"I just wanted a single kiss," the cowboy grunted, tripping through the big tear in the door. "That was it, you goddamn tease."

He held the knife out before him, a big silver knife with a smooth ivory bone handle, grinning like a sick dog.

"Now you ain't so proud, are ya?" he snorted.

Val backed into the kitchen, fumbling behind her through thin silver drawers for some weapon, a knife, a screwdriver, anything. The cowboy kept smiling and grinning, moving closer.

Pill and I were at the goddamn spare boudoir door and tore it open. We stood right there a few feet from it all, unable to muster a word or motion.

"Go back to bed, boys," Val whispered, still pleasant, still calm. "Henry and I are playing a little game."

My brother, Pill, didn't move. He stood in the doorway, staring at the cowboy's sweaty face.

"Don't move a muscle, boys," the cowboy grunted, turning toward us a little. "You both stand right there."

My hands ached with sweat. My whole head felt light and then heavy and then light again like a goddamn fever. My sweet Val had a short screwdriver in her hands, but she was shaking. Her hips shivered against the kitchen counter. Her big blue eyes were glimmering with big silver tears.

The cowboy took one step closer, knocking the screwdriver right from Val's shaky hands.

"Don't you ever tease a man," the cowboy grunted, putting the knife against her thin white wrist. "Don't ever play me for a fool." He reached his hand down between the folds of her robe, right between her breasts where her heart must have been beating like a scared rabbit. My mouth was dry and hard with terror. I felt my own knees shaking. Pill looked ready to cry. His hands were clenched so tight at his side that his fingernails were drawing blood in his own palms.

"Don't either of you boys move," he grunted. "You're gonna learn how to deal with a no-good woman."

He stood in front of her, hulking her in his shadow.

There was no sound in the whole trailer. No one was breathing. No one could breathe. Then a bit of gravel. A single spit of gravel shot up from the ground and ricochetted against the side of someone else's trailer, then another, the rumble of gravel rolled up right outside along with two thick yellow double-beams that crossed the inside of Val's trailer, lighting up the cowboy's face. The big heavy grunt of a pickup died outside. Then the pickup truck door opened and two boots slid across the dirt and up the steps and then I heard the single sweetest word I'll ever remember:

"Val?"

Still all silent inside.

"Val?!"

Then the trucker stepped through the gape in the screen, a big square-faced man in blue coveralls. His name was scribbled on a patch on one side: "Buddy." His hair was black and dishevelled a bit. He had a jug of wine in one hand and a single daisy in the other. His jaw set tight in his mouth as he stepped inside and saw my sweet Val pressed up hard against her own kitchen counter.

"You best put that knife down, chief," Buddy whispered, setting the wine and flower down on the sofa. "For you end up cutting yourself."

The cowboy turned and glared. For there were no other words needed right there. Two dogs don't need words right before they set into it and neither did these men. The cowboy turned and lunged at poor Buddy, taking a wide, drunken swipe at him, cleaving the front of his coveralls. Buddy lammed the cowboy hard in the throat with a solid punch, knocking his sand-colored hat off, then Buddy dove right at him, shoving the cowboy over the couch. The two men landed on top of each other, growling and cursing, Buddy on top, trying to wrestle the knife away from the cowboy, who spat and drooled and hissed like a snake. Buddy landed a few more blows, smacking the cowboy's nose, but then something happened that will always stick in my head because of how awful it all was.

The blade of the knife ran right through Buddy's right palm, right through, then clanked dully to the floor. Buddy howled, gripping his wrist; he backed away, bowing over in pain. There was light in that wound. The hole was that big. Light ran from the trailers outside through the hole in his hand. His face was bright red.

The cowboy picked up his knife and ran out, dove into his truck, and disappeared. He went right back into the dark night that had made him drunk and evil to begin with. His hat was still on the floor. Ol' Buddy kind of tumbled into the bathroom, gritting his teeth in pain. He held his hand under the sink, running the water bright pink through his wound. Val came up behind him and began kissing his neck and saying, "I'm sorry, so sorry, baby," and nuzzled her head against his big shoulders. He wrapped a big pink towel around his hand, shutting off the faucet.

Val hurried me and my brother back into the spare bedroom, then locked us both in. Her face was as white as her sheets and her blue eyes had still been swimming with tears. She hadn't said a word to us. She was still shaking. She stepped back into the bathroom.

Then, as usual, they began making it. Right in that bathroom, Val fell to her knees and unzipped the man's coveralls and then closed the bathroom door. Then the unmistakable sound of that man and Val, like every Friday night, cinched together, bare and cold, their bodies pressed against the wood door, created a kind of friction that hurt my tongue. That was when I wished both those men had been stabbed and died right there, that was when I didn't care that this man was hurt saving my Val. This man with the hole in his hand was no different from any of the other men who would come over after Val had put us to bed. He still had that same dumb-empty look in his eyes. He still had that same dumb look while he laid his cool naked body next to hers. Most of her men, I guess, were well-behaved. But I guess any goddamn fool can act polite if they know what they'll get in return for some lousy sweet-talk or flowers or wine.

That's what I hated most about all those men. They weren't any brighter than me. But there was nothing I could have done about any of it. I was a dumb, greasy-faced trailer park kid. All these men had snakeskin boots and red pickups with gun racks and decorative mudflaps, what could I possibly offer her besides true, unmistakable love? How could I make her feel the way they made her feel, held down against the dull red velvet, naked and used and bare? My same brother was already asleep in her bed, snoring with the same frustration, not just with tall white legs or truckers or cowboys or trailers but the whole town, and not just the ignorant little town of Tenderloin, but of all space and time that sinks down on your head when you feel like a man and still look like a goddamn dumb kid.

All that was too much for me. This man had my Val, they were making it right outside the door or on the sofa or in the kitchen, making a kind of rhythm so mean that I slipped on my jeans and shoes and climbed out the spare bedroom, down into the gravel, skidding past the fading light shot from Val's TV or Buddy's blood-shot eyes. I stared at his pickup, same as any other of these men's Valiants, Monte Carlos, Big Fords and Chevys, darkly colored in the same sense of desire and urgency. I reached down into the dirt and picked up the sharpest rock I could find and lit a match to that gasline of anger and rage that had welled up in me all night. I let that rock fly hard and straight, busting the rearview mirrors and headlights, scratching deeply honed doors and kicking in silver-chromed grilles. My whole miserable life lit up in an explosion of hate and anger, until Val's porch light flickered on and I disappeared back into the darkness, back through the window, and back into her soft, sleepless white bed, still shaking with rage. Maybe the trucker cussed or shouted and then took off, maybe he stayed and took his anger out on her again, maybe they laid together not touching or uttering a word, both wishing he had left, but the next morning the trucker was gone and I couldn't have been happier. When Pill and I finally rolled out of bed, we got dressed and sat at her small kitchen table, we wolfed down big helpings of yellow French toast and burnt bacon, no one talked, Val stared hard into my eyes and didn't say a damn word; she looked me in my face and then turned away, cold and silent. I didn't mind her being mad. As long as the trucker was gone, she could be as quiet as she liked. I know that sounds real selfish, but she knew there was nothing between her heart and his but being desperate, and me busting up that man's headlights only put a kind of picture to all that undeniable frustration anyway. We packed our stuff up and stepped outside. The trailer park was bright and silver and gray with dust. Maybe I turned around and said good-bye or maybe I was mean and stone-faced and stepped out onto her porch without muttering a thing, but Val stopped me and put her hand on my shoulder and looked down into my eyes and said something like:

"You're gonna end up hurtin' someone with all that anger, Dough. You're gonna end up hurtin' yourself and someone you love with a temper like that."

Then more than anything I felt like crying, but I didn't, because Pill would have never let me live it down, and I nodded and turned away and me and my brother walked back across the lots of mobile homes, disappearing back into our own unhospitable hell, kicking rocks at each other without saying a goddamn word.

# the veil of tigers

The night in that trailer park belonged to blood and tigers.

There in that trailer park I began to suffer through the worse nightmares I'd had in all my life. Nightmares that made me sweat right through my small bunk bed and poor white sheets. Nightmares that made my blood run cold and force me to wake my older brother up with squeals of terror. There were things out in that darkness, things born of venom and cool white innards that I could hear howling from my own bed. Nature had become some sort of strange palace of deception and terror, full of things like rabies and spitting snakes, horrors my own brother, Pill, used to try to scare me with, all kinds of real and hideous creatures, with all kinds of heads and claws and talons, beasts that fed on human blood, all kinds of real monsters and spooks that formed some mystical imperial hold over my ten-year-old heart, and then all he'd have to do was whisper the word "tiger" at night from above his bunk while I was trying to fall asleep and I'd nearly wet my drawers. Heck, I had been raised in Duluth. That was no trailer park out in the middle of nowhere. Now in damn Tenderloin I was surrounded by the threat of nature all the time. There were goddamn crickets outside our bedroom window every night. There were coyotes that howled sick with blood. Slick unthinking creatures, meat-hungry tigers, most despised of the jungle cats, would invade my dreams and waking moments with a dark and warm-breathing feeling of doom. They would lunge down on top of me in my nightmares and snap my neck. I would wake up and still feel their thick black claws around my throat. I would feel all my blood leaving my body as I became cold with death. This was something I couldn't shake no matter how hard I tried. This was a real feeling that my blood was about to be ripped out of my veins at any moment and I wouldn't be able to do damn a thing about it.

My whole world was then a poor nightmare of terror and blood. My whole life became threatened by this kind of nature every day.

The slow girl, Lottie, who sat beside me in class, the one with four pigtails that pulled the skin on her face so tightly across her forehead, with the very nearly crossed eyes and clothes that always smelled like urine, well this girl, began more and more to annoy me. Her constant jabbering was always getting me in trouble with Ms. Nelson and my grades were already beginning to suffer, me being dumb as a stump anyway. So I used to just lay my head down on my desk and try to ignore this urine girl. I'd just stare through my fingers at her; tired from not sleeping at night, I would watch her tiny pink mouth make huge spit bubbles and kissy-faces. Her tongue would shoot in and out until I would kick her or pull her hair. This girl, Lottie, wasn't all bad, she would let me cheat off her tests most of the time, but she wasn't much brighter than me, so it didn't really help. I guess I pulled her hair and spat at her because I thought I could. She was a dumb farm girl, and as dumb farm girls go, she was probably the dumbest of the bunch. This girl was the pee-kind of awkward kid who all the girls in class hated and picked on, the girl who the boys in class pushed down on the playground to cop a feel off of, the girl who the teachers ignored because she was just so slow and awkward and annoying that somehow there never was any room left to pity her.

But this one day, right in the middle of class, only three weeks after we had all started school, this girl stood up and started screaming. I hadn't even been paying attention. Maybe I'd been staring out the window dreaming, feeling the tiger's jaws around my neck, feeling my blood loss, when I turned and faced something that made me whole body shiver.

"Ms. Nelson . . . ?!"

Lottie was crying, holding her hands between her legs, and there was blood, plenty of blood, all from under her dumb blue and dirty white skirt. Her eyes were wide with terror and shock. I just froze as Ms. Nelson's face went red, too.

"Ms. Nelson, I'm bleeding all over . . . "

There was bright red blood all over Lottie's leg and starting beneath her chair on the floor. I felt myself shuddering as Ms. Nelson led Lottie out of class and to the nurse, I guess.

"You'll be alright . . . "

No one in class said anything, no one but Dan Gooseherst, this fat, round-headed kid who sat behind me, you know the one with the red crewcut and freckles. Dan Gooseherst had been held back from the sixth grade. He was all round and snotty most of the time because of it. He sat behind me grinning and laughing, making a big horse face.

"Yeah . . . she got her period right on herself. That's one dirty girl."

My mouth felt dry and hard.

They sent in Bucko, the grade school janitor, this guy in flannel with a bright red face who used to drink from a tiny green bottle behind the Dumpster in the back of the building. The janitor mopped up the mess and disappeared back into the hall. Some of the boys began to laugh and make jokes. The girls in class began to make faces at each other. How the hell was I supposed to know about any of this? They never showed a pretty girl getting her period in *Playboy*, hell, my brother sure never mentioned it. Dan Gooseherst hopped from his seat and scribbled something on the blackboard.

"Lottie is a dirty Pig."

All the boys made faces and laughed. All the girls pointed. Mary Beth Clishim, this witch who sat a few seats up, snapped her bubblegum and said, "Lottie's a fat sow."

I shook my head. This girl had bled right in the seat beside me. This girl had been dumb enough to just sit there bleeding. I couldn't feel anything but anger, I guess. This girl was really as stupid as she seemed.

Then it hit me. No one had probably told poor Lottie. Who was going to tell her? Her old man? Her dumb older sister? She didn't ever seem to speak of a mother. The rest of these lousy farm bastards sure didn't seem to talk to her. No one had told her a damn thing.

I looked around the room at all the ignorant faces. Pig-faces, that's what they all looked like. Dan Gooseherst was yukking it up alright, and all the girls in class were whispering and giggling; ignorance, that's exactly what it was, a whole pen full of imbeciles. They were all fat-faced and pig-skinned bastards, not just for laughing or giggling or whispering, but for not knowing any damn better.

Ms. Nelson reappeared with Lottie and stood behind the desk as the poor girl went and got her jacket and bookbag from the back of the room. Her dirty dress was all stained with blood. Everyone was quiet. The room smelled like disinfectant; the thick vapors ran up my nose and made me want to vomit.

Lottie's face went white as she read the blackboard. I felt a hard white knot in my gut. My hands felt wet with sweat. Ms. Nelson's face froze with shock, her thin eyebrows snapped in place as she read the words scribbled in white chalk, floating over the black space of board.

"Who wrote that?" the teacher asked.

No one offered a breath. You could even hear the nasal-kid, Ralph, in the back of class, fighting to breathe.

"I said, who wrote that?!!"

Ms. Nelson's fist snapped against the blackboard. Her eyes were black and full of fire. "I want to know who wrote that right now or everyone's staying after school."

Dan Gooseherst raised his hand. I couldn't believe it. That fat-head bastard was going to turn himself in. I kind of shrugged my shoulders. Ms. Nelson stared at Dan.

"Dan?"

"Dough Lunt did it, ma'am."

I turned and stared the fat pig-faced slug right in the face.

"You lyin' bastard . . . "

"Dough!!!"

"Take it back . . . " I grunted.

"I can't. You did it." Dan smiled.

Ms. Nelson stood right over me. I could feel the heat of her shadow boiling against my skin. I could feel the whole room swelling with all their goddamn silent stares. I looked Dan Gooseherst right into his swine-filled eyes, then around the room, searching for some sort of glimmer of honesty, for something, but there was nothing, all their eyes were black as coal and much less bright.

"You will both stay after school."

"But I didn't . . . " I mumbled.

"Not another word, Dough. Lottie, get your things, your sister will be here soon."

Ms. Nelson led Lottie out of class once more as Dan Gooseherst smacked me in the back of the head. The rest of the day was a gray blur, until everyone else got to go home, everyone but me and Dan. Ms. Nelson sat us down in front of her desk and lectured us for about a half-hour about things we couldn't even remember and sure as hell didn't understand. All I knew was that I hadn't done a goddamn thing and this big fat-head Dan was going to get his house lit on fire all right. My brother Pill and I would take care of that for sure.

"Do you understand?" was how Ms. Nelson ended the lecture. We both nodded and put on our coats and stepped out into the playground to walk home. I looked that fat bastard right in the face and smiled.

"I'm gonna burn down your house for this, fat-ass."

He shoved me, grabbing my coat.

"I'm gonna break your neck," he grunted.

I pulled free, pushing him back. He was about my height but heavier. He shoved me back and I smacked him on the side of his lousy round head.

"Fat-head."

"Homo."

The gray sky loomed over us as we traded blows, walking

down the block. At the corner, I knocked him into a bush and smiled. He sank into the green shrub, stuck, his legs and arms kind of wavered over his round body like a fat overturned bug. He looked up at me with his big pig eyes and let his jaw drop open. Then he stared behind me shaking his head.

"Shit . . . "

I shook my head. My brother was always trying to pull that one on me. This dumb farm boy must have thought I was as slow as him. I knew there was no one behind me. I kicked him in his belly again.

"Lottie . . . " Dan muttered.

He didn't move. He laid in that bush still as hell.

I turned and felt my eyes bulge.

This girl, Lottie, was really standing behind me.

This girl was holding a big sawed-off hunk of wood.

Crack!!!

She hit me fresh as spit. The board snapped down across my face, then again. She caught me right under the chin, knocking me to the dirt. I felt like a damn sledgehammer had been laid down against my neck. I gritted the dirt between my teeth hard as my head rolled on my shoulders. The whole world turned upside down as I tasted my own blood in my mouth.

I looked up into the gray sky and watched Lottie stand over Dan, holding the board tight in her hands.

"But he . . . "

SMACK!!!

She caught the side of his head, breaking the board on his round face. She hissed and leapt atop him. Her fingers dug right into poor Dan Gooseherst's face, clawing right at his dull eyeballs like one of them harpies or ravenous birds of prey you might see on a nature special. I had never seen a girl just turn like that before. This girl, this dumb, soap-faced girl, all dirty and dim with three or four pigtails and her long white neck, tore a thick red line across Dan Gooseherst's face, across the bridge of his nose, to his lip and then back at his eyeballs again. Dan just howled as Lottie dug her thumbs into his eyeballs. He squealed, trying to knock her off. I just laid there, still and afraid, stunned as hell, sucking my own blood down my throat. Lottie grabbed a handful of Dan's short red hair and began pounding his head against the dirt, bam— smack-smack-smack, his empty noggin' reverberated against the earth. I looked at her and she was actually drooling. Her eyes were all thick and white as she slammed his head once more. Lottie's face was a mess, she was screaming and crying an undecipherable language, a stutter of cries and mumbles and hisses unrecognizable to the human ear, but I had heard it all before, I had spoke it, the cry of the defeated, the speech of the humiliated, the sound you make when your older brother sits on your chest and makes you hit yourself with your own hands, that was a sound I could recognize for sure.

Her eyes were black and small. Her hands tore at his face, digging at his eyeballs. Her long thin fingers worked against his skin, pulling at his fat white flesh. Poor Dan sucked in his breath, trying to knock her off. Her nails tore up his neck and chin until Dan shoved his palm against her jaw.

Then it got real ugly.

Her mouth dropped open wide and then she got hold of his fat hand, clamping her dirty teeth down on his pink flesh. There was no goddamn sound and then Dan let out a hiss, a goddamn howl, clutching his hand in agony. He swung hard, knocking Lottie off and onto her back.

Her face poured out snot and tears in a rain of clear saliva. Her mouth was caked in blood. She pulled herself to her feet above Dan Gooseherst, sucking down her crying, wiping her face clean in her sleeve. Dan held his hand, rolling on the ground. Lottie spat something red from her tiny mouth into the grass. Her spit was bloody and gray and ran down her chin. Dan made this horrible whimpering sound like a sick animal. He uncovered his hand and a clot of purple blood ran down his wrist, trailing around his fat arm.

Dan Gooseherst, you poor dumb bastard . . .

He held his fingers as the blood spilled over his fat digits. His tongue flapped around his teeth like a dried-up worm. He couldn't even afford a scream.

There was a huge red hunk missing from his pink hand. There was a huge red and maroon wound that showed the soft pink insides and workings of Dan's fat palm. Her teeth marked where she had bitten like a wild damn animal. He gagged on an abundance of spit and terror, his face was a wreck of deep red and pink scratches. He looked up at Lottie and pulled himself to his feet, wobbling past, bleeding through his hands. He fell a few feet away, then got up again and limped toward his home. Me, I laid where I was, holding my head, trying not to make a goddamn sound, as Lottie walked away, probably still crying. There was something in her face that made my whole head feel swollen. Her dumb brown eyes had had this horrible look in them. There was no shame in what she had done. She had maimed poor dumb Dan Gooseherst and left me there bleeding because that's what you do when someone crosses you the wrong way. You tear off a hunk of their no-good hand. You draw their blood. There was no thinking to be done about any of it. She had seen we had humiliated her and just knew we deserved to be punished for sure. This was something born in her slow-moving head. This was something she was sure of inside her poor red heart. Her eyes had been black and small and clear and full of an awful kind of certainty I don't think I'd ever seen before. Her eyes had been so full of a kind of blind conviction that made my head feel a whole lot heavier with my own sweat. I remained still until she was long gone, clutching myself on someone's front lawn. I held my face and began to run home; my eye felt sore and raw as I felt some tears moving down my face, burning along the open skin. There were things in that night that made no noise as I crossed the gravel path home, there were things there that moved over my head and in the darkness that made me sure nothing was safe anywhere that night.

# the dark eye of a dog

**M**y dull red heart had become a lousy trailer of its own. Old and worn and beat and without any room for any other lousy souls to clutter or fill. But leave it to a well-meaning adult like my mother's boyfriend to give it a real unwelcomed try.

"Howdy there, guys." His pale lips curled with mischief. "I got a little surprise."

French looked around to be sure my mother was busy in the kitchen and leaned right into my ear with his hot stale breath.

"What would you boys think about going to a real-life dog-fight tonight?" he muttered so careful and quiet as my mother clanged some dishes together, preparing dinner in the kitchen.

It wasn't that French was a bad guy, he really wasn't. I mean, he never beat on me or Pill or hit my mother, he never came home drunk and knocked a kitchen table over or threatened to kick our heads in for being so unruly and all, and maybe all that was the reason it was so hard to get along with him. It had been his fault we had moved to Tenderloin. My mother had fallen for him and he somehow convinced her to uproot us and sell our house and buy a trailer and move us all to that godforsaken hellhole of a mobile home community. But there was absolutely no way you could hate him for it. We had been living with him for a little less than a month already and he was still real nice and quiet and never raised his voice at anyone even when he probably should have. He was still sweet with my mother and always offered to take us all out to dinner at the Sizzler in Aubrey. If he was watching a football or baseball game on Saturday afternoon and you said you wanted to watch a Kung-Fu movie or Horror Spcctacular, he would take a swig of beer from its cold silver can and nod and watch the goddamn movie with you. My own old man would have laughed right in your face if you ever tried pulling a stunt like that with him. He would have laughed so hard you would have wondered what you were thinking to ask to change the channel in the first place. This here French, he never made you feel like that. He was soft-spoken and calm all the goddamn time. The only thing he did that was mildly irritating was piss real loud at about six in the morning when he got up to go to work. Heck, our room was right next to the damn bathroom and he'd be in there every morning for about ten minutes of forever, just urinating away like some sort of unnatural spring fountain. But that was about it. He was quiet as hell the rest of the time and always well-mannered. Nothing me or my crazy brother did could get a rise out of him. That was what burned me the most, I guess. This guy was like a ghost or something. This guy was about as lifeless as the old man I had lying in the ground.

"What would you boys think about going to a real-life dog-fight tonight?" ol' French muttered over a warm beer in front of the TV right before dinner. Me and my brother sat on either side of French, staring at the blue-and-white flicker of the television screen.

"What?" I asked. "Mom don't know, does she?"

My mother ran a spoon through a bowl, mixing up another one of her ungodly casseroles. My mother would take any three good ingredients and make a horrible casserole out of it. Any of the leftover meat ol' French brought home from the plant, secondhand pork products that he got real cheap, would turn to ungodly things in my mother's hands. Take three foods you think you like, something simple like turkey, noodles, and celery, right? My mother could mix those things up in a way that would make you wonder what exactly happened from the time she put it all in a pan and put it in the oven and then put it all on your plate. My mother opened the oven door and popped the poor casserole inside.

French shook his head slowly. He had a long pale face with

deep blue eyes. His hair was brown and thinning and cut short in a crewcut that showed the shine of the side of his head right above his pointy ears. "Do you think I'm plum crazy? Of course your mother doesn't know." His eyes sparkled behind his brown-rimmed glasses like magic.

I smiled, nodding like a maniac. "Sure. I'll go." A dog-fight. A goddamn dog-fight. I'd never been to anything like that before. The closest I'd ever been to anything like that was when the Dilforts' big black labrador got loose and killed Gretchen Hollis's four white kittens back in Duluth. The big ugly dog had torn out all their necks and left them in a single pool of dark red blood and dirt beside the Hollises' house. The Hollises were so upset that they planted four white wood crosses in the meadow beside their house in memory of the dead kittens and all. That spot was a perfect place to go and smoke a cigarette or stare at a nudie magazine because it was dark and shady and all the little kids in the neighborhood thought the place was definitely haunted.

"What about you, Pill?" French whispered. "You in?"

Pill shrugged his shoulders.

"I don't care."

"Well, do you want to go or not, pal?" French smiled. He pushed his glasses tight against his nose.

"Sure. Whatever. I don't care."

Apathy rolled like a sermon off my poor older brother's tongue. I didn't despise him for it. He was a goddamn product of our lousy circumstance and his preposterous hormones.

"All right then. We'll leave right after dinner. Not a word to your mother now, understand?"

I nodded excitedly. Pill shrugged his shoulders and continued staring at the television screen.

"Now go help your mother set the table," French whispered, taking another slug of his beer. I shot off the couch like a rocket and pulled the dinner plates from the cabinet like a lit fuse. My brother just sighed and took his seat at the table. French flipped off the TV and followed. My mother pulled the casserole out of the oven, placed it in the center of the little round wood table with that nice checkered yellow tablecloth, and everyone sucked in their breath. The three poor ingredients were unrecognizable.

"Looks great," I lied, folding my napkin into the collar of my shirt the way my old man used to do. My mother smiled and spooned a big helping on to my plate. It steamed and congealed and oozed and permeated and folded in on itself like some sort of yellowish gravy organism, but I didn't falter. I closed my eyes and began force it down in the name of the uncanny prospect of the evening.

Pill just poked at his food, mixing it up with his fork like some sort of sculptor or dejected artisan. His own technique was to spread the poor food all across his plate in a flat plane of creamy ooze so it might appear like he had eaten most of it, but no parent I ever knew was fooled by that trick, so he took a bite and shuddered, spitting it into his napkin for cover.

"This is great, honey," French mumbled across the yellow table. "Clean your plates, boys, so we can take off."

"Take off? Where are you all heading?" my mother whispered, wiping her pink, pink lips with the edge of her blue napkin.

"Well, we were all gonna head over to Aubrey and pick up some parts for the Impala." French smiled, scraping his fork over the plate. Lie. Lie. Ol' French was lying right to my mother's sweet face. This guy wasn't all as perfect as he seemed. He might be a real bastard after we all got to know him. He might be out the goddamn trailer screen door before we even knew it. He shoved another forkful of yellowed noodlelike gelatin into his mouth and forced it down. "Mmmm." He smiled. "Great."

Pill rolled his eyes and spat another mouthful of food into his napkin, folded it up under the table, and forced it into his jean's front pocket. The horrible glob on his plate was not disappearing. It seemed to be growing actually, shifting in density and matter, it bubbled a little, expanding across his plate. He grunted to himself, shaking his head in frustration. Me, I wasn't faring any better. What was left of my horrible casserole on my plate had dried up and become a hard and thick substance that felt awful against my gums. I swallowed, nearly gagging, and started to cough. French shook his head, wiping his mouth on his napkin.

"All right, boys, let's go." French crossed his fork and knife over his plate and pushed his chair away from the table.

"But there not even done eating." My mom frowned.

"Oh, they're fine." French smiled, kissing my mother on her forehead. "Besides, we want to make sure we get there before the store closes."

French winked at me and I nodded back. This guy couldn't be all bad.

We all piled into my mother's rusted-out Corolla and drove out to the worn-out barn where the dog-fight would be taking place. Ol' French had met some guy drinking at the bowling alley a few nights before and this guy told French all about it. Sure, sure, nearly every man in town would be there. No women, no girls. Strictly a man's sport. Dog-fighting. Sure. They were pitting Lester Deegan's young shepherd against Stu Freeman's old pit bull. The way they did it was they'd beat on the two poor dogs, all the bastards there would stick them with rods and broom handles and then they'd turn these two poor dogs loose on each other to draw some real blood.

The barn was off Mill Creek Road, way out of town, in the cold gray brush behind someone's ranch. The barn was tall and shiny and red like it had just been painted. There was a line of cars, mostly pickups and big Chevy's with V-8s and some stock GMs all parked one beside another behind the barn. There was a pure yellow light that broke between the panels in the barn's walls. "This is it." French patted me on the head. He turned off my mother's Corolla and hopped out of the car. The warm autumn air hung all around us like a sweet breath, dry and still, soft as me and my brother, Pill, followed ol' French toward the barn.

"Hey there, French, glad you could make it," some round guy with a real red mustache said, smiling as we walked through the side door. French. This guy knew his damn name. Maybe they worked at the plant together. Heck, French was a supervisor. People were bound to know him around town, I guess. We stepped inside and the glare of the big yellow hanging lights made me squint.

Nearly every man in Tenderloin was packed into this barn. Thick plumes of cigar and cigarette smoke drifted in the air under the bright lights. There were old men with pale gray faces and empty pink gums and white cowboys hats sitting in chairs in the back and younger muddy boys with muffled brown hair running around, pulling each other into the dirt, there were middle-aged men with square heads and long looks in their overalls and work-clothes passing around silver flasks of booze and their big-shouldered teenagers who spat tobacco into the gray dust with conviction. Me and my brother followed French as he edged his way toward the middle of the crowd.

There in the middle of the barn was the ring. It was a small section of about ten feet rounded out by some metal chicken wire about four feet high. There were breaks in the fence at opposite ends where some crude gates had been built. Ol' French patted me on the shoulder and pointed across the ring.

"There's Lester Deegan's dog," he whispered. The dog was this big brown-and-black and German shepherd with a long, thick snout. Its eyes were nearly green and black in the middle, its nose was crusted over with some snot, and its gums were pink with blood. Its tongue flagged in and out of its red metal muzzle, keeping its jaws closed tight.

"That there's the champeen," this kid, Billy Pillick, mumbled, elbowing me in the side. Billy was a year younger than me and twice my size. He had a big round head and a pug-nose and most of his teeth were missing. He was always getting in trouble at school for eating some other kid's lunch.

The dog's owner, Mr. Deegan, had a long brown hunting jacket on and a white face that was shadowed by a white cowboy hat. He held his dog on a thick brown leather leash, keeping him at his side, right outside one of the gates. Mr. Deegan looked like he was more intelligent than the rest. He was the local veterinarian and I kind of wondered why it was he'd put his own dog through such a bloody thing other than the practice of having to sew it back up when the fight was all over. His face was stern and serious and his mouth was tight-lipped. He didn't look like a man who belonged there at all. His face was so clean and white. He looked like the preacher on Sunday. His dog had the same quiet calm, the same stern look in the black of its eye. They both looked regal. They both looked like champions, all right.

Mr. Deegan led the shepherd, Lance, by the thick brown leash into the square metal ring, tying the dog to a metal hook, still looking calm and resigned the whole way.

Then there, on the other side of the ring, was the pit bull. This dog was pale, blue-white almost, sick and pink-nosed with thick silvery trails of drool that ran from its short, square silver metal muzzle. There were pink scars all along its thick body. There were pink wounds all around his neck. This white dog was huge. Nearly twice the size of the other poor dog. It looked like its belly was full of some sort of hot-toothed rabies. It kept snorting out loads of drool from its small square jaws, flicking its short triangular ears as some tiny black flies swarmed around its head. This dog was going to tear the other dog into pieces. This dog kept yanking on its thick metal leash, trying to get free, rearing up on its big square paws, this dog was wild and ugly and full of spit. This monster was going to snap that champion's neck in two.

Mr. Freeman yanked the metal chain, leading the big dog through the gate and clamped the dog to the ring. Mr. Freeman had a red hunting cap on, with the furry bill nearly covering his red eyes. His face was dark and whiskered and some spit had dried in the corner of his mouth. He sold propane and rented moving vehicles to anyone lucky enough to leave town. He had been run down by a thresher when he was a kid and had lost one whole foot to the awful machine and walked with a limp, shifting his weight to one side of his body, then back, limping along with his huge white dog. His pit bull reared up on its hind legs, tearing at the wire fence with its huge paws.

"Down!!" Mr. Freeman yelled. "Down, you mangy mutt!!" Mr. Freeman's face was red and pock-marked where full puddles of sweat had begun to form along his forehead.

French pulled a plug of tobacco from inside his jacket, cut a nice size of chaw from its slick black mass, and planted it in my hand. Heck, I had never even seen the man spit tobacco before in my life. He didn't say a word, either, just handed me some and stared across the ring at the brown shepherd, Lance, like he had handed me tobacco a hundred times before.

"Do you want some there, Pill?" French asked, cutting another piece loose. Pill shook his head. He was about as friendly as a god-damn tick. It was beginning to piss me off. Here French was going all out of his way to try to appear all fatherly-like, taking us to this whole masculine regalia and all, offering us chaw like our own old man might, and Pill was being a real jack-ass about it all. French just shook his shoulder, sunk the chaw between his gums and cheek, and put the plug back in his jacket. He leaned in close and whispered, "Don't swallow any of that spit now or you'll get a sore stomach."

I nodded, watching how French had placed the chaw in is mouth. I slipped the tobacco between my bottom lip and gum. The chaw tasted sweet like molasses and it began to liquefy and bleed syrup down the back of my throat. I began to gag a little.

"Spit." French smiled out of the corner of his mouth. I nodded and spat a load of slick brown juice like a real pro, watching it plop in the brown dust and slowly sink in color. My face felt good. I felt like a man all right. Spitting tobacco and watching other men swear and swig from the passing flask of whiskey. This is what it felt like all right. French winked and patted me on the back.

"Who do you boys favor?" he asked.

I shrugged my shoulders, spitting again. "I like that shepherd."

"Yeah? That other dog looks awfully mean," French mumbled.

"That other dog's gonna tear that shepherd in two," Pill mut-tered.

"We'll see," I mumbled, leaning against the wire fence. I looked around the ring again. That big white pit bull was growling and snarling and drooling as Mr. Freeman jabbed it in its side with the end of a broom handle. The dog yelped and snapped at the handle, unable to open its jaws on account of the silver muzzle. Mr. Free-man jabbed the dog again in the belly. The other dog stood at the opposite end of the ring, still and solemn, scratching in the dust as it flicked its ears.

Then they turned those poor dogs loose.

My dog, the shepherd, Lance, was still and awful quiet. It hadn't even begun snarling, even when its owner began riling it up, jabbing its flanks with the end of a broom. Mr. Deegan pulled the red muzzle off and untied the leash, hopping out of the ring. I felt like closing my eyes right then. That poor dog was going to be torn to delicate pink ribbons.

The pit bull was snarling and spitting and nearly ready to climb up over the wire fence. Its owner, Mr. Freeman, poked it in its side with the big black stick a few more times, then yanked the muzzle and leash free.

My good ol' dog was as good as doomed.

There was a single moment when all the men got quiet and hushed and even the dogs were quiet, right when those two animals first locked eyes, when they first saw each other in all that slick and coated fury, there in that moment, there was a single drop of blood that climbed up my spine and made me feel like dying.

My dog lunged forward, not making a sound. Its clean white jaws clamped down on the pit bull's front right paw, clamping it right at the joint, tearing and drooling silver spit and dark red blood. The big dumb white dog just sat there. That big ugly dog just sat there, trying to pull its paw free, not snarling or biting back; it yelped a little and tried to yank itself free. Blood broke out all along the white dog's flesh, spilling to the gray dirt and dust in perfectly round dollops.

"Kill!! Shilo, kill!!!" Mr. Freeman yelled, shaking the wire fence. But his dog wouldn't move. It snarled a little, as good ol' Lance snapped at the bloody front paw again, clamping down hard and snarling. The shepherd shook its head wildly, tearing the big white dog's front paw from its joint.

"Je-sus!!" someone shouted. I couldn't move. I couldn't look away. I held my fingers through the spaces in the wire fence and held my breath in as more blood darkened the dirt around the white dog's flanks.

"Kill!!!" Mr. Freeman shouted. "Shilo, kill, you lousy mutt!!!"

There was a milky-white silence in that big dumb dog's black and pink eyes. The shepherd growled all slick with blood, tearing at the other dog's joint. Then the big white dog snapped awake, its black eyes darkened as it bled from its missing paw. The pit bull snarled and lunged, clamping some loose fur around the shepherd's neck, tearing it all free with one huge swipe.

"No!!" I shouted. The shepherd pulled itself free and backed away a little, circling as it moved. The dust in the air began to cloud my eyes and throat. I felt like I couldn't hardly breathe as tiny droplets of blood broke from the shepherd's bare neck. The fur had been torn loose. Its skin was dark and shiny. The blood gathered in a clot at the base of its neck.

"Kill!! Shilo, kill!!!" Mr. Freeman shouted, shaking the fence. The shepherd's owner, Mr. Deegan, was silent. He stood straight-faced and stern at the opposite side of the ring, holding the wire fence, biting his own lips gently.

The pit bull and shepherd began to circle each other. Their teeth were both full of blood and spit. Their eyes were black, blacker than black, almost empty. They moved close to the dirty ground, tensed and mean and snarling. I looked up and saw my older brother gripping the wire fence. His face was pale. His eyes were bright and fixed as he mumbled something to himself like a prayer, I guess. French's face was the same way, all tensed and staring straight ahead, as the dogs stopped circling and locked eyes once more.

"Kill!!!!!"

The dust and smoke in the barn seemed to rise. The voice rang out loud and clear and seemed like it should have come from Mr. Freeman's sore red mouth again, but it hadn't, it was sharp and stern and orderly, and had arrived from Mr. Deegan's thin lips. His face was all pale and solemn as he let out the command and his shepherd obeyed, lunging forward, catching its teeth on the side of the pit bull's short white face, digging its incisors square through the flesh and into the white dog's dark black eye.

"God damn!!"

The pit bull howled, rolling into the dirt, as the shepherd clamped its teeth hard on the bigger dog's soft skin and shook, tearing the malleable black eye from its socket in a mess of thick blood. I squinted, shaking my head, and French squeezed my shoulder. French's face was all tensed around his eyes, like he was having problems stomaching it all. But my brother, Pill, didn't move. He just stared ahead, dumbfounded, I guess, holding the fence tight as it held him up, too.

"No!!!" Mr. Freeman shouted, tossing his red hunting cap to the dirt by his feet. "No!!!"

The pit bull rolled in the dirt, clawing at its emptied eye socket. The eye had disappeared in a mess of blood and dirt and mud as the shepherd lunged once more, gripping the soft fleshy meat under the pit bull's throat. It tore, digging its teeth into the skin, pulling a clump of fur and flesh free, snarling in the blood and drool as the big white pit bull laid on its side, still and as good as dead.

The shepherd backed away and began to circle. The pit bull didn't move. The sides of its pink and white belly slowly rose and fell, its hind leg kicked a little, as its one black eye rolled around in its head. My mouth was dry. My heart was pounding in my chest so hard that I could feel my own blood beating in my ears. The shepherd stopped circling; some blood and drool dripped from its jaws as it backed toward its master and rested on its rear flanks. The big white dog laid in the center of the ring, still breathing, bleeding from its throat and eye socket and front paw. The dirt around its head began to darken with soaked blood.

French let out a low whistle, shaking his head slowly. My brother's face was bright red. His knuckles were cold and white as he gripped the fence.

"Now what?!" he shouted at French.

French took a deep breath, shrugging his shoulders a little.

"Now I guess they shoot the poor thing."

My brother turned back to face the ring as Mr. Deegan

snapped the muzzle back on his dog and rubbed its soft forehead slowly. He opened a small white metal case and began applying some white salve to his shepherd's red wounded neck. The dog remained completely still, unleashed by his side.

"They can't shoot that thing," Pill muttered. French laid his hand on my brother's shoulder. Some of the men stood around, settling bets, trading soft wads of green cash from big white hand to big white hand, smiling and spitting in the dirt. Other men just stood there, still trading sips from a bottle or flask. The barn began to empty out. Slowly, the stink of cigars and the gray cloud of dust began to settle all around us as my brother still held the fence, shaking his head.

"C'mon, boys, we better get on home. Your mother probably already called the state police on us." French patted my head and smiled. My brother didn't move.

"Let's go, Pill, 'fore it gets too late."

The pit bull laid in the dirt, its thick white sides still rising and falling.

"This is it?" Pill muttered. "This is it?" His eyes were red like he was about to cry. He kept holding the fence, gritting his teeth to keep the tears down inside. I knew exactly how he felt. All those men, all the men in town were nothing but ignorant bastards. These grown men were all just as dark and savage as my own ten-year-old heart. Cruel. They had made me just as cruel as hell. I had stood there and chewed tobacco and cheered along and now there was some poor dumb maimed animal moaning to itself not a hundred yards away and no one was doing a damn thing. Then I felt sure of it. I hated that whole damn town more than anything in my dull heart. I hated them for making me feel as ignorant as I ever could, for making me feel as dumb and mean and worthless as one of them. I turned my head and looked away. French stood still and stared at my brother's face without saying a word.

"What you want to do with that dog?" Mr. Freeman asked. His face was all red and greasy with sweat as he handed a huge fold of cash to Mr. Deegan, who had just finished bandaging his shepherd's neck. "I mean it is your dog now. You want me to shoot it?"

Mr. Deegan stood up and stared at the center of the ring where the white dog lay.

"Let's have a look." He tied his champion to the large metal hook and strode across the dirty ring. The pit bull clawed at the ground a little, making sweeps of dirt around its head. Mr. Deegan squatted beside the big white dog's square head, then ran his palm over the dog's side.

"Didn't fight very well, did it?" Mr. Deegan asked with a frown.

"No, it did not and I wouldn't like talking about it now if you don't mind."

"I could patch up his eye and paw and neck all right, but I'm just wondering if it's worth it."

"I'd just the same shoot it as waste the time," Mr. Freeman grunted, digging his hands into his pants pockets. Mr. Deegan stood and stared down at the dog, shrugging his shoulders.

French stared down at me, then my brother, and frowned.

"Go wait in the car," he mumbled.

"What?"

"Go wait in the car. I need to talk to someone from the plant." He raised his voice just a little, staring down into the dirt like he had just suddenly taken some huge weight on his square white shoulders.

"Go on," he repeated, and began to walk toward the ring.

I pulled on my brother's shirt. He shook his head, cussed a little, then turned and walked out of the barn. I followed, not saying a word, just watching how he kicked the dirt with the front of his shoe, then punched the side of my mother's rusted-out car as we leaned against it. The line of big trucks and stock cars began to file out, their headlights flashed on, then their engines, as they pulled away, kicking up dirt and disappearing into the dark. The big black-and-blue night sky hung right over our heads, lit up with the stars and the moon that cut through the dark like delicate bits of glass. The air was hot and dusty and blew against our backs. Stupidity. The dumb masculine stench of cigar smoke and liquor still moved through the air. Pill-Bug punched the car once more and stared back at the barn.

"I hate him," he muttered, digging his fists into his pockets. "I do. Self-righteous bastard. Tell me what to do. I'll cut his throat in his sleep."

I leaned against the car and stared up at the night sky. My hands hurt. My feet felt sore. I was anxious as hell and began running my shoes through the dirt in some attempt to stop myself from peeing on myself. Maybe my older brother was right. This goddamn French seemed awfully phony. Lying to my mother about where he was taking us, bringing us out to the middle of nowhere to watch two dumb `animals tear each other's eyes out, offering us chewing tobacco and trying to be all fatherly as hell. Maybe ol' Pill was right. This guy seemed about as sincere as the rest of my mother's ungodly boyfriends. At least all those men who got drunk and took a swing at my mom or me or my brother, at least, they were all honest about it. They never tried to hide the fact that they were bastards. This guy, French, he was a whole other story. I spat the chaw from my mouth and wiped the spit with my sleeve.

"I'll cut his throat right in his sleep," Pill muttered again. Then the red barn door swung open again and French and another man stepped out, carrying something between the two of them. They walked up to us and the car, kicking up dust, as the broken light from the stars and the barn flashed across our faces.

There was the big white dog, all bandaged and sedate, wrapped up in a thin blue blanket, resting in French's and Mr. Deegan's arms.

"Don't say a word," French mumbled, breathing hard. My brother shook his head. His face went all red and tense like he was confused to death.

"What the hell's that?" Pill mumbled, his eyes all hard and black.

"I said, don't say a word." French frowned, unlocking the blue hatchback. The hatchback door rose and extended as Mr. Deegan and French gently slid the big white dog inside.

"You can't bring that on home," Pill muttered. "What are you doing?"

"Keep quiet," French whispered, slowly closing the hatchback door shut. French wiped some sweat from his chin and dug in his back pocket. He pulled out his brown leather wallet, the same wallet me and my older brother had taken lonely bills of cash from without anyone's permission so many times before, and dug his fingers through until he fished out two crisp twenty dollar bills and planted them in Mr. Deegan's soft white palm.

"There you go, Mr. Deegan." French smiled, shoving his wallet into his back pocket. Mr. Deegan shook his head, folding the cash up and stared down through the back window at the slumbering animal inside.

"Now I can't guarantee that that animal will live for long," he said. "He's on a sedative right now, so he should be all right for the night. But if it gets wild on you or you notice the wounds not healing right, give me a call. You should bring him by the office in the next few days and I'll change the dressing for you and give you some more medication."

French nodded and shook hands with Mr. Deegan.

My older brother was dumbfounded. I couldn't help smiling, shaking my head at the crazy thought of it all, but smiling as we piled into the blue car.

"My mother's never gonna stand for it," Pill grunted, slamming the car door shut.

"She will if we tell her we found the dog on the side of the road and we brought it home to keep it from dying there."

"She ain't ever gonna believe that," Pill mumbled. He stared straight ahead with a mean, sour look, crossing his arms across his chest. "Who asked you to get that damn dog anyway?" my brother asked.

"No one. I did it for myself. I need a bird-dog for the winter."

"Bird-dog? That ain't a bird-dog. That dog can't even see. It's missing a goddamn eye. I ain't gonna lie to my mother."

"Enough already. You tell your mother what you want, Pill. I ain't asking you to lie to her. But on account of that poor animal lying back there, you might just wanna keep your mouth shut so as not to ruin our chances here."

He sounded like one of us. He hadn't even presumed he could just tell my mother that we were going to keep the dog, whether she liked it or not. He must have known her better than we had thought. French stared at the open black road, gripping the wheel tightly. He checked in the rearview mirror every couple of seconds, watching as the dark blue blanket rose and fell with the dog's shallow breath. Before long, we were home, and Pill shot out of the car and into the trailer before the car's engine even died.

"Give me hand with 'em, pal?" French asked, unlocking the hatchback. The hatchback door rose and squeaked as French leaned over and rubbed the dog's side.

"How come you did it, French?" I asked, staring up into his long white face. He rubbed the sweat between his glasses and the skin on his nose and let out a sigh.

"I don't know, kiddo, I thought it was the right thing to do. Your brother's been in a kinda slump since we moved here and he seemed pretty upset by that dog getting hurt and all so I thought maybe I could, you know, make him feel better about things, but I guess it didn't work out so well, huh?"

"Guess not."

"Can't certainly get rid of the poor thing now, can we?" He seemed to answer himself by shrugging his shoulders. "You gonna stick to the story?" he asked, leaning over the car. His face was sticky with a little sweat and his eyes were dark behind his glasses.

"I guess so. Long as I don't get in trouble for lying."

"You won't. Here, now give his legs a little lift."

I dug my hands under the blue blanket and lifted, pressing my skin to its warm white flesh. The dog stirred a little as we lifted it out and made our way up the front steps in side. The screen door clanged open as my mother shot up from the couch, raising her thin black eyebrows.

"What is this?" she asked, covering her mouth in surprise. French and I laid the big white dog down on the sofa and frowned.

"Found him . . . side of the road," French grunted. "Brought him to Mr. Deegan." French couldn't even look at my mother as he lied. He just stared down at the animal as it dug its face into the cushions of the couch. Pill was nowhere in the sofa room. He had gone off to our bedroom to pout or hide himself behind a porno magazine.

"But why didn't you leave it with Mr. Deegan?" my mother asked.

"Oh, he was gonna kill it and the boys took a liking to it so . . . "

"It's huge," my mother pleaded. "Look how big its paws are. We can't keep that thing in here." Her eyes were big and wild as she looked over the animal's soft white body. "What happened to its eye? Oh, and its paw?"

"Must've been hit by a car or something," French grunted. He stared at me and gave a little nod with his head.

"Can we keep it, Mom?" I asked, almost on cue, pulling on her housedress. "It won't bother no one, I promise. And I'll take care of it, too. Pill will help, too."

"I don't know," she whispered, staring at the pit bull's square jaws. She bit her bottom lip, thinking hard. "Where's it gonna sleep?" she asked.

"It can sleep out here," I replied.

"What about shots and rabies and all that?"

"It's got all that stuff already."

"I dunno . . . "

"Thanks, Mom!!" I gave her a good hug around her waist and stared down at the big white dog. It laid still, wrapped in the blue blanket, burying its face back under the sofa cushions. I looked up at French and nodded. He was smiling nervously, running his hand along the dog's side, patting it gently. After it all, he was a real square guy, I guess, but I started to wonder how much longer he'd stick around before he finally had enough of it all. Between my mother prone to fits of crying in the middle of the night, and me and my brother running wild all around the goddamn trailer park, I began to think that this French wouldn't stick around for much longer. I stared at his long white face and nodded to myself. Sure, one morning, we'd wake up and French would be gone, maybe the big black Impala would still be on the blocks out front, maybe some of his clothes would still be in my mother's closet, but like all the men in my mother's life, he would be gone without a right word or reason. Maybe my mother would pack up all of his things in a brown cardboard box and send it off to him, maybe he'd come by the trailer and pick it all up when no one was around, but eventually he'd be gone and less than a blurred photo in my own mind.

The big dog rolled on its other side, yelping a little.

"Somebody should stay out here with it tonight," French offered, rubbing its soft fur with his fingers. I nodded, stroking the white dog's belly.

"Well, you've got school tomorrow, pal." My mother frowned in my direction.

"I'll do it, I guess," French mumbled, sitting beside the big white dog. He patted the dog's side and smiled.

"Did you guys already come up with a name for it?" my mother asked.

"Shilo." French nodded.

"Shilo? What kind of name is that?" She smiled, rubbing its side. "What about Spot or Pluto or something canine like that?"

"No, Shilo's good." I nodded, too.

"All right then, I better pick up some dog food on the way home from work, I guess," my mother said. She rubbed the dog's sore white belly. "Good grief. Looks like it's some kind of monster."

That poor dumb dog became the biggest goddamn baby I'd ever seen. My mother didn't seem to pay too much attention to the dog after the first few weeks; she ended up being the one who fed it everyday and gave it its medicine, but then after a while, it seemed like the dog had always been there and it was another dirty mouth to feed. That big dumb dog would just lie around with its big ugly head drooling in your lap as you watched TV, or it would beg for scraps at the table like a poor animal, staring at you with the poorest single black eye you'd ever seen. Once all its wounds healed, its empty eye was a hard gray-and-black cavern that had to be sealed up with stitches. Its one leg that had lost a paw became hard and black, too, a thick bumpy wound that ended just below its joint. Its neck healed fine, but left three or four huge pink scars along its neck. That dumb dog would hop around on its three legs and rub its muzzle against your thigh or leap up and lick your face or come and lay right on top of you if you happen to sleep in the bottom bunk and left your door open a little.

I'd dare say French nearly fell in love with that dog.

The two of them would just sit on the couch for hours, French would let the animal take licks from his beer can and he'd rub its big ugly one-eyed face as the Saturday football game flickered on in front of them like some sort of honeymoon. But then if the dog knocked over a pot of my mother's flowers or ate a whole plate of fried chicken, ol' French would holler, "Dough, take care of your dog, here," like their love affair was some kind of secret our trailer didn't ever notice.

Pill and that dog never much got along. He had stared across that fence at it and cheered it to win and when it had lost it had been as if the whole world had let him down again and he held it against that dog as it hopped around our dingy little trailer, playing up to anyone that would pay it attention. Once, I saw my brother give that dog a kick, and because of its missing paw, it rolled right on to its side, but that's all it did, just laid there like it had wanted to lie right down in that exact spot in the first place. That was a dog that refused to be beaten down. The dumb thing didn't have enough sense to know the sore spectacle it was.

Me, I tried like hell to take care of that miserable thing, but it had been an old dog to begin with and wouldn't run or fetch or roll over or do any damn dog trick you could think of except sic, which didn't do much good, because that damn dog Shilo couldn't move after anything fast enough to catch it in the first place. So the dog would end up clamping its big teeth down on your pant leg or shirt-tail and would refuse to let go until it got tired of playing or tore a hole in your garment or until you finally gave in and left the damn dog your clothes to tear and chew on. That Shilo was a good dog, but for a ten-year-old, not much fun to play with. I guess I got used to taking it out for a walk twice a day in the field behind the trailer park so it could do its business all right, and then I'd watch it hop on home and return to its couch to watch whatever was on television.

Then at night that dumb dog would crowd me in my own bed.
Its cold gray breath became the smell of sleep on the bottom
bunk of me and my brother's crowded room. That dog's great
square pale face with one dark eye buried beneath the blankets beside my neck became the last thing I saw before I drifted off to
dreams of violence and gore in the beat of that dog's irregular
breath. That dog sure became as lazy and stubborn and hopeless
as me or my brother or French or my mother and soon enough fit
in the empty red hollows of all our poor hearts, all right.

# the devil in his place

**D**o you wanna see the hanging ghost?"

This damn loony girl, Lottie, was right at my screen door.

"What?" I muttered, not stepping too close. Her hair was twisted up in four pig-tails, pulling her pale skin taut around her eyebrows. She had on a dirty gray dress and big brown boots that must have belonged to some monstrous older brother.

"Do you wanna go to the Furnhams' farm? It's not too far a walk from here."

This crazy girl, Lottie, had followed me home from school. This girl that stunk of urine and had at least four hundred god-damn pig-tails, the same girl that sat next to me in class and mumbled on and on about all kinds of crazy nonsense, like how her old man had cut his thumb off and ran two miles to get it sewn back on, this same girl who had tried to maim me only a few days before for calling her a dirty pig when it had been that fat-head Dan Gooseherst, this dirty farm girl who had bit a huge pink hole into that fat kid's palm like a goddamn rabid animal, that same girl had followed me to my awful trailer and was standing outside my door, picking something poor from her tiny white ear and staring back at me with small gray-brownish eyes.

"What the hell are doing at my house?" I muttered kind of quietly so my mother in the kitchen couldn't hear. Poor Lottie shrugged her shoulders, still picking her ear.

"They got a dead horse out there. That's where Mr. Furnham hung himself. Right out in the barn."

This girl, Lottie, was sure nuts. My dog, Shilo, sniffed around the door, rubbing its pink nose and white face against the screen. Kill, I wanted to mutter. Sic. But I didn't. I just stared at her round head, looking at the way her eyes never remained still in her head.

"Well, do ya?" she asked again.

I stepped back from the screen door, itching my eyes like they hurt. This girl had tried to knock me senseless and had maimed poor Dan Gooseherst without a thought and now wanted me to go out of my dirty trailer to some barn with her, alone. This girl was the craziest kind I'd ever seen.

"There really are ghosts there," she whispered. I could hear the snot in the back of her throat as she pulled on her dress.

I shook my head. This girl made my teeth hurt in my head. Her big round head hung emptily on her shoulders, moving from side to side as she leaned against the screen, trying to stare inside the trailer.

"I gotta eat," I mumbled, forcing a lie. It was only three-thirty in the afternoon. My mother was in the kitchen defrosting a big leg of lamb that wouldn't be ready for another few hours. "Sorry." I tried to smile. Lottie poked her head right against the screen, breathing my breath. Her little round nose had a gray ring of sweat and snot underneath it. She smelled like a boy. Like sweat and dirt and the unimaginable things left in unkept ear canals that might blossom to be unholy nightmares or sticker-thorns in the spring. My dumb dog, Shilo, sniffed the girl through the door and whined for her attention.

"Is that your dog?" she asked.

"Yeah." I nodded.

"That's a pretty dog." Lottie smiled, rubbing her hand against the screen so my big dumb dog would lick her palm. "Sure is a friendly dog."

"Sure, sure, whatever."

"So you're eatin' right now?" she asked.

"Yeah," I lied again, trying to back away from the door. "I just asked my mom. Sorry."

"Oh." Her eyes became dark and sad. She backed away from the door as I breathed a sweet breath of relief.

My mother's heavenly voice rose like song from the other room. My mother, my sweet mother, the all-knowing, all-seeing, omnipotent island goddess of our lonesome trailer, shouted from the kitchen.

"You have plenty of time to go out, Dough. Just be back by six, okay?"

"But, Mom, I . . . "

"No, no, you need to get out of this trailer and get some exercise. You don't wanna end up like Joe Lunerhead, do you?"

Poor Joe Lunerhead was one of our old neighbors back in Duluth who grew up to be a no-good bum right beside us. This guy was a couple of years older then me and my brother, but he still was a teenage-kid, I guess. He had a huge white freckled face and a short red crew-cut that showed his tiny, pointed ears. The thing was, this Joe Lunerhead never left his goddamn house. There were at least a million neighborhood kids on our block who played stick-ball or catch-one–catch-all, but this dumb kid, Joe Lunerhead just stayed inside and ate and slept in front of the TV until he was nearly three hundred pounds and all pasty and white and his parents had to sell their goddamn house to put the kid in some special clinic somewhere in Minneapolis. That Joe Lunerhead was someone my mother was always threatening me with.

"But Mom, I've got homework and . . . "

"You've got all night to do it. Stop being rude and go out and play."

I felt myself grit my teeth. Humiliated. Right by mother's sweet white hand. My own mother had handed me straight over to the crazy piss-smelling girl right at our own door.

"There really is a ghost out there," Lottie repeated with a smile, pressing against the screen door. I shook my head and pulled my dirty baseball hat down over my eyes. This would be the lousiest afternoon of my short life. Worse than being at Sunday School. But I made a plan right there. Stay with her a little while, maybe walk down the long road toward all the farms then ditch her and run home and make it back to the trailer to doze in front of the TV and forget that that crazy girl knew exactly where I lived.

"You gonna come out, then?" Lottie grinned.

"Yeah, yeah, hold on," I grunted. I stole one of my older brother's shirts and checked to make sure there were some crumpled-up cigarettes stashed inside one of the pockets. There were. Three lonely squares. Enough for sure. I unlocked the screen and stepped outside. My big dumb dog lapped at the screen. I hopped down the gray cement steps and looked around. Most of the trailer park was empty. Most everyone was still at work. There were some little kids, babies, I mean, running around half-naked, wearing only their diapers, chasing each other in front of a trailer down by the end of the cul-de-sac. There was a skinny mother in a long blue dress sitting on her front porch, combing out her long yellow hair, watching her little naked babies running around in the dirt. The sun was out. The sky was pretty and blue and it was almost as hot as summer. I tightened my baseball cap right down around my eyes again. Lottie was just standing there, staring at me. She was standing beside the ugliest pink girl's bicycle, too small for her for sure, with pink streamers from the handlebars and silver noise-makers in the spokes.

"That your bike?" I asked.

"Naw, it used to be my sister's. She's too old to ride now. You can try it if you want." She smiled.

"No, that's okay, I'll walk."

"You sure? It's a good bike."

"Yeah, I bet."

"Haw. Okay, then." Lottie shrugged her shoulders and took a seat on her tiny pink bike and began pedalling around me in wide circles as we started down the dirty brown road toward the Furnhams' lousy old barn.

"You like living in a trailer park?" she asked, nearly cutting me off as she finished a big figure-eight.

"No."

"How come?"

"Because it's stupid," I grunted.

"Why?"

"Because it is, okay?"

"Okay."

She circled around me again on her crappy pink bike. Her long awkward knees hung out from under her dress as she pedalled. The lousy noise-makers in the spokes sparkled and grumbled as she rode. "Do you like your name?" she asked. I stopped walking and watched her wheel around.

"Hey, listen, I ain't gonna walk with you if you keep asking stupid questions." I accentuated that with a good solid spit then started walking again. I fumbled through my brother's shirt pocket and put a cigarette in my mouth, then took out a book of matches from my own pants and lit the square, coughing a little as I inhaled.

"How come you smoke?" Lottie asked, swerving past me.

"What?"

"How come you smoke?" she repeated.

"Because I do. Jesus," I grunted.

"You do it 'cause you think it's cool." She smiled, shaking her head. "You do it 'cause you think it makes you look older."

"Shut the hell up for a minute, will ya?" I inhaled and coughed again.

"Haw! You don't even know how to do it right." She giggled, shaking her thousands of pig-tails behind her round head.

"Forget it," I shouted and stopped walking. "I'm going home."

"No, no, don't go home," she pleaded. She stopped her lousy pink bike right in front of me. "I won't ask any more questions, honest. Okay? I promise."

"How 'bout you don't speak at all?" I asked, staring at her lousy face. She smiled, shaking her head and began pedalling again. I began walking behind her once more.

"Do you like Ms. Nelson?" she asked. Ms. Nelson. Oh, Ms.

Nelson. Long-legged pedagogue. Her stern face and short skirts were no match for my sleepiness and general lack of classroom brilliance. There was something there between us, some spark, some lust I felt as she scolded me for falling asleep again or for failing another test, but it was a kind of lust even I knew was hopeless and might fade the closer I came to graduating the fifth grade. My Val, on the other hand, well, that was love, pure and true. There was no persuasion against my poor, poor heart that could set me free from her soft-cheeked spell. No pathetic glare from my older brother or hasty curse word on her behalf could upset the sweetly disconsolate adoration that I had come to own for her.

"No, I don't like Ms. Nelson." I frowned.

"Oh, I thought you liked her. I thought you wanted to marry her."

"You're crazy." I tried to smile, offering a phony chuckle. "You're nuts, that's what you are."

"I thought you wanted to marry her and run away with her."

"Did anyone ever tell you you talk a lot?"

She stopped where she rode and shrugged her shoulders. "No."

I shook my head and kept walking, taking another drag on my cigarette.

"Do you like any girls in class?" she asked.

"What?"

"Do you like Mary Beth Clishim?" She smiled, winking at me a little.

"What?" I grunted. I stared at her round face and gray eyes. Her lips were curled tight in a little smile.

"No, I don't like her."

"All the boys do." Her lips curled in a smirk.

"Well, I don't."

"Do you like Laurie Avers?"

"No." I swatted at a fly that buzzed past my head.

"What about Jill?"

"Jill who?" I asked.

"Jill Montefort. Do you like her?"

"No, already. Jesus, you don't ever shut up, do you?"

"What about Ms. Nelson? You like her don't you? You can tell me."

"You're giving me a goddamn headache."

"Well, you have to like somebody."

"Why's that?" I asked.

"Everyone likes somebody."

"No, not me. I don't like anybody. I don't like a goddamn soul in this crummy place." I flicked the dying cigarette to the side of the road.

"Haw. What about your brother?" she asked. "You like him?" This girl was trying to be real funny.

"What are you queer? Course I don't like my brother."

"Haw. What about Texas? Do you like Texas?" This girl was a laugh-riot, all right.

"God, you're loony."

"Sure, sure." She smiled, pedaling beside me. Her eyes were all bright and shiny then she said it. "Do you like . . . me?"

I shrugged my shoulders, staring at my feet at I walked.

"I like you about as much as that rock over there." I pointed to a round little rock that was nearly covered in green moss and grass.

"Is that a lot?" She frowned.

"You figure it out."

"Oh, you don't have to be shy with me. My sister told me all about boys."

"How's that?" Her eyes were all shiny and bright. She kept tilting her head back and forth like she was singing a song to herself as she spoke.

"My sister told me when a boy acts like he doesn't like you, it means he really does."

"She told you that?" I asked.

Lottie nodded proudly, giving me another gruesome wink.

"Well, your sister is wrong. I don't like you because I don't like you."

"Haw!" Lottie smirked and shook her head. "Are you a virgin?"

"Jesus!!" I shouted, shaking my head. "What in the hell's wrong with you?"

"So are you?"

"Why the hell would I tell you?" I shouted. This girl was truly nuts. She was giggling like crazy now, shaking her head and smiling to herself as she laughed.

"Did you ever make it?" she asked in a whisper.

"Why the hell do wanna know so bad?" I asked.

"I don't think you ever did." She smiled, nodding to herself. Her big gray teeth shone under her greasy little nose as she grinned. "Do you know how to make it?" she whispered, stopping her bike in its tracks. Her face was all greasy with sweat. One of her pig-tails had began to unravel on the side of her head.

"Yeah," I kind of mumbled, looking away from her.

"Do you?" she asked again.

"Yeah, already, I said I did!!"

She stared at me hard, edging her teeth along her bottom lip. I tried to stare back, squinting a little. Right then, she had to know it was all a lie. Her eyes were all sharp and mean as she smiled a little to herself. My face felt hot. The whole back of my neck felt like it was bubbling with sweat. Then I broke. I looked away and began walking again.

"I think you're lying. I don't think you know the first thing about making it."

"So what?!!! What the hell do you care?!!!"

Lottie smiled, shrugging her shoulders and began pedaling again. She wouldn't stop grinning. Her eyes were nearly crossed from her smiling so hard. This girl had seen something about me I hadn't wanted anyone to see. This girl had squinted right past all the nudie magazine and dirty talk and stolen unfiltered cigarettes to the sap in the bottom of my gut. The goddamn lousy truth. This girl had beat me. This girl's goddamn annoying questions had won out. I was nervous as hell all of a sudden. I wanted to get out of there in a hurry. I rubbed the back of my neck and scratched my face.

"Where the hell is this place anyway?" I shouted, digging my hands in my pockets.

"Right there." She smiled. She pointed to a huge dirty red barn, worn and crooked, that stood a few hundred feet away, behind a low wire fence. The barn looked spooky as hell. There was some sunlight that poured through the breaks in the boards and roof in thick silver beams, cutting the dust in the air like the hand of god or something. There was an old red tractor parked beside the barn and a few hundred feet back was the Furnhams' old white farmhouse, graying along the porch and roof.

"That's it, huh?" I mumbled.

"You scared?" Lottie smiled.

"No, I'm not scared," I grunted. Lottie laid down her ugly pink bike in the long yellow grass beside the silver wire fence. Then she hopped over like a pro, landing on her feet with a little grunt. I followed, catching one foot on a loose wire, tripping to my knees as I fell on the other side.

"There's their house," Lottie whispered, pointing to the white building as we walked up the tiny dirt path toward the barn. "And that's the barn. That's where he did it." She frowned. Her eyes were dark and shallow. Her whole face was gray.

"Did what?" I asked.

"Hung himself," she whispered again, staring straight at the huge red door. "His crops all came up dirt and so he sold off all his equipment and then one night a man called to tell him that he had lost the land, too, and then he came out to the barn and then he did it. He hung himself right in there and his family had to move away down south and they left everything the way it was."

My mouth felt dry as hell. I kept staring at the big red door, waiting for it to swing open. The sun had already begun to set. I looked over my shoulder. There in the distance was the trailer park, not too far away at all. There was a whole line of silver mobile homes cluttered on the horizon, packed tightly together and looking dull and ugly as anything I could ever imagine. I turned back and stared at the giant red barn. Posted in huge white letters on a black sign were some faded words. I couldn't make them out.

"No trespassers," Lottie whispered. I nodded and cleared my throat and squinted at the unholy silver light that gleamed from inside.

"You ready?" she asked. I nodded slowly as Lottie dug her fingers between the two huge red doors and gave it a shove. The whole barn creaked and groaned as more dust erupted from the thin black opening, circling like silver demons around my head. Lottie stopped pushing and turned to me and winked.

"Do you wanna hold my hand?" she asked with a smile, raising one thin eyebrow.

"No," I mumbled.

"Well, it can be pretty scary." She grinned.

"Let's just go in already."

Lottie nodded and gave the door another push. The door howled and finally gave, creaking along its metal track, sliding apart. Dust spun around us like snow as we stepped inside the old red barn. The place was dark and damp and warm and stunk of sweet death, of decaying teeth and rotting bushels of wet hay and death itself, pungent and stiff and green and dreamlike. The place was quiet and stagnant and old-smelling like a church.

This was His place. The place of death.

The dark space above our heads was coated in spiderwebs. There were thousands and thousands of cobwebs all over, crossing and criss-crossing in thick gray translucent cocoons. There were husks of dead insects left dangling in the light, hung by their empty shells by a long thin strand cast by tiny black spinnerettes.

I held my breath, gritting my teeth together as I followed Lottie inside. There was a stack of wood, coated in moss now, piled in one corner. There were huge bushels of hay, tied up tight with a string that had begun to fray along its binding. There were some shovels and rakes and scythes and huge metal tools that were piled along the wall, coated in dust and dirt. Then there was something left in the corner, a huge brown and black mass, piled in a lump on one side of the barn.

"There it is," Lottie whispered. "The dead horse."

The dead animal was huge. The old horse was a device of gray and black flesh, loose skin that had begun to rot and fester with insects and death. There were flies that buzzed everywhere, darting past our heads and back, up through the thin silver webs and back down to the gray horse's head. There along one side of the animal, I could see some whitish ribs, sticking right out of its belly. Then I could see its head, long and thin, it rested on its side. Its head was thrown back with huge white open teeth that had bits of hay and insects stuck between them. I felt my stomach go sour. I was sweating like I was sick. Maybe it was the heat, maybe all the goddamn insects buzzing around and flicking off the skin on the back of my neck, but I was sweating now, sweating right through the bottom of my feet like I was in a nightmare, like I was in a horrible dream only I could ever imagine. The stench of death was sticking to me, sticking to my tongue and my breath was like oil, like grease.

"Do you wanna see its guts?" Lottie whispered. I shook my head, but this crazy girl just pulled my hand and led me around the front of this huge dead animal, pointing at its innards like rest-stops on a roadmap. The horse's belly was split open, all its organs had spilled between its legs in a variety of colors and dull, pungent odors. "There's its intestine," she whispered, pointing at a huge slick yellow and white length of flesh that looked like a bloated worm or leech. "There's its stomach. Look how big it is." Another yellowed mass spotted with red and pink and white dots that hung out emptily along its exposed belly. "There's the heart." She sighed, pointing at a huge red mass that resembled a deflated red balloon. There was a puddle of dried blood that ran in a ring around its head and belly, there was some dust and insects that rose from its emptied eyes making that damn thing seem still alive.

Lottie gripped my arm and led me deeper inside toward the

center of the barn and then she stopped. She squinted a little at all
the dust and then looked up, staring past the dark silver light into
the rafters above.

"That's it," she whispered. "That's where he did it."

I swallowed hard and looked up. There was a thick wooden
beam that ran over our heads. It was surrounded by thin eaves of
spiderwebs and dust and empty shell bodies. Silver sunlight split
between the boards overhead and poured down across its edges.
There directly above our heads was a dark black mark, thin but still
dark, a scrape, a burn caused by the rope rubbing against the beam
as Mr. Furnham swung beneath and fought hopelessly for his soul.
I couldn't move. I stared up at that beam, unable to move, unable to
blink, the dust circled around my head as I imagined the rope
cinching around my neck, getting tighter and tighter until I dropped
and my neck snapped and my teeth ran against each other in my
cheeks and my eyes fell to the back of my head and my hands
clenched and my spine became stiff and my stomach hard and I fell
straight through my body to my death and hung up there like a cold
white wood puppet, still and quiet and unmoving as the dark.

"Hey, are you okay?" Lottie asked me, but I still couldn't move.
All I could see was the dark black mark on the beam. All I could
feel was my own death being wrung straight through my neck and
eyes and my fingers and spine and then I could feel all my sweat
run cold along my skin and then a hush, like the thin silver light
overhead had disappeared and all the shadows had taken a breath.
Then the dark night settled in through the thin wooden roof and
through all the tiny silver lines and devices and designs and then
there was a face.

There was a face in the dark above.

A long thin body moved and crept, crawling along the rafters
above me where I stood, cold and quiet and careful as death itself,
with a long black-and-red cloak that spun around its thin arms and
legs and its head. Its face was like a reptile, a lizard, sharp and thin
and mean with a hood of skin that ran from its skull, darkening its
hollow black eyes in the shadows it had stolen from the night. This

creature was no animal or insect or spirit or anything like that, no, this thing was as solemn and unholy as all my darkest dreams, something that could find me whenever I was alone, something that knew me and my own poor soul and the horrible lies and things I kept inside. This thing had hissed in my ears as I fought to sleep. This thing I feared most out of all my dumb childhood droves of unfounded terrors, this thing that had trapped me in a cold spindle of nightly dread. There right above my head and out from my own burning heart, there was the Devil, dark red as blood and quiet as a prayer.

"Are you okay?" Lottie repeated, but I couldn't hear. There was cold, cold blood running in my ears and the sound of the creature's cold slippery breath ran down my spine. "Do you wanna leave?" she asked quietly. But it was too late. There were its long red fingers, reaching out, reaching down, brushing against the cold skin of my forehead, reaching past my head and spine and soul to my poor red heart that flickered and burned as the Devil hissed with delight. Fire began to burn all around my head, flames leapt from my skin and in the air behind me as the Devil hissed and laughed, the curse, the curse burned bright red in my skin as Lottie pulled me by the arm through the huge red door. My eyes were nearly filled with tears. My teeth were chattering in my head. That was it. I was as good as gone. I was good as dead. I stumbled out of the barn as Lottie shook me hard.

"Are you okay?" she shouted, shaking me by the shirt. I nodded, still staring back into the darkness that breathed within the empty red barn.

"Do you wanna go home?" she asked.

I nodded again, feeling the whole world darken and close around me. Lottie led me by the hand down the dirt path to the wire fence; she helped me over and down where she picked up her bike and walked it beside me, staring hard into my eyes like she might start to cry, too.

"Do you think you're gonna be sick?" she asked, rolling the bike beside me. "Do you want to stop by my house and rest?"

I nodded, staring at the dirt road as it drifted under my feet. My whole body felt empty. My palms were greased with perspiration. I was shaking a little, too, shivering from all the sweat up and down my back. I leaned against Lottie as she stared in my eyes, looking scared and sad.

"Here, we're almost there," she said in a sweet voice that swam past me like a song. I followed her down a little road that winded beside a wire fence and led up to her house. There right over my shoulder was the unlit night. The sky was blue and black and moving slowly with clouds. Behind me was the dark red barn, blossoming with blood, trembling with hellish silver lights, and to my other side was the pale sallow flicker of the pathetic trailer park, burning with sparks of yellow and blue as a TV or an oven light snapped awake. Then up off the road a little was Lottie's house. It was gray and white, a big A-frame farmhouse with a nice rising porch and a tire-swing hung off a brown maple tree out front. There were some small white chickens that pecked and scurried about. Their eyes were blue-lit in the dark as they squabbled and fluttered beside the front porch.

"Nobody's home," Lottie mumbled, throwing her bike down in the dirt. "We'll go around back." She pulled me by the shirt and led me around to the back of the house. There was a gray wood porch and some darkened cement stairs that led down to a shadowy basement. Lottie led me by the shirt sleeve down the gray cement steps and pushed open the basement door. It creaked and swung open, knocking some dust loose as it moved. Lottie stepped right into the blackness, sure as hell, and found the small silver chain for the lightbulb, then gave it a pull. The lightbulb snapped awake and swung from her movement, teetering back and forth on its wire.

"We can sit down here for a while before my dad comes home." She smiled, squeezing my arm. As the lightbulb swung, shadows moved all along the walls, creaking back and forth, moving all around. There were eyes. Thousands of still silver eyes. I felt the spit run dry in my mouth. My eyes fluttered in my head.

"Trophies," Lottie whispered, still holding my arm. "My dad's a taxidermist. He stuffs them."

There were mounted creatures all around my head. There was a huge purple and brown and white quail mounted as if it was in flight along the wall. There was a thick black-and-white badger poised at my feet, its huge triangular teeth bared in a snarl. There was a buck's head raised on the wall, its shiny black antlers branched from its brown skull. There were some fish mounted on brown bits of wood and rock, there was huge white skull that had been bleached and emptied, thick brown and black skins that had been stretched along the wall, there was a huge wooden desk that sat in the corner, glimmering with silver tools and knives and a hundred glass bottles of all sizes.

"What are those?" I asked.

There within some of the round glass jars were silver and green stars, shimmering as the lightbulb swung over our heads.

"Eyes," Lottie whispered.

The lightbulb came to a stop. The shadows became still on the wall.

"Eyes?" I mumbled.

"Glass eyes."

There in the shiny silver jars were all kinds of glass eyes. Blue eyes, big black eyes, tiny silver eyes, small brown eyes, all smooth and cool as pennies, cold to the touch, but hard and strange and mysterious.

"This is my favorite," Lottie said, opening one of the glass jars. She dug her fist inside and lifted up a tiny black cloth and pulled out two perfectly round glass eyes. They were big enough for a person and green and hard and shimmered brightly like jewels, stealing light from the white bulb overhead.

"They're beautiful, aren't they?" Lottie smiled, holding the eyes in her tiny white palm. I nodded. Those glass eyes were the most wonderful things I think I had ever seen. I reached out to touch one. It was cold, cold and warm from Lottie's soft sweaty skin. The glass cornea was black and radiant inside, staring out as Lottie moved under the light.

"It's for a person," Lottie whispered. "For Ms. Dubuque when she dies."

"Who?"

"The lady who lives on the other side of town. She's going to be stuffed when she dies."

"What?" I mumbled.

"She already paid my daddy to do it. And she wants these green eyes." Lottie placed one in my palm. It fit perfectly in the tiny recess of my hand, rolling around gently as I stared deep down inside. They were perfect. They were the perfect death-eyes for a lady who hadn't even died. The thought sent a shiver down my spine.

"What does she want green eyes for?" I asked.

"Who knows? My dad says she's got more money than she knows what to do with."

I held the glass eye in my hand tightly. The thing felt heavy and indestructible against my skin.

"Don't break it now," she whispered. Her eyes were bright and silver as she stared at my face. "Nice, huh?"

I nodded again.

"Bet you think I didn't have anything good at my house," she said. "Here, I better put them back." I held the eye for one more moment, then handed it back to her, staring as she gently placed it back in the glass jar and covered them in a tiny black blanket, to help them sleep, I guessed. There in the other corner of the room was a huge brass and silver drum that dripped water into a dirty brown bucket. It dripped, dripped, dripped quietly, splashing against the shiny liquid inside.

"That's my dad's still." Lottie frowned. "Supposed to stay away from that. Moonshine." She winked. I nodded, exactly sure of what she meant. One of my mother's old boyfriends, Joe Brown, had been a real bastard and drinker, too, and would take long angry sips from a huge gray jug he kept in the trunk of his car. He had been a real bastard all right, and nearly sent my older brother, Pill, to the hospital for breaking the antennae off his beloved El Dorado. I looked at the still again. That thing looked like a shiny open wound ready to rust or turn ugly.

"Lottie?!!!"

There were heavy, clumsy footsteps that pounded against the floor overhead. I flinched as the footsteps clambered around a little then stopped right above our heads. Someone dropped a glass bottle that broke and spilled all across the floor above.

"Lottie, get down here and clean up this mess," a cold gravelly voice shouted. Lottie froze, then held her breath.

"That's my dad," Lottie said, staring into my eyes. "I'm not supposed to be down here." She sighed, staring up at the floorboards.

"Lottie?!!" he called again. "You better not be down in my things!!" he shouted.

"You better go," she squeaked, opening the back door. I shrugged my shoulders and nodded and ran up the back stairs and around the side of the house and stopped and looked back over my shoulder to make sure I was alone. There in the front window, along the faded blue curtains, was a huge black shadow, tall and square, the shadow of a man that knew how to use knives to cut and sew and sever and probe the poor frail body from its glassy silver soul. There behind that window was a man who kept the eyes of a rich woman in a glass jar on his desk, a man whose voice was hard and mean as if his throat had been overgrown with rust or metal spines, a man whose eyes had to be two cold black pits along the side of a long narrow serpentine head. Here was a cold hollowed man that belonged in that hellish unholy town. Here was a man I could hate without a single thought. He stood in the front window and watched me go, running along the dirt as my shadow skittered from dark spot to dark spot as I disappeared down the gravel path and out to the long road that led home.

There ghosts all along that awful night.

There were spooks of all kinds that hissed from the woods and trees and shadows, spirits of the lowly Devil, the creature that had taken my own poor hope. Cold black shadowy hands moved along my neck, touching my sweat, reaching out to pull me back into the darkness, back into that house, back where that devil stood, gauging my heart. My teeth were chattering in my head, my whole face was covered with sweat as I turned and looked back into the darkness, back at that poor crazy girl's old wooden house that rose on a gray little hill. My breath was coming hard, my legs felt weak right at the knees, but I stopped and turned back and stared hard, hoping that poor girl was following me, wishing she was right behind me right now, but she wasn't, she was trapped in that house, trapped worse than a ghost, alone there hiding in the basement, holding her breath to save her soul.

# the birthday surprise

**M**e, I turned eleven without a sound. That was my first birthday away from our own home and I felt hopeless as hell spending it alone with ol' Pill and my folks. There would be no nicely decorated party with streamers and foil, no sincerely dubious party games like spin the bottle or five minutes all alone in the closet, no nice birthday kisses from the fat sweet girls on my old block, and worse of all, I guess, no extra presents all wrapped up nice and neat in bows and newspaper for me from all the other dumb kids I might invite. This birthday would be spent with my lousy family in this crummy damn town. This birthday would surely be the worst I'd ever had. It just happened to fall on a Saturday, so my mother was real sweet and made everyone keep quiet to let me sleep in late. But that damn dog woke me up anyway. I sure didn't care. My mother was going to prepare me a huge dinner: big thick red pork chops and real applesauce and a huge chocolate ice-cream-topped cake. That sounded great. I was going to lay around the trailer all day and watch a Kung-Fu movie or old black-and-white monster show because it was my damn day and ol' French said I could watch what I pleased, but then about two hours after I woke up and was just settling in on that lumpy ol' sofa with a nice can of grape soda and my brother, Pill, and ol' French and my big dumb dog, well, then the most awful surprise happened upon our lousy screen door.

"Hello?!!" I heard her whiny, rouge-covered voice. "Is anyone home?!!"

Then I sat up and rolled my eyes and just knew it was going to be a birthday worse than any I would have spent alone.

"Hello, Marie!!" my mother screamed, placing the big yellow cake within that dull gray oven as she dropped her big green cooking mitts to the floor. My mother fumbled at the door latch and pushed the dirty screen door open wide and I shook my goddamn head because just then I could smell that horrible pink perfume like some sort of insidious vaporous flower-laden claw and I knew, oh, brother I knew, it was my big, white-faced relative Aunt Marie and her lousy kin.

My Aunt Marie was my own father's older sister. They had both been born and raised in Duluth, children of a big burly cattleman and a pink-faced lady that played organ in Our Lady of Perpetual Sadness Church, but only my Aunt Marie had ever been baptized in a real ceremony signifying her damn holy ways. My aunt had been born first and by the time my own old man had been delivered and it was his turn to be inducted or indoctrinated or christened or whatever, my grandparents had lost their land and cattle and means of living so their son was never sent clear and pure into the world. That whole thing might seem pretty useless, but between him and my Aunt Marie it made all the difference in their dark little world. By the time my old man was old enough to drive, his poor father was gone and laid in the grave and my big Aunt Marie thought it was her duty and right to help raise a young man who took more pleasure in fistfighting and kissing young ladies than anything else in his devilish life. Then just a few short years later, my old man ended up marrying my own sweet mother and knocking her up with my older brother, not directly or necessarily in that order, and that was the beginning of a life my Aunt Marie could never approve. My older brother, Pill, was conceived out of wedlock in the backseat of my old man's stock Futura; my mother had been a cocktail waitress and table dancer at a rustic saloon, dubiously named "Vollie's Nudie Bar," and after their son was born, my old man began doing odd jobs, mostly fencing stolen goods to put food in all their sweet mouths. My mother stopped dancing on tables and started going to church and tended to her baby, and a few years later, I guess they had me and by then my old man had gotten his transcontinental trucking license and was working steady and all was pretty as pie. But the way my aunt saw it my old man had been born in sin and, like the heathen he was, it was only a matter of time before he died in it, too, sealing his and the fates of all his poor, ignorant family.

"Where's the birthday boy?" My aunt grinned. Her face was so round and big and white and pink and fat that her eyes seemed like two soft black dots pressed into a mold of dough. Her nose was tiny and all snub, her damn perfume made me sick as she squeezed me around my neck. I could feel the cold gray ridges on her lips as she hugged me hard and planted the most awful greasy kiss on my cheek. "How does it feel to be eleven?" She grinned again.

It felt like dirt.

I shrugged my shoulders. There's never an easy answer to get you out of a dumb question like that. My aunt stopped squeezing my neck. Pill grinned like a bastard, shaking his head. He was lucky. He was thirteen, too old and too ugly to be hugged. But not me. Me, I was still short and kind of pudgy in the face and old aunts and ladies thought it was a real goddamn cute thing to go and squeeze your cheeks or smother you with their lousy goddamn made-up makeup lips. I wiped her grease off my head with my sleeve and stepped aside. Two plump girls stood behind my aunt glaring with big dumb smiles.

"Now don't be bashful. These here are your cousins, Dough. This is Hildie. You remember her, now don't you?"

This girl looked like no cousin I could have ever had.

Her hair was short and blond and curled loose down around her ears. Her face was tiny and round and white. She had on a nice red plaid skirt and black shoes and thigh-high tights. This girl seemed clean and well-mannered as hell. Maybe I hadn't seen this cousin in a few years. Maybe until then that girl had been nothing but a runny-nosed little goat, fiddling at her mother's huge skirts. Now she was different. Now this cousin of mine was twelve. Now she was pretty and soft and clean as a pearl. Her tiny white hands were fidgeting behind her back and her eyes glimmered bright blue as she flashed me a real polite smile. Looking back on it now, it seems there was always some sweet-faced older cousin I felt some small ardor for, illegal or immoral as it might have been, there was something very nice in sharing some of the same stock with a delicate young lady like that. I had two second cousins who had met at a wedding and then gotten married themselves, and the whole thing caused a real row on my mother's telephone. Kissing cousins. It just seemed to me a kind of mysterious thing, something you knew you shouldn't do because you've been told not to, making it seem just as forbidden and pleasant and dangerous and attractive as hell. I just couldn't get the thought of kissing that girl Hildie out of my head. I didn't really know why. Maybe it was just that having a pretty girl-cousin like that was a way of knowing at least one pretty girl who had no choice but to talk back to me. It seemed my chances were better kissing a girl I was related to than one who wasn't so close and might decide I was too ugly or too heathenous.

This girl Hildie was a real pearl. I smiled back at her, feeling my face race with fire.

"And this is Pettina," my aunt said. My god. Poor ol' Pettina sure got the short end of the beatific stick. Pettina. This poor girl had been named after ol' Richard Petty. Number 43, racecar driving king, because my Uncle Dirk, Aunt Marie's husband, was a real stockcar fan and had some abscess on his penis and had to have it lanced and subsequently lost his powers of fertility and having bore only two girls and no son, it was the least concession my fat aunt could make on my uncle's behalf. This cousin, Pettina, sure was huge. Next to her slender older sister, she looked like some kind of pink pear or piece of fruit. Her head was round and heavy and full like some sort of fleshy balloon, her eyes were two tiny black dots that looked ready to disappear behind her two huge pink cheeks. She was biting at her fingernails, which rested at the end of five of the fattest digits I had ever seen. Each little finger looked like a plump little pork sausage that she kept nibbling from. I began to wonder if her awful name had somehow led her to such a portly place of humiliation and shyness.

"Hello, Dough," Pettina kind of snorted all in a huff, like it cost her a lot just to get those two lousy words out. This girl Pettina was chunky and lacking any kind of charm I could imagine. She wore a white-and-pink dress with yellow ribbons in her hair, which pulled her shiny red hair up away from her fatty little porker face.

"Here you go, sweetheart." My Aunt Marie smiled, pulling a thin present from her huge black purse. "Just a little something for one of my favorite nephews." This gift looked sad even all wrapped in its dull yellow paper and lousy silver bow. It was too small and thin to be anything good. She handed it to me and I gnashed my teeth. French pinched his glasses against his nose as he patted me on the back.

"Well, go ahead, pal, open it," he whispered. My brother, Pill, shook his head. Not another goddamn wallet. Not another goddamn wallet.

I felt the lousy gift in my tiny dirty hands.

No. There was no luck in my world.

This gift was going to be another goddamn plastic wallet. I could tell. Too thin, too light to be anything else. For a moment I gave up a hopeless prayer that what lurked inside was not a horribly stitched piece of vinyl but a knife, a red Swiss Army knife I had seen with my brother at the hardware store in town. I gave up an empty prayer that my fat aunt had somehow read my dreams and the thing waiting in my hand was exactly that sweet new knife. I peeled off the thin yellow paper and forced the worst fake smile I could ever give. That lousy gift was like a blow to the head. Another goddamn plastic wallet. Plastic wallet? My lousy Aunt Marie had gotten me a goddamn plastic wallet for every birthday ever since I was about three. I never used them. Heck, I didn't have a thing to put in them. They all just ended up collecting in the bottom drawer of a dresser full of old junk, like shark's teeth and arrowheads and old holy scapulars I had forgotten how to roll. This real nifty wallet was vinyl brown, not even simulated leather, but shiny brown with gold trim. There embossed in one corner was the single word, "Hawaii." The damn thing made me sick.

My older brother, Pill, let out a squeal. He laughed and made a real smug grin. Sure, this was all a regular riot. Another lousy gift from my fat Aunt Marie on my lousy eleventh birthday in a lousy dump of a town. Nothing was going to go right for me ever again.

"We got that for you when we went to the islands last summer." My aunt smiled. I nodded, not saying a damn word. "We know how old you're getting and a man needs a good wallet." Or a hundred crappy plastic ones, I guessed.

"Say 'thanks,' Dough," French whispered. I shook my head like I suddenly forgot how to hear.

"Say 'thanks,'" he whispered again. I clamped my teeth together and folded my lips in. There was a dull silence in the air, waiting, waiting, waiting for me to say "thank you" or "thanks" or "what a great gift, gee, thanks, you big old pig," but I didn't say a damn word, I just held it in and didn't breathe, until my big dumb dog, Shilo, marched right up and licked the back of my hand.

"What in God's good name is that?" my aunt whispered.

"That is our dog," I grunted, scratching the top of its ugly white head. Good ol' Shilo rubbed its face against my leg and then sniffed at Aunt Marie's feet. Its gray empty eye rubbed against her fat gray thigh as it laid its big paw on her chest.

"It sure is the ugliest thing I'd ever seen." Aunt Marie frowned. "Well, what happened to it?"

"It got hit by a truck. They had to sew its innards all back in and its eyeball got knocked outta its head and . . . "

"Dough . . . " French mumbled, staring at me hard. I frowned and shrugged my shoulders and didn't say another goddamn word.

My aunt's face went all sour. Her big red lips turned gray as she tried to afford a smile, but turned away.

"June, what kind of dog is that?" she called into the kitchen.

"Oh, you know, the boys found it so we gave it a home."

"Certainly doesn't seem healthy to have a dog like that just roaming around."

My older brother, Pill, shook his head and got up off the sofa and pulled on his gray sweatshirt to leave.

"Where you going?" I asked in a plea.

"Need to take the dog for a walk," he lied, pulling on Shilo's big black collar. That bastard Pill had never taken that dog for a walk before in his life. But now my damn aunt was there and her awful flowery scent and disapproving voice had begun to fill all of the poor trailer's air and my older brother was looking for any way out he could find.

"Why don't all you kids take the dog for walk? Give you time to get reacquainted?" my mother said, stirring something in a big yellow plastic bowl. Her face was sweet and thin and white and suddenly I thanked god my mother smelled like sweat and permanent wave hair products and grease instead of that goddamn phony floral nightmare that kept pouring out of ol' Aunt Marie.

"That sounds nice. It will give the a-dults a chance to catch up," my aunt said, grinning, phony as all hell.

"Christ," Pill muttered with a frown.

"Language! Watch your mouth!" my mother hollered. My brother shook his head and kicked the screen door open and all four of us stepped outside. The sky was pretty blue and bright and warm and full of big white clouds that hung over our heads like blots of fatty half and half cream. Poor ol' Shilo hopped down the stairs and back around the trailer to the big wide brown field that began just a few hundred feet away. There right in the distance was the dark red barn, a dark red dot at the very end of that field that stuck out from the blue sky like a scar or a wound. There in that barn lived the Devil and the cause of all the worst nightmares I had ever dreamed. I turned from its awful sight and stared down at Hildie's black shoes.

"I'll wait here." Ol' Pettina frowned, taking a seat right on our gray cement steps. Her face looked all round and sour like a goddamn prune. This girl seemed like it was a real problem for her to breathe without a frown. This girl seemed to be the unhappiest thing I knew. She seemed to fit right in our crummy little town.

"Fine by me, stay here if you want," Pill muttered, pulling his blue stocking cap down over his scabs. He dug into his pockets and pulled out a pack of smokes. He kept mumbling to himself, kicking at the dirt as he fumbled for a match. I paid my brother no mind. I kept staring at my cousin Hildie's tiny black shoes. Her black socks ended just below her bare thighs. That thin white space seemed like some kind of infinitely mysterious thing.

"Do you smoke?" Pill asked my girl-cousin, lighting up the cigarette. He took a long drag and let the gray smoke run around his head like he was some sort of real tough guy, like it might physically hurt him to be outside the trailer with such goddamn squares.

"Sure." Hildie smiled, plucking the cigarette from his lips. She fit it in her tiny pink mouth and smiled, taking a short drag and exhaling like a pro without choking on a lung or coughing up any smoke. Her face was a little sweaty and red around her cheeks. This cousin sure seemed like the nicest thing I'd seen in a long, long time.

"Did you ever smoke any grass?" she asked, taking another drag. I felt my eyebrows shoot up over my forehead. Lord. Grass? One of my mother's old boyfriends, Lenny, used to come over and smoke it all the time. Me and my brother used to sit at the top of the stairs and try to get high off all the smoke. Never did any good.

"Did you ever?" she asked again. This pretty cousin wasn't a clean little pearl at all. Her lips were curled tight around the cigarette, making her whole round face seem kind of shiny and a little older. This girl seemed as cheap as all the other high school girls I'd see walking home in town; smoking with their long thin hands bent just at the wrist, laughing with their big gray horse-faces, trading beauty secrets and about who made it with who behind the football field the night before. This sweet cousin of mine wasn't so sweet at all. It made me want to kiss her even worse.

"You've never smoked grass?"

"Sure," Pill lied. "I've done it a couple of times." Hildie finished off the smoke and flicked it into the deep brown dirt. Then she just took a seat, right in the goddamn grass, and spread her skirt over her pale white thighs. Then she ran her tiny white hand over her blouse and unsnapped the top snap. Then she reached down there to her faded pink training brassiere and pulled a pink stick of bubble gum out from beside that palest-looking skin and folded it right inside her tiny red mouth. My god, this girl was trying to be cute as hell. My older brother stared at her hard, not saying a word. His hands were dug into his coat pockets. His eyes were gray and big. He looked worried and kind of confused.

"I'm going back to the house." He frowned. Hildie shrugged her shoulders in reply. My brother backed away slow like he was trying to think of something else to say but then ran out of space to walk. So then he just shook his head and turned away.

"What do you do around do here for fun?" Hildie asked, snapping the gum on her lips. My own hands began to blister with sweat. My whole chest sure began to feel sore.

"We don't do anything," I whispered, not sure if my voice really could run that high or weak. Her nose twitched a little as she frowned and blew another perfect pink bubble-gum bubble. Her lips made a gentle kiss as the bubble blew and then snapped and disappeared back in her mouth.

"Do you got a girlfriend or anything?" she asked.

"Not me." I frowned. I wanted to sit down beside her bare white thighs. More than anything in my life. I wanted to hold her hand and sit down right there.

"Did ever kiss a girl, Dough? No, wait. Did you ever French-kiss a girl?"

"Nnn . . . no." I had wanted to lie, but it felt like she had pulled the words right out of my mouth. My lips felt dry as I finally got up enough nerve and sat on down.

"Why is that?" she asked.

"I don't know."

"Did you ever see a girl naked?"

Then again I knew what I wanted to say, but it came out all wrong.

"No."

"No?!"

Her plaid skirt was moving right over her thighs. I could hardly keep the spit in my mouth from turning to dust. I had seen a million naked girls in a million different nudie magazines. I had seen every beautiful inch, the cool wide hips, the nape of the neck, the back of the thigh, from bare toe to bare nose and not one centimeter from any girl I'd ever met or known. My heart felt low in my chest. Now this pretty girl had to know. I was eleven and hadn't even touched a girl beside my mother and all the damn lust in my heart filled my poor body ready to burn.

"Do you wanna kiss me?" she said with the prettiest singsong kind of little voice. Her eyes blinked under her soft curls. Her hand ran along my wrist. I could feel my hands curdle with sweat. I could feel my spine tingle up through my brain.

"Heck, I dunno." My tongue felt heavy and dumb. I could feel my heart moving, all my blood leaving my dumb round head. Her breath was right beside me. Her lips moved right beside my poor white ear.

"That's the only way you'll ever learn how. We can kiss right here."

Her nose seemed very prim and straight as she moved it beside my cheek. I shot to my feet and backed away, rubbing my face. Then all I could think to say was:

"Maybe next year."

I smiled and backed away, tripping over my clumsy feet. I stared at the thin white space of her thighs were she sat, holding my hand to my cheek where her breath still burned.

"You all ready for dinner?" my horrible fat cousin Pettina called from around the side of our trailer. Her face seemed to bloat up as she spoke. This girl didn't need another damn meal. She needed to do a lot less scowling and maybe take a walk or something. Her lips curled over into the ugliest smile as I nodded and walked around the trailer to the front door. Pill sat there on the steps with a scowl, tightening his fingers into tiny white fists at his side. There were voices, loud harsh shouts as he stood and put his hand against my shoulder to keep me from going in.

"It's a surprise they don't run away or go off hog wild! Young poor boys like that! Lucky they don't end up to be convicts or career criminals!"

My mother and French didn't say a word.

"Have you been taking them to church?"

"Sunday School every week, Marie." That reply was the awful truth. Every damn Sunday morning of mine and Pill's was spent with Mrs. Heget, the deacon's wife, and a roomful of godless heathens who couldn't tell the difference between our sinful ways and Jesus' sweet homilies.

"Well, what kind of a man goes around cheating on his wife?" my Aunt Marie screamed.

"We're not married, Marie," my mother whispered, banging a pot or pan. "And French here is the best man I've ever met."

"Well, why do you let him do those horrible things? Him with someone else's wife? You with another man? Parties in this trailer like that? I never heard of such wicked, wicked things."

My older brother Pill's face turned bright red. He stared hard straight ahead. That was one thing he could never stomach, one thing he couldn't stand. Maybe it was the real reason he didn't like French so much. Maybe it was the real reason he hated that whole crummy goddamn town. My mother and ol' French were swingers all right. They used to have their swinging sexy parties in our lousy silver trailer every other Friday night and smoke some green cigarettes of grass and drink some purple flower umbrella drinks and end up kissing someone else's soft-mouthed husband or pink-lipped wife. There were a few other couples who lived in the trailer park, a few other couples from town, all good god-fearing people, all plain and nice and bored who would meet in a trailer or home and sit around and laugh and joke and then get all drunk and kiss someone's spouse on their pale delicate neck and roll around with them on the floor until all their awful clothes were gone. The whole thing sounded like an elaborate game of Spin the Bottle to me and not worth the goddamn trouble of having to send us to Val's every other week, but both ol' French and my mother sure seemed to enjoy it and there was no way I was going to ever petition against the sweet smell of Val's warm white bed instead of mine.

"The whole thing's unnatural," Marie argued. "It just isn't right."

My older brother, Pill, gritted his teeth, clenching his fingers tight to the bone. He stood up and spat hard onto our neighbor's, Mrs. Garnier's, back porch. I pressed my face up against the screen, pushing my nose up against the door for a peek. My fat aunt had her arms crossed, all indignant and sour, hovering beside my mother, who mixed something in that big yellow plastic bowl. Her face was thin and sad as she turned the wooden spoon against the mashed potatoes inside.

"Do the children know what you both do?"

"No," my mother lied. She stirred those potatoes in that bowl slowly, keeping her eyes on the floor.

"Carrying on like that. You're gonna warp these kids worse than they are," Aunt Marie mumbled through her perfect white teeth. I turned away from the screen and shook my head. My older brother kicked the porch steps and then threw open the door. He ran into the trailer and snarled, staring up into my aunt's fat white face.

"Get out," my brother shouted. "Get out now."

"Pill!!" my mother mumbled.

"I mean it. If French is being too quiet to do it, then I sure as hell will."

"Pill!!!" French hollered, shaking his head.

"Get out!! Take your lousy daughters, too!!"

"Pill," my mother muttered. "Not another word."

"Well!" my Aunt Marie mumbled. Her face was all flustered and bright red. The fat on her face started to bloat and tremble as she held her hand over her chest like she had never heard such harsh words before. "It's no wonder these boys cause all the trouble they do. In a madhouse like this, I'm surprised they're not worse off!!" My fat aunt fumbled around for her purse, then stood by the screen door.

"This unclean life is not worth living!" Marie shouted. Her fat pink lips shook all across her face. "And you're all unclean as rags!! Filthy rags!!" Her lips stopped moving as she turned and wobbled down our front steps and back into the dirty brown station wagon that had delivered that ungodly woman to our door. Her poor, poor girls followed her into their car, not saying a word. The little ugly girl, Pettina, had begun to cry and mumble, pulling on her mother's huge white dress, but my other cousin, Hildie, just frowned and turned, popping the pink gum in her mouth, staring at my face as my aunt pulled their car back down the gravel drive and back onto a civilized road. There was something so sad and resigned in my cousin's sweet white face, something so cold and lonely, something I couldn't understand at all. Her face seemed tame and small like a dove, her eyes were tiny and blue and sad, and for once since we had moved, I was glad as hell we lived there, dirty and unclean the way we were.

My mother had begun sobbing, her face was all red and full of tears. She locked herself in the bathroom, crying to herself, running the water so we all couldn't hear how bad she felt. French shook his head, staring out the open screen door over his open can of beer.

"Jesus, Pill, what did ya do that for?" French asked, shutting the screen.

Pill stood beside me, still clenching his fists at his side.

"You weren't gonna say a damn thing," my older brother mumbled through his tightened teeth.

"There's a time and a place, pal. A time and a place, and this sure as hell wasn't the time."

My older brother glared at ol' French hard and then turned and disappeared into our dull blue room. I fell onto the sofa, staring at the black TV screen.

"Sorry about all this, Dough." French frowned. "It ain't right to ruin a man's birthday. This didn't have nothing to do with you at all."

Me, I just shrugged my shoulders and stared at the blank screen. That's exactly how I felt. Hopeless and empty and sure sick of my whole lousy lot in the whole lousy empty town where I had been moved to live.

"I'm gonna go talk to your mom," he muttered, patting me on my head. Shilo, my big dumb dog, came and sat beside me and laid his ugly white face on my lap. I scratched his thin white fur, rubbing my finger along the empty black space where his one black eye should have been. Then I felt sure of something. Right there, that moment, I just knew in my gut I was hopeless and doomed as

my dumb white dog. Half-blind and hopeless, that was all of us in
my lousy trailer. Too dumb to notice how awful and pathetic we really were. Sure, I loved my mother and my older brother and
maybe even ol' French, but they all just didn't care to see the truth.
We all were really as unclean as filthy rags. My fat Aunt Marie was
right. Right the way she had been about my own old man's pen-
chant for sin. We were all dirty and full of ignorance, with my
mother crying all the time and French drinking cheap beer from a
warm can and the both of them really having sex with other peo-
ples' husbands and wives and me and my older brother being rest-
less and wicked and godless and, above everything else, doomed.
All of us in that forsaken trailer were surely doomed.

My poor, poor heart felt full of black sap and drool. I stared
down into my dog's big white face. It had fallen asleep in my lap,
its big white hind legs were kicking in a dream, maybe some nightmare of being chased by a dark black force or being torn apart into
too many pieces to count. Its only good eye flickered around under
its white eyelid, dull and useless as it twitched and breathed heavily against my tiny legs. I shut my eyes right there and felt most like
crying, crying alone on a lousy couch all lonely in that godforsaken
ignorant town, without a single friend in the world. I was sure that
would be the perfect way to end the worst birthday an eleven-year-
old had ever had, but I didn't, I just kept it in and kept my eyes shut
and tightened my hands into hard white fists.

Then there was a knock at my screen that startled me right out
of my glum.

"Hello, Dough," that crazy girl, Lottie, whispered through the
door, pressing her big white forehead against the screen. "Are you
at home?"

This girl was sure crazy.

I smiled and shook my head and unlatched the door and
stepped out onto the porch. Lottie's face was all white and sweaty.
Her pig-tails were all crummy and coming loose along one side of
her head. Her eyes were bright gray and her cheeks were bright,
bright red. There in her hands, she had something hidden, closed
tightly between her tiny dirty fingers. Her ugly pink bike sat at the

bottom of our gray steps. She was smiling, smiling big and wide like some kind of crazy fool.

"I came 'cause I have something for you," Lottie whispered, leaning in close enough for me to breathe her sweaty breath. "I didn't make a nice box or wrap it up in paper or anything sweet, but I hope you like it just the same."

Her tiny white hands opened up in front of my face. There in the round part of her dirty pink palm was the most mysterious thing I had ever seen. The green glass eye. The glass eye that was to be embalmed into the richest lady in our town. My mouth dropped open and my throat dried up like it was sore.

"But . . . "

"My dad won't notice it's gone. That lady isn't gonna die for at least another forty years."

Her fingers moved against my skin as she placed the glass eye in my hand. There, cool and smooth like a dream, I could feel its round weight and strange gravity fill my palm.

"I shouldn't take this," I tried to lie. "If your old man found out . . . "

"Shush." Lottie smiled. "It's your own present now."

My whole face felt red as fire. I wanted to say something, to sum it all up in some nice words, but they wouldn't come, my poor tongue had somehow been betrayed and made stupid in my mouth. My lips were kind of heavy and trembling and I felt lucky enough to muster out, "This thing is sure neat as hell."

That crazy girl just smiled, all red-faced and embarrassed I guessed. That girl just smiled and didn't say a word but sure let out a sweet kind of squeal and hopped down my front porch steps and down onto her ugly pink bike and rode on home, shaking her head and singing right to herself all along.

That green glass eye was all mine.

I held it in my two hands. I laid on the old red sofa and placed it in my palms and watched it roll on my skin, glittering with light, shining with some sort of preordained beauty I didn't think I'd ever understand. I hid it in my front pants pocket as my mother and French came out of the bathroom. My mother's face was still all red and her eyes were pink and swollen. French had his hand on her shoulder and tried to serve us all dinner as best as he could, tying my mother's blue-and-white apron around his waist and spooning out huge helpings of my mother's badly burned food. My brother stayed holed up in our room, even for the cake, which sagged all on one side and was blackened on the outside but still somehow wet inside and not fully cooked. But I ate it all, I didn't give a damn; I forced it all in my mouth and after dinner sat out on the porch by myself, grinning at the way that glass eye seemed to glimmer and glare and shine and steal all the light from the dark silver stars that hung so low and awful in that blue-black sky.

Then after a while, I kissed my mother and French shook my hand and I went off to bed, careful not wake my damn older brother, who laid curled up in his bunk, mean and cold and facing the wall. I slipped under the covers and placed that gorgeous glass eye right on the sheets above my chest, staring at it as the light from my bedroom windows sparkled in through its perfect sight.

That glass eye was sure the best gift anyone could have ever given me. That glass eye was the best gift I think I ever got. No one could really understand it. Maybe not even Lottie. Maybe not even me. There was something golden there, something powerful and mysterious about that thing. Sure, there was nothing I could really do with it. That poor girl was probably going to get the whipping of her life for stealing it for me. But there was something about it, something priestly in that green and white blown glass, something I could only see and stare into as a moment of untold and unlimited possibilities. Even though it wasn't real, even though no one had ever had it loose in their head or set free in their skull, that glass eye, all round and green and shiny, was as perfect and full of insights as anything I had ever held. There was something so strange and wonderful about its cold shape in the palm of my hand. A third eye. A third glass eye that belonged to a lady rich with wealth. A lady who would have worn that eye to stare right through her own awful death. That glass eye couldn't help but see the truth through the murky darkness that hung above our trailer thick as the night. That glass eye was the keenest instrument of incorruptible hope I could imagine in my small mind. It made it seem as though the future was still a faraway thing, something I might not be able to ever clearly see with my own cold and immovable eyes.

"Look at what I got," I whispered, holding the glass eye beside my brother's sweaty head. I tried to wake my brother up to show him my prize, but he was more interested in his own rotten sleep than the wild ramblings of his younger sibling.

"That thing sure is stupid," Pill mumbled, rolling over in bed. He coughed a little, then yanked the covers up to his head. My big dumb dog sniffed the glass eye once, then laid its ugly face beneath the covers of my bed.

They couldn't see.

But me, I didn't care. I placed it on the sill of the tiny glass window right beside my bed and stared at it until I fell asleep, sure of all the ways everything would be different from that lousy night on, all right.

# the king of the tango

The dark had a single red beat.

That red swollen sound would rumble through the window beside me as I fought to fall asleep, turning within the blankets of my own bed. I guess at first, I didn't know if I was losing my mind or hearing some kind of spook or having another goddamn nightmare, but I began hearing this single beat-beat-beat-beat moving through that parted shade at night and then all I could do was yank the dirty blanket up over my head and mumble to myself that it was only a dream, sure, it was all just a bad dream and if I held my breath and that sound was still beating there, then all I could think was that I was surely going crazy for real. But then I began to hear singing, someone singing, and I stared out my bedroom window to the new silver trailer that had moved next-door and then I watched as a square black form moved in the dark to the beat-beat-beat-beat of the night.

That old man was dancing in his trailer naked again.

Mr. El Rey del Perdito. King of the Tango. He had a long gray face and a shiny full black pompadour that didn't look like it belonged on his withered old head. He was thick with big shoulders like an old athlete and moved very slow, except when he was dancing, and then, then he was dynamite. I had never seen anything like it before in my life. This old man was somehow unbelievable. I had lived in that trailer park for nearly two months and by then I had just about refused to be amazed, amazed by anything, when this strange old man just happened to move next to our door.

I pushed open the red curtains that hung from the tiny window in our small blue bedroom. I stared across the lot to the old man's big square mobile home. It still hadn't been bricked into place with mortar and cement blocks. There were still four huge black rubber tires that were slick with the dew of night. He had moved into the lot a few days before. This old man was crazy. Every night at about midnight, he'd put on an old tango record and shut off all the lights in his house and light some candles and just dance there naked in the cool dark.

His bare feet shuffled and slid across his bare floor. The mobile home rocked a little as he moved, stepping in time to the exotic muffled music that boomed through his shiny yellow curtains. I could see the flicker of candles along the glass of his windows and his shadow moving along the walls, back and forth, back and forth, swaying in time to the rhythm of the music and his sad, heavy heart, his wide feet sliding across the flooring as his thin shadow spun about.

"Jesus," I heard French mumble through the thin wood panelling. "It's past midnight. The damn boys have school tomorrow. What is that old man, a maniac or something? Doesn't he have any goddamn consideration?"

El Rey's feet moved without regard as the tango singer's voice peaked, shaking the windows in the old man's mobile home. I flinched as I caught a glimpse of the old man's great gray bare back and naked behind as he crossed in front of some of his windows. Pill snored in the bunk bed above mine, his poor heart lost in some lusty dream, unaware, dead to the world.

"That's it. I'm going over there," French grunted. I could hear him shift in bed.

"Oh, don't be silly," my mother whispered. "It's really kind of romantic."

I rolled my goddamn eyes and laid back down in my bed. My mother let out a giggle. I shook my head and pulled my pillow over my face as they began doing it right behind the damn wall. I gritted my teeth and stuck the corners of my pillow in my ears. Not again. This would be the third goddamn night in a row that they did it while I was just on the opposite side of their thin fake wood wall. Heck, I wasn't stupid. I knew my mother and French made love. I knew my mother and French had wild swinging parties on Friday nights so they could share their love with other couples from the trailer park. That didn't bother me. My mother had had boyfriends ever since my old man died. They would come over and kiss my mother on her lips and pat me and my brother's heads and send us up to bed and get sexy right on our old black sofa back in the old house in Duluth. They were always as quiet as hell at least. Ol' Pill would stand at the top of the stairs and listen, to try to hear if they were making it, so he could open up a nudie magazine or light a cigarette without having to worry about my mother intruding. But living in that goddamn trailer, having to listen to my mother and French do it, do it right in the middle of the goddamn night, and with the old man next-door dancing and starting to sing along with the record, it was more than goddamn a little frustrating trying to get to sleep.

I woke up the next morning, got dressed, ate some cereal, and watched as my mother gave ol' French a long kiss good-bye right in front of me, then she sighed as he took his lunch bag out of the fridge and disappeared out the screen door. Pill-Bug sat beside me, gulping some cereal down, dripping milk all over his shirt as he drank from the bowl.

"What the hell was that last night?" I mumbled.

"What?" My mother glared at me with a mean look in her blue eyes.

"All that noise?" I knew what I was trying to do. I was trying to embarrass her so that that kind of horrible undelicate consummation never happened in that trailer while I was there again.

"The new neighbor next door," my mother said, "is a dancer."

"No, not that," I grunted, staring my mother cold in the eyes. "The other noise."

"What other noise?" My mother dropped her gaze and poured herself some coffee from the cruddy blue coffeepot. She looked over her nails as if they were the most interesting things in the world.

"You know, the other noise."

"I'm sure I don't know what you mean." She took a sip of coffee very smugly, still staring at her nails.

"C'mon, Mom, you know what I mean. It's disgusting."

"Excuse me?"

"You're grossing me out," I mumbled.

"Well," her face blossomed bright red, her eyes searched all over the rim of her coffee cup, "I am sorry. I forgot whose trailer this is."

"It's gross as hell," Pill grunted, staring her in the face. "You're supposed to be an adult and all that. Can't you wait until we ain't around to do that stuff? It's sickening. Really."

"Well, some of the things you boys do gross me out a little, to be quite honest. All those nudie magazines in your bedroom. Don't you think that makes me feel a little ill?"

Pill's face went bright red. My mother stared right at him and he lowered his head, finishing off his breakfast in one quick gulp.

"I'm gonna be late for school." He threw his cereal bowl into the sink, grabbed his books, and shot out of the trailer like a rocket. My mother smiled a little, whistling to herself, washing out my brother's dirty white cereal bowl. She scrubbed it clean, then placed it in the dish rack to dry. Her eyes met mine in a sweet shock of uncomfortable silence. There was nothing to say. Somehow my mother knew everything I thought I had kept hidden in my own room and heart. There was no way I could keep a thing out of her magical big blue-eyed sight. I looked away, shoving another spoon full of Crunchy-O's in my mouth. The lines of her shoulders were soft and round as she wrung out the dishtowel and stared out the kitchen window, still whistling to herself. There in our own kitchen, my own sweet mother seemed like a still kind of mystery to me. Here, I had known her all my life, but there sure were plenty of things about her I couldn't ever hope to understand. There were things in her soft white face I couldn't even begin to imagine to see.

"Tomorrow you better come with me to the parlor," my mother whispered, patting me on the head. She pulled her fingers against my unruly brown hair. "You really need a trim."

My god.

That beauty parlor made me squirm with unholy sweat.

It was another goddamn horrible place of mystery and womanly order I couldn't even try to begin to figure out. The cackle of those ladies' awful cigarette-sweet voices was enough to make me squeal in pure agony.

"Be still, darlin'," my mother warned, snipping the scissors along. My own sweet black-haired mother worked at the Curl Up 'N Dye Beauty Parlor located in town a few blocks from the Pig Pen supermarket and a few streets over from the hardware store. Every other Saturday afternoon, my mother would cut my damn hair and I'd have to endure that awful parlor of pink and silver and cheap spray perfume from blue tear-shaped bottles and those voices, those damn whiny voices full of slim, unfiltered cigarettes and fork-toothed gossip I wasn't supposed to quite understand.

My mother's scissors tickled my neck. Clip. A breath of brown hair curtseyed to the shiny white tile floor.

"Well, when I told Danny, my first husband, God rest his soul, that I was pregnant for the first time, he said, 'What if I don't want a kid?'" Mrs. Larue whispered from under her green cat's eyes glasses and a mouth full of smoke. Mrs. Larue had had at least ten million ex-husbands. Heck, I wasn't even sure if they were all dead or she had just been divorced half-a-million times, but from all the different stories she had about different men, I kind of guessed her marriages only lasted until after the first act of connubial consummation. Mrs. Larue sat in a silver salon chair, smoking her long meaningful drags. Her face was long and white, her own hair was a kind of feat of beauty queen stature, like a great blue tuft of cotton-candy stuck in place by a thick coating of shiny hairspray. Mrs. Larue wasn't so much beautiful as she was glamorous. There were big black-and-white photos of her pasted up all around the store from when she was younger and a Miss Teen Queen and from other beauty pageants like that, and her hair looked the same in all of them. It was as if she had applied a thick coating of makeup and some everlasting styling spray to her face and hair to preserve their beauty. For me, though, her true beauty lied in her tight pants. Mrs. Larue wore the tightest pants I ever saw, bright pants, too, like polka-dot pink or bright green that showed her wide and divine hips.

"So I say, Danny, if you don't want a kid, you better split town now because it is on its way, honey, and there ain't a damn thing to do about it now."

All the ladies nodded and took drags on their smokes. There was Mrs. Larue in the silver salon chair, and Mrs. Darve in the chair beside her, and the deacon's portly wife, Mrs. Heget, who didn't even work there but came on Saturday afternoons just to gossip and who stood next to my mother, admiring the job she was doing on my head.

"My husband, Lucky, he was the most stubborn man I ever knew," my mother whispered. I cringed, gripping the silver metal chair. "When my first boy was born, he insisted on naming him Pill. Pill-Bug. What type of name is that for a boy?"

"Terrible," Mrs. Heget muttered. Her fat face crossed over a frown.

"That's what I thought. I asked him if it was some relative or friend or someone he was naming our boy after, but he said 'No. Just like the way it sounds.' I said, 'Why the do you wanna name your first born that?' And he said, 'A name like that will make the boy tough.' He named Dough here for the same reason."

"What?" Mrs. Heget whispered. "I don't think I quite under-stand."

"He figured these boys would grow up tough and mean from other kids teasing them about their names all the time. He thought they'd get in plenty of fights and then they'd have to grow up strong and learn exactly how to be men or die from trying. He was a fool. My Lucky, oh my, he was a fool all right."

"Men," Mrs. Larue mumbled.

"Do you know what?" Mrs. Darve whispered. Mrs. Darve was thin and had a white, pale-looking face. She had no eyebrows of her own. Instead, she drew them on for herself. Two deep brown smudged marks than ran over her blue eyes. It didn't make a damn bit of sense to me. Mrs. Darve smiled. Her fingers pulled the cigarette away from her mouth. "Last weekend when I went over to Aubrey to visit my sister for a day, I forgot to make a dinner plate for Eddie and so he ate half a jar of mayonnaise instead."

All the ladies let out a horrible, wheezy laugh all at once.

Mrs. Larue grinned. "Men are sure the dumbest animals I've ever met."

I gripped the silver swiveling chair tightly, squirming under the huge white plastic bib that fit me like a dress, tied too tight around my neck and too long for the rest of my body. My mother snipped again, leaving a few freshly cut hairs stuck to the sweat on my neck, reddening to itch for sure.

"Don't squirm, Dough," my mother whispered. My own mother was a pretty lady, not pretty like Val or even Mrs. Larue, she was pretty like a mother ought to be, like the Virgin Mary or a mom you might see on TV. She had her black hair nearly cut to her shoulders in a nice bob and she never wore any tight pants that I ever saw. Most of the time, she was quiet and gentle the way you'd want your mother to act, but sometimes, sweet Jesus, sometimes she'd just surprise the hell right out of you.

The sweat on my neck began to itch all right. I could feel my mother's breath against the back of my neck as she worked the sharp edge of the scissors around my ear.

The shiny silver and pink door flashed open, slamming against the door post as ol' Mr. Darve strode in, shaking the whole parlor with the fervor in his sweaty blackened eyes. He wore a blue-and-gray work-shirt from his job at the service station. His hair was greasy and black and stood up in the back. His face was all whiskered and red and hard-looking right around his eyes. He looked dumb and mean and drunk as hell.

"Where is it, Dolores?!!!!!" He strode right up to his wife and gripped her by the front of her puffy pink sweater. Mrs. Darve's smudged eyebrows seemed to tremble.

"Where the hell is my liquor, woman?!!!" He shook her hard, snapping her head back and forth on her thin shoulders. He raised his hand back and swung, cracking her with the back side of his fist. Mrs. Darve's face was bright red, red from the mark, and sore from the awful humiliation running down her spine.

"It's gone," she mumbled, trying not to cry, but the tears were already there. "It's all gone."

Mrs. Larue had snapped to her feet and had forced herself between Mr. Darve and his wife, inching her wide hips in front of him with some sense of control. My mother had stopped trimming my hair.

"Just a minute, Eddie, you aren't bursting into my store and starting some trouble."

"Can it, Edna. This is between a man and his wife."

"Like heck it is," my own mother muttered. "This is Edna's place. You can't just come in here drunk and start trouble."

Mr. Darve shot my mother a cold, mean look, still gripping his wife by the front of her sweater, stretching out the neckline so his bride's faded white skin showed down to her square shoulder.

"Where's all my goddamn liquor!!!" he shouted, shaking his wife again. The deacon's fat wife, Mrs. Heget, had backed away, standing in the shadow of the big blue bulbous hair dryer that arced behind her.

"You let go of her, Eddie," Mrs. Larue warned. "Before I call the police."

"You call the police. 'Cause theft of a man's liquor is a crime, too."

"She didn't steal your liquor," my mother whispered, her hands on her hips. "She poured it out."

"Poured it out!!! You poured it out?!!!" He shook her hard, accentuating each word. Tiny blue streams of tears ran down Mrs. Darve's face. She held her husband's arm, not trying to break free, just holding his arm, as if it was his awful arm and not him keeping her rooted in place.

"Now you're gonna pay back every damn red cent you owe me for that hooch," Mr. Darve shouted. "You understand?"

Mrs. Darve nodded through a sob.

"I said, do you understand?"

Her blue eyelids flickered with tears. "Yes."

"Good." He let go of her sweater. "Go get your purse. I'll take what you got now."

Mrs. Darve trembled to her feet and ran in the back of the store, sobbing. Mrs. Larue followed, pushing open the tiny pink curtain and disappearing into the back room. Ol' Mr. Darve's face was bright red. He sneered at my mother, holding his hands on his hips like a proud fool. He made me feel a hard black knot in my stomach.

Mrs. Larue stepped from out of the back, holding her hands behind her back.

"Well, where the hell is she?" ol' Mr. Darve asked.

Mrs. Larue squinted hard and stepped right up that poor dumb bastard then shoved a shiny silver pistol right in his face. It was a small shiny .22, but sure powerful enough to blow a hole right through Mr. Darve's thick white skull.

"Don't move," Mrs. Larue warned, sticking the muzzle right in his eye. "Don't move or poor Dolores will be a widow."

Mr. Darve let out a little squeal.

"It's okay, Dolores. Come on out," my mother whispered. "Come on out." Mrs. Darve appeared from the back room, holding herself. Her face was red and puffy from crying, her pretty pink sweater was all stretched out and hung off her shoulder completely. She stepped in front of her husband, staring at his face.

"Now you tell this poor woman you love her. Go ahead. Tell her, you bum," Mrs. Larue shouted.

"I love you," Mr. Darve repeated, squinting hard.

"Tell her she is the only one for you," my mother muttered.

"You're the only one for me."

"Tell her you're sorry for ruining her prom for her by making her cry," the preacher's wife shouted.

"I am sorry for ruining your prom for you by making you cry."

"Now kiss her hand." Mrs. Larue smiled.

Mr. Darve reached out and kissed his wife's hand. The horrible black fear rested in his dim, empty eyes. My mother took a tube of dark red lipstick from the beauty counter, uncapped it, and pressed the tip against Mr. Darve's forehead. Mr. Darve grunted a little as Mrs. Larue dug the pistol harder into his eye, keeping him still. My mother pressed hard, smearing some dark red letters across Mr. Darve's shiny white forehead.

"D-R-U-N-K," my mother muttered, finishing the job. "Now everyone will tell before they have to take a whiff of you."

Mr. Darve clenched his fists hard. Mrs. Larue jabbed him in the eye with the muzzle, backing him toward the door.

"If you ever lay a hand on poor Dolores again, I swear to God the last thing you hear will be me laughing over your old dead bones." Mrs. Larue shoved the gun hard against his cheek.

"Now go home and sleep it off."

Mr. Darve shot out of the beauty salon and out into the street, holding his eye, mumbling to himself stupidly. All the ladies let out a breath. Me, I let out a breath, too. I reached back and wiped a handful of sweat from my neck. Those ladies were crazy all right. My own mother, too. She was just as brave and tough and ornery as the rest of them and I hadn't known it all along. It was a real surprise to me to see her handle herself like that. I had always thought it was my own old man that had kept everything in our lives straight and in line. Now I wasn't so sure.

The beauty parlor was definitely a place of some sort of mystery. My mother was as foreign and unknown to me as any other woman I knew. She might seem strong and brave one day, hollering at me or my brother for lighting something of hers on fire, but then maybe late at night I'd hear her crying, out in the sofa room all by herself, with her knees buckled up to her face, crying all alone in the middle of the night until French would wake up and comfort her and lead her back to bed. My own old man had told me that my sweet mother had nearly died when she was a baby, and it had been a real danger for her to have kids, especially two ungodly boys, but she had insisted and my mother could be stubborn and hard as anyone I knew. My own mother had been born with an abnormally large heart, too big to fit on the inside. When she was born, the doctors had to keep her in one of those glass tanks for a few weeks and shove that damn heart back inside before it grew any more. My mother's big swollen heart could make her sweet as pie or make her break down and cry at any moment of the day.

Then there was her and her poor, poor Jesus that forced me and my brother, Pill, to go to Sunday School every week on account of our old man's soul lost somewhere in Purgatory or Hell and our own souls seemed about sure to follow. The Sunday School was a real horror show every week and part of my mother's plan to save her hell-bound boys before it was too late.

"What do you mean kissing is a sin?" Elroy Viceroy shouted. He was tall and thin and fourteen with all kinds of swollen red pimples all over his face and the real smart-ass in Bible Class. "That ain't one of the Commandments."

Mrs. Heget smiled. Her round pink face blushed. Mrs. Heget would surely go to Heaven for trying to instruct us blasphemous fools every Sunday afternoon. Her soul was good as gold for sure. She was a round woman; her waist was thick and quivered as she spoke. She tried every Sunday to get a bunch of trailer park and farm kids to understand the true nature of the human spirit and to understand God's unconditional love for all of us, but it wasn't easy, maybe it wasn't even possible. No one in the class wanted to be there. I knew I'd rather be asleep or at home watching a game with French or out running around with some matches or trying to teach that dumb dog Shilo how to kill. Mrs. Heget's voice was sharp and brassy like a kind of trumpet. That voice may have been the only thing that kept any of us awake. To me, Mrs. Heget's sharp-toned warbling was nothing less than the voice of a God I'd surely never know.

"First of all, kissing before marriage can lead to sex and masturbation. And well, sex, well, sex is sex. And masturbation is not proper behavior for a growing boy. It could lead to damage and injury and even night blindness."

Mrs. Heget tolerated our lack of enthusiasm with a certain degree. She was always polite and calm, but to be quite honest, I didn't want to be there and I didn't care for a word she said. All of us in the class were born sinners according to her. We were all destined to burn. Nothing could save us but our repentance and God's love. I don't think I even knew what that meant. The thing that got me was the way she was so damn condescending all the time. Telling us what we were and weren't supposed to do and think and say. Heck, I was eleven. I was having a dirty thought every other minute. Jesus seemed real nice to me, so did the rest of all the saints and prophets, but I guess I didn't understand much more than that. My own soul was a mysterious thing to me and no amount of time in Bible Class had helped me shine a light on any of the gloomy darkness born in my chest.

"Night blindness?" Elroy muttered. "How long does it take before you go blind?"

"Not very long." Mrs. Heget frowned. "But it is still a sin and something you will either have to confess or pay for in the afterlife."

"Well. I can still see fine so I'm not worried yet."

"Any other questions about Purgatory?" Mrs. Heget asked.

"I got one," I mumbled, raising my hand.

"Dough." She smiled, crossing her wide white legs beneath the big blue billowy dress.

"If you're a good person, right, and you commit some sins, but mostly you're good, do go to Hell or not?"

My brother, Pill, rolled his eyes in the desk beside mine. He shook his head and resumed staring at the back of Lulla Getty's neck.

"Well, Dough, that is an interesting question." Her round face bubbled a little as she figured up an answer. Her lips fluttered a little before she spoke.

"I think if you're basically a good person, and you've accepted Jesus into your life, well, I think then God would surely find a place for you in Heaven."

"Okay, well what if you were a good person and committed a crime?"

"What kind of crime?"

"I dunno. Stealing stuff."

Her face blustered a little around her pink eye-shadowed eyes.

"I think if you're truly sorry, then God will forgive you. God will always forgive you. He cared so much about all of you to send his only son to die for all our sins. He'd forgive you if you really wanted to be forgiven." She took a breath and nodded to herself. "Any other questions?"

"Okay, so what if you die in the middle of a crime? Like you're robbing a bank or something, then you get shot."

"You're probably going to Hell then." Her answer was curt and full of frustration. Who the hell else was I going to ask? The spiritual depth of my older brother, Pill, ended with the pages of all the nudie books he kept hidden under our bunk bed, same with French, whose true religion rested somewhere between a cold beer and the sofa and the old dog and television, and my mother, my poor mother was so filled with the Holy Ghost that it sometimes kept her up at night, and I was afraid if I ever asked her about mine or my old man's soul, she'd split apart like a beautiful broken painting or vase.

"Well, what about Purgatory and all that? Doesn't that count?"

She let out a little sigh, trying to gather herself. She made a little smile and stared at me.

"Like I said, Dough, if the person truly wants to be forgiven, then God willing, they will be forgiven and granted a place in Heaven."

My face felt warm. Maybe this fat lady was all right. Maybe she knew a thing or two about the in's and out's of all that spiritual darkness. Maybe there was some hope for me and my brother after all.

"Does anyone else have any other questions now?"

The whole tiny classroom was silent. I felt like asking her about my mother and French, if hearing your own unwed mother make it with a man was some sort of prenuptial sin, but I just gave a sigh and held that question in. Pill was staring at a single freckle on the back of Lulla Getty's neck. This Lulla was a real sinner all right, too. You could feel it when you looked at her. She made you feel kind of dirty and mean. This girl made you feel dirty for all the things she could make you think you could do. I had seen her walk home smoking with her hand bent right at the wrist, gossiping about something with her dark red lipstick burning like a wound on her lips. Then some nice new red Camaro drove by and then stopped and ol' Rudy LaDell got out and hollered a thing or two and Lulla swore something back and then she just shrugged her shoulders and they both hopped into the car and then they both just sped away, down to the old gray road that led to the drainage ditch by our trailer park, and it was there that I saw the two of them wrapped in some unconnubial lock of lust, her long sixteen-year-old legs wrapped tight around his back, rocking the car as I stared from down in the ditch, shaking my head. This girl, Lulla, was as lost as me or my brother, all right. Her poor neck would have swelled up on fire if the heat from my brother's eyes ever touched her skin. I stared at him and smiled. He was hopeless all right. His mouth was dropped open a little, his eyes were all full of hopeless sin and fantasies as he made little kisses with his mouth, dreaming of Lulla's lips.

"Pill? Are you all right?" Mrs. Heget asked. Pill snapped awake. He sat straight up and knocked the nicely silver-bound Bible to the floor and rubbed the side of his face. Everyone in the Bible Class stared at him and laughed. Lulla turned around and shook her head. Her curly red hair hung over her face as she shot my brother a dirty look.

"Creep," she mumbled.

He reached over and picked up the Bible and started staring at the back of her neck all over again. No doubt about it. He was doomed for sure.

Then after about an hour of Mrs. Heget's mumblings of sweet poor Jesus and protests of all our indifference in her sharpening warbles, the whole class ended with Sunday service in the dark gray pews of Our Queen of Holy Martyrs Church. That steeple seemed less like a place of God than an awful empty funeral parlor and made my teeth feel sore in my head, staring up at that skinny man slung up on that wood cross, all disemboweled and dead and left there to hang alone. There right above the altar was a thin bloody mess of a man I couldn't ever fight to turn my stare away

from, a thin long-haired man who would have been a union car-
penter or son of an unwed trailer park couple if he had lived in our
town and time for sure.

Then as the service moved on, through kneeling and posturing
and silent prayers, all I could think about was my own old man's
funeral and how cold and gray his long black casket had looked,
how the flowers had dried because of the heat, and my mother had
cried without a stop until someone gave her some Valium to fall
asleep and my fat Aunt Marie wailed as they heaved the coffin out
of the church and that forever kind of sound of that big black box
disappearing down, down, down into that shallow bed of dirt and
earth. All those kind of memories could make me feel about as unwelcomed in that holy place and the thin eyes of God as anything
could, besides the fact that neither me nor my brother had ever
been properly christened or baptized and then all I kept waiting
for was that thin man on the cross to part his perfect gray lips to
cry out, "There will be no sinners in my Church! No sinners in my
church!!" Then maybe a tongue of fire would spring from my head
and I'd run out of the church in tears, now sure in my heart there
was no hope from Jesus or Saint Peter or the Virgin Mary or God
or the pope or the church or anywhere.

That day I came home from service and stopped outside my
new neighbor's newly erected tiny white picket fence. It surrounded the front of his trailer, making it seem more like a home.
My brother had decided to go and walk down the road to the filling
station to try to pick up some smokes and new porno mags to wipe
all that holiness off his clean skin, but me, me, I stood outside Mr.
del Perdito's white picket fence and stared at the old man lying
nearly naked right on his own gray front steps. These things with
my mother and French making it every night had to stop. Mystery
or not, it was a thing that was keeping me awake and by then I was
pretty sure hearing your own mother making it with her boyfriend
was at least some kind of venial sin.

"Hey, you live here right?" I grunted, staring at his bare olive-
colored chest. He had on some white-colored pants though his feet
were as naked as the day he had been born. They were hard and

gray looking and looked well-worn out. There was a tattoo of a brilliant green snake that wrapped around one of his bare upper arms and another tattoo of an angel praying just below the opposite shoulder.

"Yes, sir. My name is El Rey del Perdito. I am the undisputed King of the Tango of the new world. What can I do for you, my friend?"

I got right to the goddamn point.

"Do you think you can cut that noise out at night?"

"Perdon?" the old man said. He stared at me, a little shocked by my lack of politeness. He sat up and rubbed some sweat from his face with a small white towel.

"All that music. It's driving my mother crazy," I mumbled.

"Oh *lo siento, perdoname*. I am sorry. I didn't think anyone minded my dancing. Let us talk about it over a cold soda, shall we?"

His white teeth glimmered in his head like they had been shellacked.

"Sure, I guess."

"What's your name, sir?"

"Dough."

"Very wonderful name, my friend. Let us retire to the mansion, Dough, to secure some soda, eh?"

"All right."

He opened up the screen door and held it for me as I stepped inside. El Rey's entire motorhome was empty as a church. There was a small record player in one corner, a cardboard box full of records beside it, an old gray refrigerator in the opposite end of the place, and some pillows and blankets thrown in the middle of the floor. There were all kinds of candles planted along the windowsills and along the floor in some sort of mysterious pattern that dribbled wax in tiny beads of gray. El Rey walked across the bare floor with his bare feet and opened up the refrigerator. He pulled out a cold can of soda and placed it in my hand.

"Hey, who's that?" I mumbled. There was a black-and-white picture of a beautiful dark-eyed woman with long dark hair that hung above her shoulders in a mystical arrangement of jeweled combs. The photo sat right on the floor beside the old man's makeshift bed. Her dress was a tight corset and sparkled with more jewels around the bodice. I picked up the picture and stared at her round face.

"That was my wife. Dolcita. The Tango Queen of Santa Anna," he said, staring up at the ceiling. "Her feet were made of tiny hummingbird wings. The way she moved when she danced, it was like flying."

El Rey made a little dance move, holding one hand to his hips, his other hand gripped the hand of some imaginary dance partner as he turned in time to the rhythm in his head. "Da-da-da, da-da-da. Her feet were glorious. They were like angel's feet. Better than angel's feet. They were like the feet of God." He turned and stopped and stared down at me.

"She died last April. Cancer. It ate out her whole belly. There was nothing we could do to save her. There was nothing we could do to stop it all from happening." He stared down at the picture and smiled. "Sometimes I feel like I am in the middle of a horrible dream. That I am caught in the worst nightmare of my entire life and there's no way to escape it and suddenly everything is gone and I feel so hopeless and alone that I don't ever want to sleep again. Did you ever lay in your bed too scared to fall asleep? You feel like the whole world is on your head and you'll never be able to sleep again."

I shrugged my shoulders.

"That's the time I dance, my friend. That's the perfect time right there." He strode over to the tiny black-and-gold record player and pulled a shiny black record from its sleeve then set it in place. Then he dropped the black arm and needle into the proper plastic groove. "That is the best time in the world to let all that agony right out through your feet."

The tango music boomed on. His bare gray chest began to get sweaty as he moved.

"C'mon, Dough, dance. Dance with me!!"

He grabbed my tiny hand and set me into motion, swinging me about. He was old and gray but still kind of strong. He danced be-

side me, then spun me across the room. I suddenly froze in my
spot. I was altogether unrealistically and positively afraid my older
brother would come in and see me dancing there and call me a
"homo" or "faggot" and then the whole thing would be something I
would never be able to live down.

"That's it, my friend. Now you've got it." His bare feet slid
across the floor as he began to hum along.

"This is the only way to keep her alive. The dance," he shouted
over the music. He gave a little hop, then did a quick turn and
bowed just as the music ended. He held his position and blew a
kiss to an imaginary audience.

"Bravo!!" he shouted, taking another bow. He picked up the
tiny white towel and began to wipe his forehead and bare chest.
"*Bien. Muy bien.* You're well on your way to becoming a great
dancer."

He patted me on the back.

"Hey listen, Mr. Rey, you're making my goddamn mother some
sorta sex pervert and all. Do you think you can cut that music out
at night or not?"

"Do you really want that?" he said. "Don't you want your
mother to be happy? In love? Don't you want her to feel young
again?"

"No."

"But how can you sleep at night knowing your own mother is
lying awake unhappy? How could you sleep knowing I am in here
lying awake, too? I need to dance, Dough. I need it. I need to shake
the old age loose off the skin of my feet. I need to shake all the old
ghosts loose. I need to dance in the dark until I think I might die,
too, then I know I'm ready to go to sleep and dream about my
sweet."

I shook my head. This old man was entirely confusing. He
wiped some more sweat from his forehead.

"Don't you worry, son. Love will find you, too. You have so
much time, though. Don't worry." He patted me on my greasy head
and sent me out the door.

"I'm sorry you must leave now, Dough. I must practice the cha-

cha-cha for tonight." El Rey closed the door behind me and I cringed as I heard the needle strike the record and reverberate within the empty motorhome. There would be no sleeping again tonight.

I opened up the screen door and stepped inside our own trailer. My mother and French were at the kitchen table with the old lady that lived in the lot behind us, Mrs. Garnier. Old cat lady maniac. Her face was tiny and gray and tight-skinned. There were a number of fleshy carbuncles that grew under one of her eyes. Her hair was long and white and gray and pulled tight in a bun on the top of her head. Ol' Mrs. Garnier had at least three million cats, all ugly, underfed, scrawny gray cats with rotten black faces and worms that bled from their rectums, ugly cats that scratched at her screen door all night and hissed and dragged bloody woodland creatures home to her front door and fought each other in the gray, gray gravel dirt of the trailer park the same way me or my brother did. Old Shilo had nearly torn one of those cats apart a few weeks before, catching the poor feline in its short gray jaws before me and my brother could pull the damn thing loose. Shilo had pulled a hunk of fur and skin from its mangy neck, though. That was a whole other affair. Mrs. Garnier came stomping over, threatening to sue and all that, unless we kept poor Shilo chained up. That big dumb dog was not too happy about sitting on the end of a length of chain. Now during the day, the dog hopped around in front of the trailer on his three legs howling and snarling like some awfully deformed unnatural marionette.

My mother smiled at me as I slumped on to the sofa and stared back at what they were all talking about. Old Shilo came up and dropped his head into my lap. I rubbed him under his neck and strained to hear. Mrs. Garnier had a piece of paper all knotted up in her tiny gray fists and she was talking so excitedly that spit kept shooting from her mouth. Maybe she had been living with so many cats for so long that her rotten old head had begun to take their triangular-shaped form. Her rotten old head perched on her shoulders like a horrible little cat-skull, darting back and forth with spit and a little hiss as she talked.

"It's indecent." Mrs. Garnier frowned. "An old man like that doing those kinds of things late at night, it's indecent. There's children running around all night and day, what would happen if they saw what was going on over there?"

This old lady, Mrs. Garnier, had caught me and my brother smashing blue bird eggs from a nest we found in a small tree in the field behind the trailer park. That old lady had grabbed me by my ear and my brother, Pill, by his hair and led us around the front of the trailer and told our mother exactly what kind of degenerative heathens we were to be torturing such poor unborn creatures. "Heathens!!" that's what she had called us. "Heathens!!" I had seen at least half of her brethren of felines murder, maim, and mutilate nearly an entire species of robins, rabbits, and any other small unlucky creature that passed the dark gray shadows cast by the old lady's trailer. I had once seen two or three of her cats tear a rabbit into several bloody parts, strewing its remains all across the front of her steps in streaks of red and black. I had urinated right outside her bedroom window in some sort of revenge to it all, I guess, but I don't think it did any good. Her entire trailer stunk of cat piss and overfilled litter boxes anyway.

"Now wait a minute." My mother frowned. "No one said you had to watch what that man does at night. You can just close your curtains if you want."

"What about the noise? That horrible music blaring. Him banging around all night. It's inconsiderate to say the least. Don't you agree?" Mrs. Garnier turned to French this time for support.

"I guess," he said. His face was long. He looked like the old lady was wearing him out.

"I'm an old woman, and all I have left is my sleep. We pay too much to live in this park to be disturbed by the likes of some pervert. I guess, when it comes down to it, it's a question of morals. I'm sure you wouldn't want your boys to see the things going on over there, would you?"

"No," my mother said. "But . . . "

"But, nothing. Are you going to sign the petition or not?"

"No." My mother frowned.

"It is a shame your boys don't have better role models to look up to. Bad apples don't fall far from the tree."

"Good day, Mrs. Garnier," my mother announced, opening the screen door for her as the old woman waddled out.

"Hmphh," the old lady grunted, wobbling down the front steps.

"Witch," my mother mumbled as she shut the door. French shook his head, taking a swig from his silver can of beer. "Who does that old bag think she is to go around bothering people like that?"

"Doesn't look like it matters. There were enough names on that petition without us." He sat the beer can down and stared out the kitchen window. Mrs. Garnier pounded on El Rey's screen just once, then slipped the petition between the door and the frame and wobbled away.

"I guess I'll go work on the car." That damn black Impala was sure to never get off those four concrete blocks. I think French had taken several strange steel-colored parts out of that lousy car that must have belonged to some kind of airplane or boat. He opened up another can of cold beer and patted me on the back.

"Feel like giving me a hand there, pal?" French asked.

My mother smiled at me dumbly, proud as hell at her good taste in men, I guess. French's face was all wrapped up around his big dumb smile. There was some kind of stupid shimmer in his teeth and some real paternal glimmer in his eyes.

"Sure," I grunted, digging my fists into my pockets. French pulled a six-pack out of the fridge and stepped outside. I followed, helping him yank the dirty white tarp off the useless black car. We folded it between the two of us and set on it down beside the rear blocks.

There it was. Oh, '72 Impala. Absolute vehicle without hope. Even the thick red rust on the wheel wells looked like it didn't quite have the heart to set in and completely eat out the doors. We stood there before it, me, shaking my head with a frown, French grinning, patting his belly, eyeing that ugly black prize.

"She's a real beauty, isn't she." French sighed, taking a sip of beer. Jesus. This poor bastard was blind as hell. There wasn't anything on those concrete blocks but a corpse, a goddamn derelict left up on an empty tomb.

"Let's see if she'll turn over." French grinned, propping open the driver's door. Turn over? Turn over? That car had never ever started before. He must have sure felt lucky, making it with my mother three nights in a row, dreaming that that poor hollowed-out empty vehicular nightmare would ever turn. I leaned against the side of the car, shaking my goddamn head.

French slid the dull silver keys into the ignition, closed his eyes, and gave the ignition a quick turn.

There was a sputter somewhere deep inside.

"No hope," that damn thing seemed to whisper.

Ol' French gave it another mean crank.

"Give up," the damn engine block wanted to reply.

French let out a sigh and leaned back in the lush vinyl seat, then took a big swig from his silver can.

"Doesn't look like it's our day, does it, pal?"

He finished off the beer and crushed the can in his one hand in a true show of raw human power and skill. He yanked another silver can off the plastic ring and tapped the top three times, staring at me with a dumb wide grin.

"You ever split a beer with your old man?" he asked.

I felt my teeth snap against my lips. Old man? Who was this guy to even mention my own dad? He must have been feeling drunk as hell or right at home to even make those lousy words come off of his stupid thin lips.

"Do you feel like tasting a sip?"

I stared at him hard and shook my head.

"C'mon, it'll put a little hair on your chest."

I shook my damn head again and spat into the dirt. French shrugged his shoulder and pulled himself out of the car with a grunt, then propped up the hood and dug his head under that greasy black sheet of metal, searching for the indiscernible cause of the mechanical commotion that prevented his fine automobile from performing a proper start. I leaned against the back of the car, hoping the damn hood would drop and lance off his big thick head, maybe leaving his body under the wheels of the damn use-less machine that was sure never to roll. I stared over at El Rey's big mobile home and watched as the old man was hunched over, applying the second coat to his tiny new picket fence. There was sweat all along his bare chest and back. His face looked tight and solid and stern as he moved the thick black brush over the slots of wood, singing to himself some tango or cha-cha-cha. Here was a man who could understand. Here was a man who had seen the lurid ghosts of his quiet life moving all over his old grayed skin but still found a way to move ahead. Here was a man who was quiet but knew all the right words when he spoke. I smiled to myself, then turned and watched French tear out some big slinky silver mechanical device from under the hood.

"Here's our problem all right." He smiled through a face full of grease. I shook my head and turned back. El Rey ran the brush against the wood. His greasy pompadour shimmered and shined. He looked old and content and fine. He looked right at home. Then a thin, dumb-looking man walked up to my new neighbor's white fence.

"Yer the man that lives here, then?" the tall man asked. There was a glare off the tall man's square white head. His hair was long and black, his eyes glimmered gray with light. His single eyebrow formed the bottom of a wide sloping forehead. He wore a dark blue pair of overalls and had a wide silver shovel in his hand. It was Mr. Deebs. The funeral director from two lots down. He was no director of any funeral at all. He was the man who dug the ditch they dropped you in after dreaming your last dream. He lived alone in a big baby blue trailer on the other side of the tiny gravel road. Mr. Deebs was some real kind of strange bastard. He was the guy who used to stand behind his screen, cleaning his gun, while he watched me and my brother sit on the side of our trailer, smok-ing our squares or shooting the bull, and he'd just stand there be-hind his screen with a thin little smile, swabbing out his rifle's firing mechanism, wondering exactly how long it might take to en-tirely dissect me and my brother limb from limb. Maybe he wasn't that bad, but you can tell a lot from the way a lousy bastard like that makes a smile. Well, that Mr. Deebs sure had the exact loony grimace and wide-eyed glare and thin metal wink of a real child-murdering type. The kind that would split you up into parts and dump you in a plastic bag somewhere in the woods for a lonely woodsman or farmer to find when he had to take a leak. Heck, even my mother didn't think it was right that a funeral director, gravedigger, whatever, a man who dealt in the finality of this mortal life, a man of his supposed spiritual stature and all, lived in a goddamn trailer park like the rest of us hopeless heathens. That Mr. Deebs just wasn't right. I don't think I had ever heard him mutter a word, except once, when me and my brother must have walked past his trailer, and I swear on my mother's grave I heard him whisper something like, "Sweeeeeeet . . . "

"You're the pervert that dances there in the nude at night. This is your place then?" Mr. Deebs frowned. He gripped the shovel tight in his one left hand.

El Rey put down his paintbrush and smiled. He wiped some white enamel on his pants and offered his hand to shake. Mr. Deebs just kept frowning, tightening his fist around the shovel's handle, holding his other hand at his side like it hurt.

"When you plan on leaving?" Mr. Deebs asked.

"What do you mean?" El Rey grinned. "I just moved in. I just put up this fence. I guess I don't plan on leaving for some time."

"That 'tis a shame for sure, my friend."

Mr. Deebs clenched his jaw and shifted his weight, tightening his shoulders in place. He twitched his lips a little, then looked down at the tiny white fence. Then there was a moment when I could see the dark gray slots in that bastard Deebs's eyes turn black, when his whole white face just twisted in a scowl and he let out a terrific shout and gave that old man El Rey a shove and swung that silver shovel hard into the tiny white fence. The old man tripped backwards, sprawling on his side along his concrete steps as Mr. Deebs kept hollering and spitting, tearing up the brand-new, half-painted fence, kicking at the tiny white posts, snapping the wood with the edge of the silver shovel he swung so hard in his hands.

Then ol' damn French was over there before I could even blink. He ran up to El Rey and grabbed the old man under his shoulder, helping him to his bare gray feet.

"You all right?" I heard French ask.

"Yes, yes," old El Rey said. His face looked tired and gray. He held his side like he was out of breath. Mr. Deebs smashed one end of the fence under his foot, pressing right it into the dirt.

"Now why don't you cut that out?" French mumbled, dropping his hands to his side.

Mr. Deebs looked right up and stopped swinging. His big wide forehead was caked in sweat. His teeth were bared and shiny.

"Mind your own business there before I cut you on down next." Mr. Deebs nodded and frowned. He cleaved the top of the rest of the fence with another angry swing.

French shook his head and gave Mr. Deebs a shove, pushing him in the chest.

"Now I said cut that out!!" French shouted.

Mr. Deebs gritted his teeth and brought the shovel up over his head, then down, catching ol' French on his shoulder with the flat side of it. There was cold dull thud in my ears that sounded like the sudden arrival of someone's dirty red blood. French fell to his knees with a grunt, gripping his neck in pain. Goddamn Mr. Deebs shouted something in some strange language mixed with spit and brought the shovel up to swing again. Then French started and gave a little grunt and lammed that bastard hard in his gut, then cracked him a good one right in the jaw, knocking some blood loose from Mr. Deebs's white shiny teeth. Mr. Deebs raised the shovel to swing once more, but French wrapped his big arm around that thin bastard's throat and wrestled him to the ground, pinning his face into the dirt, getting him in an ol' hammerlock.

"Don't make me snap your goddamn neck!!" French shouted. "Go on, be still!!" French kept squeezing hard until Mr. Deebs gave in and just laid there still as hell, kicking his foot in little circles in the hot gray dust.

"Don't make another move or I'll crack your goddamn neck!!"

My mouth was dropped open was wide as it could go. My teeth

had dried with spit and nearly punctured my lips as I tried to breathe.

"Don't ever come around here again, do you understand?"

Mr. Deebs grunted something through the dust. French let that Mr. Deebs-bastard go and the thin dirty man took off down the little street, into his blue trailer, leaving his shovel and blood and mess all in the dirt outside old El Rey's house.

"You okay?" French asked El Rey. El Rey smiled and nodded again, then patted French on his back and then coughed and climbed on into his mobile home. His face looked empty and old. The way he was holding his side looked like he had been stabbed. The tattoos on his arms suddenly looked tired and thin and dull and drab, the grace in his step looked cold and ill. Then French turned, holding his shoulder, and looked me right in the face. Me, I didn't move. I didn't say a word. He kind of stumbled toward our trailer, clenching his shoulder and gritting his teeth.

"C'mere," he whispered, tightening his face in pain. I wiped the sweat off my face and wandered over to where he stood in front of our trailer door. His long thin face was covered in sweat. His eyes were small and dull like was about to fall asleep.

"Be a sport and go get me my beer."

I shrugged my shoulders ran over and pulled the rest of the six-pack off the roof of the black car and placed an empty plastic ring in his hand. He sat down on our unfinished porch with a groan, then took the four cold metal cans and placed them against his neck, rubbing his shoulder with a frown. I stared at him, watching as a trickle of blood ran from the collar of his dirty white shirt on down.

"Don't think this is the way you're supposed to handle things, pal," French mumbled, wiping some blood from his neck with the palm of his hand. "Because it's not. You should always try to talk things out. That's what a real man does." He took a deep breath and stared over to where that nice little fence had been. "But sometimes I guess it just ain't that easy. Sometimes people are just dumb and make you do something you don't wanna do and you can't back down because that's the exact problem of being a man."

Poor French was still breathing hard. I guess he was as stunned as me. He had knocked that poor bastard down like some sort of prize fighter. He had taken care of business all right.

"Let's go inside now and tell your mother what happened." He stood and spat hard out into the gravel. That was the first time I realized exactly what he meant. He had punched a man out over a tiny white fence and a crazy old man right in front of our home and no bloody shoulder was shaking him loose. He had put up with me and my crazy brother and my mother crying by herself at night, and for some stupid reason, he was still standing around. Maybe that was exactly what it was all about. He was no quitter. He was in for the long haul and the best thing I could do was just get used to it.

I opened up the screen door for him, watching as he stumbled inside. My mother was on the sofa and turned to smile, but then caught sight of French' sorry frown.

"June," French mumbled. "There was some sort of fight."

"What happened to your neck?!!"

My mother broke into tears right away, but at the exact same moment put some ice on the neediest part of French's swollen skin. Unmysterious as hell, my mother opened him a cold beer and helped him to their bed. There was nothing confusing in her movements. Everything she did for us was out of her big red swollen heart. Every time she hollered or cried or burnt a meal was out of her incessant undeniable love. French let out a groan as he fell into bed, maybe hoping his wound would profit him some sound sympathy love.

Sure enough, in the middle of that night, I heard my mother laughing through the walls and their closed bedroom door. I kept waiting to hear Mr. Deebs breathing at our windowsill, shiny shovel in hand, but I guess ol' French had given him a real scare and he didn't ever poke his thin greasy head in our trailer's direction again.

Then the very next day El Rey's empty mobile home was gone. No one said a word.

No one really could understand. Not even my poor mother or

ol' French, who had both stood up to help him stay right next door. Maybe in both their parental hearts, they might have never known what the King really meant to me. He was someone who might have been able to see right past all my hate and anger and fear to the cold dull spot where my treacherous nightmares burned. He might have been the best thing that ever happened to that god-damn town or trailer park, and all our neighbors were either too dumb or half dead to understand. They were all either too blind or too tired to see. He was a ray of light in a gray and miserable place. He was a ghost no one wanted to believe because a nice thing like that makes an empty space whenever it leaves.

Two nights after he left, I stared out the window late at night to try to see if he might return. I crept out of bed and pushed the red curtains aside and pressed my nose against the dirty glass and stared out at the empty gray lot. He was gone. His mobile home was gone. There was only the dark and the cool blue shadows of the clouds overhead that didn't move in any time to any music of our lonely night.

# the dollar-eighty-nine story

**P**ush not pull, pale-face."
Me, I pulled on the big silver door handle for the hundredth
time, shaking my head in a nervous confusion. The old Injun grumbled at me from behind the counter through the glass door.

"Push!! Push, fool!! Push!!"

Me, I kind of shrugged my shoulders, and gave the door a good
solid push, smiling at the tall, red-faced Injun as he shook his head
and turned away. The bell above the door rattled as I stepped inside, right past the sign that read:

"Real-Life Injun Artifacts" and the rows of old Mars Bars and
rotten candy that lined the shelf in front of the gas station counter.
Chief's Filling Station was the only goddamn place in town that
would sell cigarettes or porno magazines to minors. It was a gas
station about three miles away from our trailer park and a good
hike even on a clear day, but depending purely on the mood of ol'
Chief, the only clerk and a lousy goddamn drunk, you might walk
all that way and not return with either a pack of cool smokin' Marlboros or the latest glossy issue of *High Society*. He was a real bastard and the only Injun I ever knew, except the ones from TV, and
those were about as real as those naked ladies all spread out in the
nudie magazines I surely loved. This would be my first time trying
to buy smokes without my older, still underaged, brother, Pill. But
now I was eleven. For nearly two full weeks. Almost an adolescent. Almost pubescent. Almost a man. To be honest, I guess I
thought the chances were about as likely I was going to walk out
of there with some kind of cigarettes as me or any kid my age

might have trying to become an astronaut, but I felt like I owed it to myself to give it a try. There was nothing to lose but a swollen amount of budding pride.

"Gimme a pack of Marlboros, unfiltered," I kind of stammered, staring up into the Chief's thin, porous face. His whole face was wrinkled like a gnarled old tree. There was a big bulbous knob right between his eyes that jutted out of hard skin and all kinds of crazy lines that ran down and around his face in thick, branchlike wrinkles. His eyes were bloodshot and red as hell and he stank like a goddamn open bottle of sour mash. He had long black hair that was all knotted behind his head in a pony-tail, gray all along the edges, that ran down his back. He wore a black shirt with a string of beads looped around his neck. He would have been spooky as hell if he wasn't drunk and I sure wouldn't have tried buying smokes from him if I ever thought he might actually be standing behind that counter stern-faced and sober.

"Show me some proof of age," he grunted, all in slow, single-syllable words, the only words he could muster from his swollen red tongue. That drunk bastard had to be kidding. Kids like me were the only ones keeping him in business anyway.

"Oh c'mon, man, don't be a drag."

His big gnarled-up face remained cold and expressionless. He pulled a silver flask from his back hip pocket, uncapped it, and took a long draught. A single bead of liquor ran down between two hard wrinkles on his chin and disappeared somewhere inside. The gaps between his reddened flesh led somewhere dark and deep like the roots of a tree. "Do not think I do not know how old you really are," he whispered, leaning over the counter. "You are nothing but a baby to me."

He let out a loud thick laugh that echoed in his wide throat and sent liquor-stained spit right in my face.

"Oh, c'mon Chief, stop busting my balls. I'm old enough already."

"What do you know about being old? What do you know how to know about being old?"

I rubbed my face with frustration.

"Listen, man, I just want some smokes."

"You listen, little boy, and I will tell you a story about what it means to be old enough to call yourself a man."

He took another shot from his flask and leaned his big red face closer to mine. I could smell his hot, sweet breath. I could feel it moving upon the bridge of my nose.

"Three full days before my thirteenth birthday, my father took me out of our home and out into the woods. My father was a great warrior and chief of our people. He had helped get a new school built on our reservation and running water in our homes. His white name was John Cloud. My people called him Great Gray Cloud."

The Chief's eyes were black and stern. The folds on his face had tightened into a serious plain of red flesh. The perfect cylindrical taste of a Marlboro was beginning to fade from my poor lips with the Chief's seemingly unrelenting bullshit. Don't get me wrong, as far as all the other bastards in town went, the Chief seemed like one of the few people I wouldn't want to set fire to. He had a quiet kind of nobility about him. But it was hard to respect a man who couldn't finish a sentence without a goddamn shot from the flask. My own old man was said to be a drinker before they found him pinned under the back wheels of his big rig, and if it was one thing I knew, liquor was just another of one of man's many ruins.

"My father took me out into the woods to observe an old ritual among our people. The passing of boy into manhood."

He took a swig from the flask. I didn't look away. I wanted to see if he would cough. He did.

"He lit a sacrificial fire and asked the great earth spirits to welcome me into manhood, to help me break from my childish ways and become a leader of our people the way my father had. My father took me to the sweat lodge and we sat there for two days where we prayed to Coyote and the Four Winds and there we had visions and he told me of the promise I would fulfill to our people. On my birthday, my father took me on the great hunt."

His eyes were twinkling like stars in the sky, far away and silver and blue. He was drunk for sure.

"There was an old wolf that had raided our chicken coop ever since I was a child. This was no ordinary wolf. No. This was a great spirit wolf with the marking of Coyote, the trickster. He would leave only two paw prints, side by side in the snow where he tracked. Two prints like a man. He would wring the chickens necks and not touch their eggs, and when my mother would go to collect the eggs and crack them open, there would only be blood. My father had been tracking the wolf since I was a child. My father was a great hunter. But he would set traps for the wolf and when he would go to check the traps, they would always be empty. He had raised a whole litter of dogs to track the wolf. The pack he had raised had fought with the wolf a dozen times, but the wolf would always escape. Only once had my father ever really seen the wolf, and it was that time that I was ten and my father had taken me with him to hunt pheasant. This all made it clear for him. This all made sense in his clear mind. The wolf was waiting. The wolf was waiting for me."

My mouth was empty and dry as the Chief took another swig.

"On my thirteenth birthday, my father and I set out to kill the wolf. He brought his dogs along and I had my mighty Winchester and he had his compound bow and we tracked the two-footed wolf down into a shallow canyon all covered with snow. There down the canyon ran the two paw prints, side by side. The walls of the canyon were too steep for the wolf to climb out of. The canyon ended in a old brick dam that was also too steep to climb. My heart was filled with fire. I felt humbled. If I shot and killed the wolf, I would be made a man. If I somehow missed, I would for-ever lose my father's favor. My father stopped at the ridge of the canyon and nodded to me. He unleashed the pack of dogs and the dogs ran down the ridge. They tore through the snow. They barked out loud. They disappeared into the darkness. They had the great wolf trapped. I could hear it. I marched down the canyon and then looked back at my father. He stood there like a mountain with his hands in his pockets. He could tell me nothing more. Everything had to be already learned. I switched the safety on my gun off. The mighty barrel had turned to sweat in my cold hands. The dogs were silent now. The cold white wind was silent now. All was quiet. Everything was waiting. Would I be made a man like my father? Or would I fail and bring shame upon myself?"

My own hands were covered in sweat. I couldn't move. The Chief leaned in even closer, his big gnarled nose nearly touched my ear.

"The dark shadows of the canyon fell upon my back. There was the end of the canyon. There was the old dam. There my father's dogs were silent. They sat on their haunches completely still. They sat beside one another in a kind of half-moon. There in the darkest part of the canyon was the wolf. The wolf was white and silver. He was black. He was huge. His head was huge. His front haunches may have came up to my shoulders. His snout was long and sharp. His eyes were the deepest blue I had ever seen. There he stood completely still, staring right back into my own weak eyes, his sides breathing with the cold in my own chest."

"Then he moved. A silent move, a move of grace. He ran right through the dogs, right up the middle of the canyon toward me. I felt my finger along the trigger. I felt his heart in my own throat. His eyes were my own eyes. His breath was my own breath. The wolf bounded right before me. I closed my eyes. I heard him whisper. I pulled the trigger. There was no sound. There was nothing. Then there was only a sigh like snow falling on soft ground. The sky above me turned black. The wind whipped against my face. The game had ended and I turned back."

My face was bright red. My whole face was bright red.

"What the hell happened? Did ya kill it? Didja?!!" I kept asking. The Chief leaned back, lowering his head. His eyes sparkled like mine, then turned deep and dark and black, something welled up in his face that made him look fine and dull and old. He stared down into my face and shook his head. He pulled a pack of cool smokin' Marlboros from behind the counter and slid them across to me.

"Dollar eighty-nine," he mumbled.

"What? Well, what the hell happened?!! Did you kill it? Didja?!!"

"Do you want the cigarettes or not?"

I stood there, dumbfounded, staring up into his dark face. His old black eyes ran deep and hollow. I placed my money on the counter, still stunned. He hit the cash register and placed the money inside. I backed toward the door, feeling all the weight of my body in the back of my knees. My hands were greasy with sweat. The little bell above the door rang as I pulled it open.

"I killed the wolf," I heard him whisper to himself. He let out a hard little cough that made my own lungs hurt in my chest.

"That was the worst day of my life."

The cigarettes felt like a thousand pounds in my hand. The cigarettes were slick with sweat. Somehow I was already outside my trailer. Somehow I had already walked home.

There was nowhere else in town I would even consider trying to buy cigarettes or porno magazines from after that. Even if some other place would have sold them to me, the Chief's Filling Station had some mystical hold on my heart. I used to go there about every other day after school, buy some smokes like an old pro or maybe just a candy bar, and old Chief would always be there behind the counter, drunk as hell, stern-faced as a priest. He was one of the few people in that goddamn lonely town that seemed like he had any kind of heart at all, drunk and swollen with the hooch as it may have been.

"Do you know what is out there waiting for me?" the Chief whispered one day as I placed a Mars Bar on the counter. I stared up into his cold gray face and shook my head.

"Nothing. No one," he grunted. He took a long pull from his flask, licking his lips as he swallowed. "No peace. No sleep. No father, no mother, no wife. No baby. There is no great meetingplace. There are no feasts. Those are poor dreams a fool believes so that he may feel better about being dead."

I shrugged my shoulders. "You don't believe in heaven?" I asked.

"No." He hit the Sale button and the cash register drawer flew open. "If there was a heaven, it would be a cold, cold place. There is nothing good waiting for anyone when they die. There is only your fear. Only your fear."

I counted out my change, dime, dime, quarter, and slid it across the counter. He was breathing heavily. His breath was rolling around the air in great gray fumes. He was drunk worse than I had ever seen him before. Then I noticed something. There was a tiny blue baby shoe sitting on the counter beside the register. There were two small silver bells tied to at the end of the laces. Those laces were untied and frayed, dangling and worn. The rest of the shoe looked nearly new. I stared at it, biting my lip. The Chief stared me in the face then pushed the shoe away, dropping it in a drawer.

"My boy," he whispered. His eyes were filling with tears. He began to scare the hell out of me. He reached across the counter and grabbed my shoulder.

"How old are you?" he gasped between breaths of tears and snot.

"Eighteen," I muttered. His warm liquored breath ran right in my face. His eyes were dark black and huge. His lips were pink and looked dry enough to bleed.

"How old are you?!!!" the Chief shouted, shaking me hard.

"Eleven!!" I let out like a coward, dropping the candy bar from my hand.

"Eleven." He smiled. "You've had eleven years to yourself. Eleven years all to breathe." He held me in place as I began to feel my knees knocking together. His forehead was huge and sweaty and enormous and wrinkled. His skin branched out all over his face in thick grooves of flesh.

"There is nothing to believe," he whispered. Thick silver tears broke down his cheeks. "Tell me what am I supposed to believe . . . "

His fingers were digging into my shoulder. His long fingers were gripping my collar. My bottom lip was trembling. My eyes were filling with tears, too. He was right inside my heart. He was right in all my dreams.

"There is no good. No good in this place, is there? There are things you love and things you have that all go and burn and die. There are things that are part of you and your heart that fall to pieces and leave you stranded like a dog."

He shook me once.

"Tell me what will help me . . . "

"Just let me go," I whimpered.

"Tell me who will help me . . . "

"You're hurting me," I whispered, trying to pull free. He let go, his long thin fingers let me free as I tripped backwards, spilling to the floor.

"I am sorry," he whispered. "I am sorry. Take whatever you want. Take it all. You can have anything you want."

He laid his head down on the counter and began to sob. I pulled myself to my feet. I didn't move. His voice was like an old woman's as his shoulders shook. His sobs were dry and hard and empty. I began to back toward the door. My fingers moved along the silver door bar. I began to pull it open slowly. The bell above the door gave a little twinkle. The Chief lifted his head and stared into my eyes.

"Don't go to sleep. There are ghosts. There are ghosts waiting for you there."

I felt a cold shiver run down my spine as I ran out and home and into my bedroom, trembling under my covers until my older brother, Pill, came home and told me to get lost so he could look at his nudie magazines alone. I went outside and crawled under the trailer, right between the thick gray cement blocks, and lit a cigarette and waited for all the mobile homes around me to light up and for my mother to call, "Supper's ready," and for my brother to give me shot to the arm so that none of that whole afternoon would have really happened and everything would seem dull and warm again, but it didn't happen, my mother called, then again, and I just sat under the trailer until French came out and stared at me and asked me, "Are you okay, pal?" and I nodded and felt all the ghosts in the world moving toward me in the dark that had just fallen.

"Do you believe in ghosts?" I asked my older brother as we washed up for dinner in the tiny white-and-silver bathroom.

"No, what are you some kinda baby?" he snickered, rubbing his wet hands on his tee-shirt.

"No, I just . . . " I didn't finish and Pill stared me in the face and squinted a little.

"You alright?" he grunted. I nodded. "There's no such thing as spooks."

"What about Jesus all that? Souls and all that."

"Jesus? You mean, spirits? You mean like . . . the old man."

I nodded.

"He's dead. There's nothing else to it." He wiped his hands on his shirt once more.

"But you think he's in Heaven, right?"

"I dunno." Pill's face looked mean. "He died stealing something. I dunno how it all works. He could be in Heaven. He might in Hell, too. It doesn't matter. It ain't your problem." He patted me on the shoulder.

"But you said there ain't ghosts, right? So what about God? You believe in him still, right?"

"Sure. But I think he doesn't do anyone any damn good but himself." Pill opened the bathroom door and stepped out. My hands were still wet. I sat on the toilet, wiping my hands in the towel. My older brother didn't understand. We were both cursed. My old man's sins were running right in our own blood right as we moved and breathed. The Chief had been right. There was a ghost moving right from my old man's darkest dream right through me, through all of me.

"Dough, you coming to dinner?" my mother called.

"Sure." I hung up the towel and made completely sure I was

out of the bathroom before I reached around blindly and flicked off the light. The darkness made a sound behind me like a whisper, like a cold black call I could hear straight through my own weak heart.

# the devil lives in texas

**M**y nightmares had gotten worse the longer I lived in that damn town. Forlorn in Tenderloin since the end of that lousy summer. I had gone from having cruel lonesome dreams about tigers to wetting my goddamn bed like a little cry-baby every night in the thin two months we had been there. My nightmares were now something else. They were dreams so full of brimstone and hellfire that I'd wet all over myself in terror before I could even wake up and feel my own humiliation running down my leg. The Devil had begun to appear in my dreams. My old man was there, too. They would both meet somewhere on the road in Texas, a desperate black strip of mile, cast in blue and gray stones that ran straight through my head while I slept. There was no beginning to my dream. There was only an end.

They came down on my old man straight like the night. Three of them. My dad was a cold black shadow in the dark. He could hear the sound of blood in his ears that hummed like a silver engine, throbbing out of control. He turned to face his shadows, his maker, and then they came on down through my old man like a goddamn knife.

CRACK!!!!!!

They caught him under his chin with a thick black crowbar. They knocked his teeth straight up into his head. My old man was a lumped shadow on the slick black ground. Everything would turn to black blood under his hands, sticky and hot like tar. There was nothing around him but the thick square shadows cast down by his idle truck and trailer. There was nothing around him but blackness that spun above his head in sharp-cornered slates of dark sinewy muscle. Night had fallen, night had fallen straight through the top of his head.

My old man had been a highwayman. My old man's name had been Lou. Everyone called him Lucky. Even my mother. His face had been long and thin and whiskered black and his eyes had been bright blue and sad and there had been a long red fat scar that hooked from the corner of his lip around to the corner of his eye cut right by a spur into his hot flesh. My old man had spat tobacco all the time. He would let his lips fold over to the corner where the scar began and then he'd squirt a big load through the air with a smile. He had been a trucker. He had been a man of the open road. My old man had been a smuggler of stolen cigarettes. He had been a real cowboy and the most honest man I think I'll ever know.

They had found his body beneath the big black wheels of his eighteen-wheeler somewhere on a nowhere road in Texas. I had been seven. Pill had been ten. They wouldn't let me or Pill see the body when they brought it back up by rail. But me and my brother had listened. Pill had overheard exactly what had happened to my dad and then he knew some things himself that he didn't bother to offer to anyone but me. That's the real benefit of an older brother. The deliverance of an overheard truth.

My old man had lost his soul in some sort of deal. Maybe it sounds stupid to you, but I was only seven at the time, and when they shipped my dad home in a big mahogany box like some sort of present or gift, it somehow made more sense than anything else anyone was telling me. My old man had been a troublemaker and fighter just like me and my brother, and he had gotten himself into trouble with the law, or maybe the people who hired him to run the stolen cigarettes from town to town, but my dad ran into some real problems in his life and had been too proud to ask for help so he sold his goddamn soul to keep from getting arrested or shot and left in a ditch to be swallowed by coyotes or to have me or my brother or my mother torn to pieces and left on our shiny kitchen floor. He had sold his soul, and down there in Texas is where the Devil best decided to collect. My mother was still real religious, even before my old man got killed, and there was no way a spook could afford to come into our old house. She had had this real beautiful statue of the Virgin Mary, folding her hands in prayer, all silver and white and gold, with a crack right along her throat where she had been dropped. Her feet were bare and treading right over a snake. That was just beautiful. A barefoot lady standing on a snake like that, so calm and sweet; I'm sure a powerful thing like that will scare off any kind of evil, but my mother's faith could only last so long and far and I guess it just goes to show you everything will catch up with you, sooner or later.

They came down on my old man like the night all right. Three of them. My old man yanked his short silver knife from his belt, leaning against the big cold rubber wheel.

Three of them. Circling around. Three of them. Three black shadows like crows. My dad lunged and cut one down, cleaving the knife through one of their hands, sawing three full fingers straight off. The fingers landed in a perfect circle of blood with three drops each. The black blood soaked into the ground and vanished. The three fingers became white worms and crawled away. The wounded one stood without pain. They were not men. They were spooks or ghosts or devils or whatever you might want to call them. They were things I knew to be true outside my own sleeping heart.

My old man nodded, gritting his teeth. "Let's go," my old man grunted. "Let's go!!!"

They caught him with the crowbar again, poking him straight through his gray belly.

Breathe, old man, breathe.

He let out a grunt, clutching his guts, trying to strike out with the knife, but his blood gave in. His belly tightened and pulled, heaving him to the ground. Big black dollops of his own innards broke frantically from his insides. His hands were covered in his own blood. His teeth were floating loose in his heart. The Devil had finally come to take his soul. He could feel his spirit slipping down and out his great black wound. There were sharp-eyed angels with knife-edged wings floating in a halo around my old man's head.

The three men drew tighter around him. He howled, trying to fight. The knife sweated through his hands in fingers of blood. Breathe, Pops, breathe. He coughed, feeling a shaft of light burning through his spine. The three men pulled the shiny silver trailer keys from my old man's front pocket. He coiled like an empty snake at their feet. He was shivering. He couldn't move. His black cowboy hat blew off his head. He could feel his own sweat which didn't feel like his own at all. He could feel his soul leaking through each of his pores into the dust.

Depart from me, ye cursed, into the fire prepared for the Devil and his angels.

He gurgled up more blood, trying to offer a curse word. They had stolen his heart. They had taken his soul.

The Devil appeared suddenly, a shadow twisted into another, spiralling into a single velvet form right in Texas. The Devil was the same awful creature I had seen in that lonesome barn, a tall thin man with the head of a hooded lizard, a monster who wore a shimmering cloak of red dripping with blood. The Devil's spiny mouth deepened as he set his tiny white teeth into my old man's chest. My old man was going to Hell. His ventricles pumped out fire. Pride. Goddamn pride. He had been a fool of his own pride. His teeth turned to dust and disappeared in the highway gravel. His skull became a stone in the pavement road. His ghost disappeared and folded in a flash of sulfur, leaving a little black mark in the dirt. He was gone. But his curse sure wasn't. It passed through all the streams and rivers and stones and blood right down to me and my brother and that was exactly why I was having goddamn nightmares about it four years later.

My own father had been taken by the Devil and me and my lousy brother were sure to go next.

Ol' Pill didn't like talking about my old man that much.

He'd rather talk about girls.

Me and my brother used to go down to that awful drainage ditch every day after school. It was about a mile from the trailer park and we'd smoke cigarettes and look at dirty magazines and just sit there and talk. There was one long gray-silver pipe that leaked green sewage water down into a small gray stream, right along this real steep gorge where brown sticker-bushes and some trees grew. There would be small blue racer snakes and stick bugs and things like that there, mostly we just went there to get away from the goddamn trailer park, because in a big silver tube there isn't anywhere to go to do some thinking but to your room or to the bathroom, and you can only spend so much time in either place before you start going crazy.

My brother passed me a cool smokin' Marlboro and I choked on it as he passed me a light. I let the smoke charge down my lungs until I thought I was going to die, then I tried to puff it out real smooth and cool, but it always came out in a cough. Pill just laughed, shaking his head, not doing much better with his own smoking technique, I'll tell you.

"Did you make it with a girl yet?" I asked. I felt like it was my duty as his kid brother to keep on top of these things on a daily basis. To be honest, I had no idea when it could happen. I had no way to tell if he ever made it or not.

"Nope." He said this like it really hurt him, his eyes got real thin and black and small and he stared down into the green creek like he was thinking something so heavy that there was no way he could manage to keep his head up.

"But I'll tell you about the time I fingered Gretchen Hollis."

He took a long drag, fighting to keep himself from coughing.

"We were at her pool party last spring, everyone had gone on home so there was just three of us, me and Gretchen and Bobby Shucksaw, but he had to go on home 'cause he had to go to the bathroom and he wouldn't use anybody else's toilet but the one in his own house so then it was just me and Gretchen sitting there all alone drying off."

Now don't me wrong, I had heard this story at least a million times, but every time, every goddamn time, it made my palms sweat and my head feel a whole lot lighter.

"So it's just me and Gretchen. Then she goes:

"'Wanna make out?'

"And I go.

"'Yep.' "

Now you might think my brother was making something like
that up, but I knew Gretchen Hollis. This girl was the one who was
pretty and round-headed with yellow hair, the one who ran around
naked through the sprinkler right on her own front yard and used
to skinny-dip or make out with any goddamn boy her age. She was
the first girl I knew in my old neighborhood in Duluth who got a
hickie and her old man, being a real drunk, beat the hell out of her
for it and sent her to school with a black eye that she wore for a
few weeks, not far from the red love-mark on the side of her neck.

"So we start making out."

"What's that like?" I asked.

My brother shook his head, like I was a total amateur.

"Listen, I'm telling a goddamn story here, you can't keep
butting in with your stupid questions, okay?"

He rubbed out the half-smoked cigarette and lit another, heaving up great plumes of smoke.

"So we're making out and Gretchen has on a two-piece and I
decide to go for first base." He accentuated this last remark by
making a real ripe gripping gesture with both hands, giving a good
squeeze with both mitts.

"So by now we're in the garage, right behind their car and
we're still making out and I got my hand up her top and then I hear
her old man hollering from her back porch."

Her old man was a goddamn monster. He had a big ugly square
jaw and plenty of whiskers. I'd seen him kick a dog once, not even
his own goddamn dog, it was our neighbors', the Gulls', he kicked
it square in the side and then cussed it out as it ran away. That's the
kind of man this Mr. Hollis was.

"And he keeps calling for her and by then I had both my hands
up her top and she was still trying to kiss me and I was starting to
get scared. I could hear her old man out on the porch looking
around and all so I try to stop. But she won't stop kissing me."

That's the part of the story I always had trouble believing, but
it's Pill's story so I'll keep it to myself.

"Then I can see Mr. Hollis's shadow, he's standing right in front

of the goddamn car, hollering and cussing. I can smell the goddamn stink of the bottle on him, he's staggering around, spitting
and screaming for poor Gretchen, I could feel his goddamn breath
right on my neck, he's right there and poor Gretchen is trembling
in my arms and my hands are all stuck up her top and I'm worried
as hell, too, now but I can't make a move and I feel his cold
shadow pass right over us, it passes right over us and goes back in
the house."

He let out a breath like he hadn't breathed all day, shaking his
head with a horrible grin.

"That's when she told me she wanted me to make it with her
right there."

Gretchen Hollis's tiny red lips would make those words over
and over again in my head.

"Make it with me."

"Make it with me."

"Make it with me."

Her eyes would be silver as stars and her head would be perfectly round. Her neck might be covered in some drips of pool
water and her curly blond hair might still stink of chlorine. Her
tiny white fingers would lock with my brother's and show where
she had bit down to the nail. Every time I heard that story I'd feel
my stomach tighten and my palms get greasy whenever he got to
that part. There was something magical about it. A poor blond girl
in her garage, half-naked, sweet as chlorine and the words, "Make
it with me," that always seemed like a moment of endless possibilities. Those words always seemed like they were the start of something great I understood a lot better back then.

My brother flicked his dying cigarette into the dim green creek
and looked away to finish the story.

"But I didn't wanna get her pregnant or anything like that, so I
just fingered her instead."

"What's that feel like?"

"I'm telling a goddamn story if you don't mind."

He shook his head, staring down into the creek as a tiny paper
cup floated by.

"Then she went in the house and as I was leaving I heard her old man screaming and hollering and I took a goddamn brick and threw it against the side of their house and I shouted, 'I fucked Gretchen Hollis!!!' loud as I could."

His voice cracked a little at the end. My brother's face was tight and gray. He lit a few matches and tossed them down into the creek to sizzle out. His outline was black and dim as he sat on a flat piece of broken concrete. He had a look like he had just said too much.

"God, I hate this fucking town. I wanna get the hell outta here."

He sounded helpless. He had started down a road that had been set out for him by someone else, maybe my old man, maybe the Devil, he was walking down this black, unlit highway, all alone, and even now he knew he had gone down too far to turn back.

"C'mon, we better get on over to Val's." He stood and stared down into the creek. My whole head felt empty. My whole spine felt loose. I could still feel the sweat drying on my palms.

The dark sky had just become to come on down all across the tin roofs of the square mobile homes in the distance. The trees along the drainage ditch had begun to become thin. Their leaves gathered in tiny piles at our feet. There was a cold snap in the air. There was the taste of burning wood in our teeth. Summer was surely over. A desperate sort of fall was already on its way.

The bare ugliness of all my dreams broke right through my poor pink flower, Val, all undone in some ungodly chiffon gown she had just been forced to buy for two hundred stiff dollars of her own sweet money, money she had raised piles of greasy plates above her shiny white tiara for, money she had endured the stares and sticky smiles of truckers all across the greater Minnesota highways to lay her poor fingers upon.

"No, it cannot be this gruesome."

My god, her beautiful white head seemed to be floating above some thickly unreal pink nightmare. Pink. The color of that peppermint antacid my mother made me swill after eating too many sweets. Pink. More sore to my eye than any color in the whole kingdom of colors. Val's whole tiny white bathroom seemed to fade around the unsightly pink ends of her unwholesome bridesmaid's gown. Her awful reflection flashed in the mirror as she turned, trying different poses and views for one that didn't seem so offensive. No position worked. The pink dress was haunted.

"No, it can't be this ugly, can it, Dough?"

Her face was warped into a still kind of horrible grin. Her long black eyelashes fluttered with fear. Her younger sister, Dottie, was going to be married in a matter of two weeks. Two weeks of having that awful pink gown floating around her sweet trailer house.

"This is the most repulsive dress I've ever seen," Val muttered, standing before the full-length mirror. "Pray this is my sister's idea of some kind of bad joke."

Her bare shoulders shone cool and pale like baby powder in the breeze. Beneath that dress she was bare naked. Bare naked. Her lacy black panties and brassiere fluttered along the shower curtain rod. My heart pounded in my chest as they moved a little, like whispers or some kind of foreign sighs. My Val. All alone in my sight. My brother had walked down the road to pick up some chow. Now it was just me and me dream. Val, so delicate, so sweet, made up like a chiffon clown in the worst parade of my mind. I eyed the way her skin rose like a flat plain of white flesh all across the round edges of her body and up along her neck and back down her bare white spine and ran down all the way to the godawful pink bow that sat at the bottom of her back. That bow was huge, a monstrous, puffy and kind of authoritative knot, like a huge fleshy pink scar. There in the spot where her wide white back became the pink dress there was some sort of confusion. Some sort of sinister magic. Val's pretty blue eyes began to well up with tears.

"This feels like I'm wearing some sort of punishment."

Val turned and glanced over her shoulder at the monstrous pink bow that rippled at the base of her spine. "What in god's sweet name is that supposed to be?"

I sat on the edge of the tub, trying to smile, but my sweet Val was right. That dress looked like some kind of pink curse. Her sleeves were like two huge pink cotton balls that nearly bloomed up around her ears. The huge lacy pink bodice ended in another huge nightmare pink bow. Then more goddamn pink bows along the skirt that ruffled like white icing above her feet. My poor Val looked less like an angel than some kind of unnatural pink sugar confection.

"I look hideous. Hideous. Like some sort of hooker. I look like some awful kind of trailer park trash."

Then my poor Val began to cry. Sweet Jesus, help me, she began to cry. That was something I could never ever hope to understand. A beautiful woman crying was some sort of force of nature a thing as meager as me could never hope to fathom or control.

"No, it can't be this wretched," my poor sweet Val muttered, holding her hand over her mouth and saintly sweet lips. Then she just kind of collapsed right there and fell to her own bathroom floor, sobbing into the folds of her awful gown. "I look horrible. Horrible . . . like a . . . "

Her sweet blue eyes blossomed with tears and ran down her smooth white cheeks, turning the pink gown darker where her teardrops landed. My bottom lip kind of trembled as I fought to think of some words I could use, something I could say that would make her stop crying, but none of those words came. My beautiful Val did look horrible. Horrible. There were no words in the world that could change that. Somehow dressed up in that nauseating chiffon gown, Val's sweet white face and long white legs and big blue eyes were somehow made cheap. Cheap as she might have always been. Cheap as that lousy town of ignorants might have always thought. This poor, poor lady was now no better than the rest of them. She was still pretty as hell, but different, somehow more hopeless, more desperate. Under the wraps of that awful pink dress, the truth was now as bare and stunning as the tiny black mole on her smooth white shoulder. My Val was indeed some kind of trailer park whore. My Val was as unwholesome and cheap as that collection of pink bows and slip of fabric. There in the mirror and along her blue, blue eyes was stitched the truth.

Then her pink lips split between one of her sobs.

"I heard Mrs. Heget in the supermarket whispering to Mrs. Groves. She called me a tramp. She said, 'There goes that little whore!!' "

Her eyes beaded with tears as she dropped her face into her hands.

"Do they really think I'm a whore?"

That sounded more like a strange answer than some kind of question, so I figured to keep my mouth shut. There was nothing I could think to say that wasn't what seemed to me to be the ugly truth, so I kept it all in to myself.

"I hate it here. I hate being a whore. Why can't I find a nice man? Why can't I meet someone who wants more than a body?"

My teeth began to ache. There was nothing I could say. There was a stitch undone in her pretty white face. The truth. The truth had fallen loose and now it hung around her long neck as open and unsightly as her sister's pink wedding dress curse. I tried to think of some way I could suddenly escape, like maybe by stopping my breath I could knock right myself out, but I just held my hands in my lap, twisting my fingers until they felt sore.

"I wish I could just leave. I wish I could just pack up all my things and leave this all behind. Go to a town where no one knows me. Where no one thinks I'm some tramp."

Her big black eyelashes flashed with tears and runny gray mascara that dripped down her cheeks. Then she pulled my hand to her sweet round face, holding it beside her lips. Then she kissed each finger, each of my fingers just once, still crying, still dripping her lousy makeup all from her puffy pink eyes.

"I'm sorry, Dough. I'm sorry to make a fuss."

Then she kissed each of my knuckles and tried to afford a smile. Her face was now gray and lined with tracks of her own shiny mascara and tears. Her lips seemed dull and less pink than her awful dress. Val pulled herself to her feet and stared into the mirror, gritting her teeth.

"I need to take this damn thing off."

Her fingers fought around behind her back.

"Do you think you can unzip me?"

My mouth went dry. Both my ears felt red hot.

"Sure," I mumbled, trying not to collapse.

There at the base of her back, beneath the ungodly pink bow was a thin pink zipper. I held my breath and pulled the zipper to its lowest point, nearly fainting as the two folds of dress fell open and showed the top of her bare behind.

"I'm going to take a bath," she whispered over her shoulder, holding the pink dress against her naked flesh. Then right there, more than anything in my life I wanted to touch her cool white skin and tell her all I things I thought I felt, that she was more beautiful than any gorgeous dream I had ever had, that no gown could ever make her charm die in my poor heart, that beneath her warm white shoulders and pink, pink lips, beneath it all there was a kind of beauty, a kind of truth, no faded pink dress could ever disguise or remove. But then in my fingertips and along my teeth, there was something I could feel, something I knew. It was all a lie. A lie that felt truer in my heart than in my head or my eyes. I pulled my hand down to my side and backed out of the bathroom, holding my fingers in a tight fist that I rubbed against my teeth.

Then right there the rest of the night became a sad kind of dream.

I did not stare through the keyhole to watch her take her bath. I did not even try to marvel at the wondrous sight of her bare white thighs or shiny blond hair. I held my face in the folds of her red velvet sofa, gritting my teeth. A little while later, my older brother arrived home with some horrible greasy gray fried chicken I couldn't even taste along my mouth or tongue. Everything seemed dull and sounded dumb.

"Don't you like fried chicken?" poor Val asked, cleaning off her plate with a smile. Her eyes were blue and dark, but still swollen and pink from crying.

"Not much, tonight." I frowned. We all cleaned up the plates and silverware and set them in the sink. Then it was time to sit out on the porch and whisper jokes and take tiny sips of Val's cheap gin, but somehow I just couldn't watch the awful way the liquor ran down her long narrow throat or taste the hollow smell of her lone sweat breath or listen to the sweet nothings she might then sigh, so I decided to fake a stomachache and wander off to bed alone.

"Do you want some medicine?" Val asked, kissing my forehead so sweet. "A cup of tea?"

"No thanks." I frowned and closed the thin white boudoir door. I climbed into bed and held my fists to my eyes and felt like crying again because I was sure they were both listening to hear if I was going to throw up or be ill. So I laid quiet in her soft white bed and just stared at my fingers under her sheets. Then a little while later, Pill followed, opening the bedroom door slowly to see if I was asleep. I looked him in his eyes and he shook his head to himself.

"You ain't really sick, are ya?" he asked, undressing in the dark.

"No, I'll be okay."

"It's that damn dress, ain't it?" ol' Pill asked.

"Sure is," I nodded.

"That thing is awful enough to keep you from looking at her again, huh?"

I didn't make any reply. He nodded to himself, instead. But he had seen the same thing. He had realized that we had both been fooled.

My older brother settled into bed and we both waited there, under her covers, listening for her nightly caller to arrive with flowers or wine or the taste of greasy drool upon his clean-shaven lips.

There in Val's soft white spare bed, beside my dumb sleeping brother in the dark, I felt more betrayed than I had in my whole life. Not by Val's sweet face or that awful pink dress or the cowboy or trucker who would soon arrive, but by something of my own, something that had made me a fool my whole life. My own heart and damn foolish eyes. I had been made dumb by my own sweet skin. I had stared at Val like a fool and held her close to my heart and it had all been a lie. A lie. That lady was no sweet dream. She was as cheap and empty was all the men she led to bed. I pulled her soft comforter up over my head, mumbling to myself through her big white pillows and sheets, hoping it was all a kind of dream I could somehow forget.

But then I couldn't sleep.

I just held my breath and listened and waited for one of her men to arrive. I held my teeth set together and waited, hoping they would somehow both exhaust all of the emptiness of their cold dark skins and hollow red hearts and somehow just wither away and die.

Then the sound of big tires rang against the gravel and the sound of an engine died outside. I gritted my teeth, rolling on my stomach, staring at the way the headlights seemed to flicker then dim, as awful and in time to the beating of the blood in my head. I held my breath and waited for the knock, then the sound of muffled laughter, then flesh, and then the sounds of her own stupid sins.

There was the knock.

But no reply.

No reply.

The knock came louder, a full-knuckled fist against the closed metal door. But there was no sweet whisper as an answer, no tiny laugh or sigh. I sat up in her bed, staring at the bottom of the closed boudoir door. There were no lights on. The whole place had been made dark. I squinted a little as another knock rattled the frame. Nothing, no one, not a single sound.

I looked down at my older brother, Pill. He was lying on his back, wide awake, listening to the stillness that rang from under the doorframe.

"Maybe she's passed out," Pill muttered through a frown.

"Let's find out," I whispered, hopping out of the bed. My bare feet struck her cold tile floor. I winced and tried to keep from shouting a curse, shoving my fingers in my mouth. My warm palm felt along the gold doorknob as I gave it a little turn. My older brother, Pill, stood behind me, wiping his eyes. I opened the door slowly and stepped into that soft lurid night.

There was nothing but darkness all around. No sounds, no movement, no drinks or records or laughs. The pickup and man had already left. There was not another knock. The sound of gravel rolling under slippery black rubber tires disappeared as that trucker or cowboy drove back into his lonesome violent life.

We stepped across her trailer, not whispering a word, staring at the dark soft lump sighing on the couch.

There in the darkness were her bare white toes.

I smiled a little, holding my breath, listening to her sigh in her sleep. Her golden hair shined as her chest dropped and rose. Her breasts moved with each sweet breath. Then I saw something terrible in her arms. She was not sleeping on the sofa alone.

There she was, undone like a dream, fast asleep, holding her warm white face to the billowy pink nightmare dress right at the seam of that awful pink bow. I stood above her, watching as her eyes moved beneath their lids, turning in her sleep. Her face was round and white and pure. There in her nose was a little snore that whispered like a tiny beautiful bell. My hands began to ache. I bent over and kissed one of her bare white toes. I felt her own skin upon my lips and held that breath in and turned to creep back to bed, unable to keep the taste of her soap from swimming around in my head.

My older brother stared at her bare feet with a frown, watching as her breasts rose up and moved. He held his breath in his lungs tight, moving his hand over his eyes. He followed me back toward her boudoir but stopped at the bathroom door.

There hanging in the darkness were Val's precious underthings. The dark blue light from outside shone upon their thin shiny lace, showing their soft identical curves and gaps and ridges and places where they would lie against her soft white skin. My brother stared at the way they hung there, hopeless and free, still holding his breath, trying not to breathe, trying to touch their soft threads with his eyes. There on that silver shower rod was ungodly mystery. Mystery and magic, the soft cursed fabric of illusions and kisses and lies. My eyes were fixed along those underthings' magical seams. I could feel their weight upon my sweat and skin. Then

I blinked and Pill had stepped inside the bathroom and had raised his hand to her thin black brassiere and touched their silk with one of his dirty fingertips. His face was red and dark, his mouth was dropped open and hard as he ran his fingers along its soft, smooth satin. Then in a single beat, he turned and snatched the brassiere from its clothespins and shoved it under his shirt.

"The worse kind of person is a goddamn snitch," Pill mumbled, glaring at my dumbfounded stare. "Keep your damn mouth closed."

So I did.

We climbed back into her bed and I looked at him as he folded the black brassiere up tightly and stuffed it in the folds of his shirt. His face looked long and white and mean. His eyes darted into mine as he sneered a little and laid back down into her soft white bed. I didn't say a word about it. Not then, not ever. He was my older brother, he was my only older brother and I was sure I'd go to the grave and straight to Hell before I ever turned a word against him about a personal thing like that. Maybe he had felt the same way, staring at Val all warm and lonely and passed out on that red sofa, sleeping so close to that awful pink gown. Maybe seeing her asleep and so delicate and all alone made him think she could somehow be touched. Maybe he thought he could just take her and fold her up under his skin and make her disappear down into his lousy black heart. He tucked her brassiere up under his shirt and rolled over, turning away in the darkness with a snarl.

I held my breath, staring at the back of his greasy head. His goddamn fingers must have felt the warmest they ever could touching that thin black fabric against his own dirty skin. That brassiere must have made a whisper, a small quiet sigh against his body, cooing like a tiny trapped dove under his weight.

I shut my eyes and felt the night moving over me, rolling like big black clouds, mumbling things I couldn't quite hear, moving in the empty light, trembling in the air around me, until I gave in to all that darkness and let myself fall into a deep hollowed sleep.

My body must have laid like the dead.

There were no nightmares that night moving around behind

my eyes. I slept in a dark black sleep deeper than I had ever slept in my short life before. I slept past all my dreams and desires and worst fears, down to the cold white marrow of the things I had always known in my own weak flesh and bones. There in the design of my skin was the truth I could see but couldn't ever hope to understand, a message, a sign maybe, a word passed from my dead old man or his sin or curse, something dark and still like a collapsed lung or heart, something I knew I could never hope to make right in my waking mind. I slept in that dark sleep until I woke and found myself covered in my own guilt and humiliation and sweat.

Just before dawn, I had wet poor Val's sweet white bed.

I laid there under her beautiful white sheets in my own pool of filth, too embarrassed to move or make a sound. So then I began to cry. I don't know why just then, but eyes began to fill up with tears and my brother rolled over and snapped awake when he saw my awful goddamn mess. My pajamas were soaked all the way through. So were parts of her nice white sheets.

"Don't tell her," I prayed to him. "Don't tell her please."

His face was the worst cold look of disappointment and shock I had ever seen. He stared hard into my eyes, checking himself to be sure he hadn't been hit. He cinched his lips together like he was about scream, but he didn't. He held his disgust all in.

"Change into yesterday's clothes," he grumbled. "Hurry up. And stop making so much damn noise crying like a baby."

I nodded and climbed out of the soiled bed. My face was all hot and red with guilt and my pants were wet with my own humiliation and just as I was fully undressed I was sure my poor sweet Val was going to just happen to walk in, but she didn't. My heart beat hard in my throat until I had on my dirty dry clothes and I stood staring at the big gray stain on the one side of her soft square bed.

"What'll we do?" I kind of mumbled, trying not to sound terrified.

My brother just let out a sigh and helped me strip the sheets off her bed and we sneaked it all out through her window and down into her garbage cans. Then in a few hours before we got up

to eat, he helped me make the bed real nice and after some breakfast, heck, Pill-Bug was the one who offered to take out the trash,
and Val said, "That sure is nice," and he tossed it all out in the big
metal dumpster five trailers away, not letting her know, not telling
a goddamn soul that his own little brother was a damn bed-wetting
eleven-year-old flat tire who nearly cried in his sleep every goddamn night.

# the star of silver is
# just plain lousy

Then the love for a dangerous thing broke us apart.
Tore us up by my awful lips and my open mouth which I couldn't ever hope to control under the cold-eyed glare of Deputy Lubbock with no blessed spirit or living heart and no capacity to appreciate a gentle kind of adolescent burgeoning love like the one my older brother had somehow found.

My older brother, Pill-Bug, fell in for a brand new shiny red knife. No, not just any stupid old knife. Really, this knife was sharp and neat as hell. A brand-new glistening Swiss Army Knife model 109, red and trimmed in silver, with miniature scissors, fork, spoon, miniature saw, and magnifying glass. They had taken Pill's old knife away a few days after we had moved to this lousy town. But this new knife, he believed, was some sort of weapon sent to him from God or the Devil, whichever, it didn't really matter, it was meant for him and him alone. This poor knife was kept behind a single pane of spotted glass right in the hardware store in town, right by the register, completely impenetrable, completely guarded right under the damn clerk's one-armed gaze.

But my brother and that knife was just like every other love affair I'd ever seen, unlucky and sure as hell not meant to be. That knife was another kind of love a meat-eating swine like Deputy Lubbock, that bastard, was sure to put an end to, not because it was his job really, it was, but mostly I think it's the nature of most men to foul the love of every other man if his own heart is a black, twisted knot like a gall on the side of tree, full of slick sap and angry wasps, just waiting to bleed more of the same. People might say there ought to be some respect for officials of the law, and maybe there should be, but there's no way I think anyone could find any small swallow of respect for a man that would bust your older brother's nose over a stupid old expensive knife he didn't have a real chance to own.

Thirty-six dollars. That's how much that knife cost. My brother didn't have thirty-six dollars. My brother didn't have a job, either. Back in Duluth, he had been a paper boy and had lit our neighbor's hedge on fire the day before we left on account of the old bastard next door holding out on paying for his subscription until we nearly left town and poor ol' Pill got stiffed out of twelve dollars, twelve dollars he was sure to never see again, twelve dollars that might have inched him a breath closer to that knife. Heck, he was not about to start working at the lousy Pig Pen supermarket like every other scrawny pimple-faced teenager in town, and so he devised himself a plan.

"We're gonna steal that knife."

That was the dumbest thing I think I'd ever heard him say. But it was so full of frustration and hope that there was no way I could tell him any different. Frustration. I guess that's a force that'll ruin any man. And I guess that was exactly how we first made Deputy Sheriff Lubbock's unsaintly acquaintance.

This Deputy Mort Lubbock was a real bastard, all right. There are some things you can tell about a person right by the way he looks. Deputy Lubbock was a real handsome man. A handsome man your mother or sister might call handsome, but for some reason you just happen to know this man is a goddamn snake that might never show it any other way. But I could see it in his smile. His smile was a smile sure full of too much spit and hard around the edges like it was something he had practiced to make him look like the nicest guy in the world, but like I said, this deputy was a bastard and my brother and I were sure never fooled. His face looked tight around his eyes, like he had done a lot of squinting. He looked like he had spent a lot of time squinting and smiling at himself in the dark, all alone in his lousy white

squad car, maybe listening to Johnny Cash, looking into the
rearview mirror like he was trying to convince himself of something. There's nothing in that rearview mirror there, pal. There's
nothing back there but the dark. Sure, this deputy was one of
those poor cursed men, the kind who spent most of his life running away from the awful things he had already done, the things
that hung back in the dark, moving around in the shadows, whispering his name over and over again. Sure this deputy had a
thing or two to hide. He had been an all-state linebacker back in
high school, a real winner, all right, with scouts coming out to
the games and making offers for schools all over the state, but
this here deputy had been forced to let it all go just when the
golden trophy was so close and nearly right in his mitts. He had
knocked up two girls in his senior year of high school, one the
buxom head cheerleader, a half-Chickasaw and half-white girl
named Tiger-Lil, a girl of reputedly easy virtue, who he took
pleasures with in the backseat of his daddy's Bel Air, more or
less against her will, certainly without worrying about ruining
her already tarnished name. This girl got pregnant and this bastard drove her out of state in his daddy's car for the abortion and
threatened to snap her neck if she ever spread a word about it to
anyone. The other lucky girl was his prom date and steady
sweetheart, June, who was nearly the girl-next-door and hadn't
even thought about sex until the last song at their senior prome-
nade had been sung. This girl June got pregnant and ran right
over to that poor bastard's house and spilled it all out to Mort
Lubbock's folks before he ever arrived home from football practice and it was decided right there that the boy do the honorable
thing. So ol' Mort married the girl and took a lousy job in town,
tow truck operator for two years, until the baby was walking
and the wife settled in a nice duplex by the meat-packing plant,
and just then ol' Mort got the phone girl at the towing service,
Ms. Jurlene Marita, knocked up. He planned to take her on the
same drive he had taken the cheerleader on only a few years before, but Ms. Jurlene split town, without a forwarding address
and most of the tow truck service's cash, and then that poor fool

was sure that the glory and golden trophy of his hopeless life was long gone. Then he'd stay awake at night, wondering what bastard son was out there, practicing his aim on empty cans of Coca-Cola, waiting to catch up with the man who had knocked up his sweet mother and let her go on the run with a couple of grand in towing money all alone. Then he could feel those dark things creeping up on him, waiting along the edges of all his shadows, sitting there ready to wait for the rest of his lousy life, so this bastard decided he needed to make a real change and went to the police academy over there in Aubrey. Then the trophy was close once more, but always slipping right out of his hands, there it goes—nope, there it goes again—nope, and there were those things that kept him looking in his rearview mirror all the time, this kind of desperate searching and waiting, this kind of squinting back hard into the dark and him holding his breath. There was something in his lousy face that showed all his fear, no matter how many shining teeth he shone, and those things were just out of step, just a delicate touch away, waiting out there in the dark, hoping and breathing for the chance to catch up with him at last.

This deputy sheriff, he was a ladies' man, all right. He got more tail than a toilet seat, for sure. This deputy sheriff would swing by other men's houses while they were hard at work at the meat plant, up to their elbows in raw red flesh, heavy with sweat as they labored through the night and this deputy would be sweaty and laboring through the night, too, right in their soft, clean beds, right with their soft, clean wives, maybe searching for that lost sparkle somewhere twixt these ladies' voluminous thighs. Maybe he'd find it there, too, maybe just for a moment, and then it'd be gone, it would fade and dry and he'd strap his gun belt on and wink at these doughy-white wives, kissing their foreheads like he was surely the most gentle man they could imagine, or the sweetest lover he could imagine to be, but in a man like that, it was a true thing that any kind of imagination was desperately wanting.

"'Bout time I hit the road," Lubbock mumbled. Debbi, the

counter girl at the Sizzler, only twenty-two and living in a shack along Plank Road with her husband who worked the night shift at the plant, wrapped her arms around Lubbock's waist and pulled at his belt. The bed was a mess of sheets and her loose-fitting clothes.

"Just stay, Mort."

"Got to move, sweet-thing."

He pulled away, buttoning up his shirt. His raw white belly was bare with sweat and greasy body hair.

"C'mon, Mortie-baby, stay the night."

He lowered the wide brim of his officer's hat right above his thick black eyebrows. He sat on her small white bed and slid his large white hand over her bare breast.

"Not a chance, sugar. June's 'bout to wake and I need to be there to clean up the puke." He kissed her hard, smacking his mouth against hers, then bit her lip fiercely.

"Don't ever call me Mortie." The deputy shot to his feet and disappeared out the bedroom door, maybe practicing his smile.

This deputy sheriff wife's name was June all right and she was bedridden with some sort of cancer, lung cancer probably. I guess they had pulled two big fistfuls of black cancer out from her chest during her last operation and there was no clear sign of remission. This dumb bastard of a sheriff made it a goddamn duty to be there to clean up ol' June's vomit after a bout of the chemotherapy. And that was exactly what I meant. That was the kind of lonesome bastard this guy was. He'd ball every lady with a back to lie on and then tend to his wife's sickness like a real right nurse. There ain't a name for that kind of ruthlessness, I'm sure.

Yep, this deputy was fond of the ladies. Not just the pretty young ones, either; there was Gert at the Pig Pen who worked in the bakery in the back, her face had been cut by a loose steer when she was a girl and her front teeth had been jerked out of her poor head in an accident some years later, but ol' Lubbock could somehow find a moment of sparkle in her sad face, too. Then there was Sally, the short-cook at the truckstop, and Mrs. Darve, from the beauty salon where my mother worked, and I guess most surprising of all was Mrs. Beaumont. Hennie was her first name, I ain't lying, Hennie—like a chicken. This woman was huge, I mean huge, her whole head and arms and belly and legs and toes, even her goddamn pink toes which she showed off in open front sandals, were fat. This woman was round and had bright red hair and wore tons of thick green makeup right over her tiny blue eyes. Her husband was one of the heads over there at the plant, but he worked during the day. They had a fat daughter, Candy, and a house right by the plant. Big Mrs. Beaumont didn't work, either, she just sat around the house eating big steaks and rump roasts and all kinds of meat sausages that only added to her roundness. But there was something about Mrs. Beaumont the deputy must have liked, because one night a week he'd meet her in the parking lot of the Pig Pen and they'd drive down the darkest, most secluded place they could find, and right there in his squad car, they'd get all hot and bothered, I guess, fumbling through each other's clothes and skin until they were both exasperated or frustrated, and then ol' Lubbock would drop Hennie off in the parking lot and cruise around, cussing at himself for being so dumb. Because the real killer was that Mrs. Beaumont was so distressed about breaking her hallowed wedding vows that the farthest she'd let ol' Lubbock go was sticking his hand up her ungodly, sweatstained shirt. Then finally one night, after a horrible argument with her husband, she conceded to the final act of consummation and they drove out to Mill Creek Road, all alone under the stars and moon, surrounded by nothing by farmland and the musty blackness of night.

"This is gonna be the best night of your life, I promise." Ol' Lubbock was so relieved, his hard face nearly sank. He unbuckled his gun belt and yanked his shirt out of his drawers.

"I hope we're doing the right thing." Hennie ran her hand down her huge white blouse, popping the buttons open. There was a huge wave of flesh that undulated as her nervous belly heaved in and out.

"Believe me, sugar, this is something you ain't gonna ever regret." Lubbock unzipped his pants and shoved them down around his ankles, pulling himself on top of Mrs. Beaumont's girth, pushing up her huge black shirt that could barely hide the lurking flab beneath. Lubbock yanked the seat release button, sliding it back; Mrs. Beaumont moaned a little, trying to giggle. There was heat there, there was heat all beneath her raw pink skin, there was an odor, a thick musky odor that was not perfume, an odor that bled from Mrs. Beaumont's pores in ovules of sweat, creasing down around her bare skin. The deputy jerked his drawers down around his knees and tried to maneuver her great white thighs apart. They wouldn't budge. There wasn't enough room for this woman in the car. He pushed harder, digging his thumbs against her rubbery legs, his fingers sunk into her flesh, smooshing her one thigh against the vinyl seat, the other against the steam-covered window. He grunted a little, trying again, cussing some under his breath, but the woman's hefty mass would not give. Damn, this wasn't going to work. He stared down at her raw pig face decorated with all kinds of awful shades of red and blue, her makeup was like some sort of exhibit in kindergarten, it was horrible and exaggerated, he let out a sigh finally, forming that phony smile on his face, breathing hard through his nose.

"What's wrong?" she mumbled, opening her eyes.

"Nuthin'. Here, let me drive you home."

"But . . . "

"Naw, naw, naw." He looked her in her big, piggy eyes. "You know you're a big beautiful flower and the thought of me defoliating such a perty thing in this awful ol' car like this just makes me sick. I'm taking you home."

He jerked up his drawers and pants and tumbled back into the driver's seat. His face was slick with sweat. His head was all red with anger. He left his shirt unbuttoned and started the car. He dropped her off at the supermarket, then drove himself by the old deserted Furnham farm and fired his pistol into the side of that dirty old barn.

BLOOM!!

BLOOM!! BLOOM!!!

His teeth rattled in his smile as he hissed, baring his teeth like a snake. He was lost. There was no hope for him in this godforsaken town. His life was already lost. His whole life was already gone. No fat lady or young sweaty girl could change his luck. He squeezed the trigger again, blowing a hole clear through one of the wilted red boards.

This here Deputy Sheriff Lubbock wasn't only a philanderer, not only a cheat and liar, he was a man full of anger, anger for the golden moments he had lost, angry because of his own dumb lust and greed. This deputy was a bad man to have around when you planned to steal a knife you were pretty sure your own legal guardians didn't want you to own. But this was all before we had ever met him, and I only mention all this as a kind of lesson for you as some real valuable foresight I wish me and my own brother sure had had.

My brother had decided he was going to steal that prized knife all right. That was it. He didn't have any real plan or anything like that. He wanted something, something he knew he'd never be able to afford on his own, and just decided that it should be his. I guess I kind of thought the whole idea was pretty dumb, sure not worth getting caught for, but the knife itself was something spectacular, and if he wanted to risk it, then I thought I should just let the damn fool alone. Besides, if he did steal it and didn't get caught, I was kind of hoping I could borrow it from him.

Ol' Pill picked a Saturday to pull the crime. We stepped out of the trailer late that morning, sneaking past French, who was watching TV on the sofa in his underwear with an open can of delicious Pabst Blue Ribbon Beer cooling in his hand. That big dumb, one-eyed dog, Shilo, was lying right beside him, with his big white head lying in French's lap. Those two were a real picture of happiness just sitting there, grinning to themselves, dazed as all hell in front of that worthless picture tube. I followed Pill out under the great rolling belly of the sun as it just began to push on west in the sky, some time close to noon maybe I guess, we stepped through the gray gravel and dark shadows cast by the looming mobile homes, not really saying a word to each other until we were out on the unpaved dirt road that bloomed with puddles and led into town.

"How you gonna do it?" I asked.

Pill kind of shifted his blue stocking cap down over his scabby eyebrow.

"I dunno. Stick it in my pocket, I guess."

"How you gonna get it in your pocket?"

"I dunno."

"What happens if we get caught?" I whimpered.

"We ain't gonna get caught."

"Well, what if we do?"

"If we get caught, we'll steal a claw-hammer down from an aisle and tear out all their goddamn eyes."

I kind of nodded quietly. That sounded like a real plan, all right. I could tell even Pill wasn't so sure. He kept flipping his silver lighter open and closed, snatching the spark, then slamming the Zippo closed. I had no idea where he had gotten that dandy lighter from. Stolen, for sure. I looked at my older brother. He seemed like he had about as much faith as I did in any of it. Nothing had really worked out for either of us since we'd moved to this goddamn town. Misery was beginning to be a familiar taste on our tongues, worse than anything French or my own mother cooked when we were poor in Duluth but living in a house, with a backyard and at least one goddamn tree you could climb. The only thing Tenderloin had given either me or my brother was a huge dose of reckless and impudent bravery. We had learned we didn't have a damn thing to lose, and no matter what we were caught doing, nothing could bring you down any lower than the sad state you were already in, living deep within a big silver steel drawer without any goddamn backyard or baseball card swap for miles.

We walked into town that afternoon and down to the main street, where all the businesses and stores sat along the road in fat square buildings propped right beside one another. The hardware store was on the corner. It was a kind of red brick store with a nice green metal awning out front. There were some green lawnmovers and heavy tilling equipment sitting out front beside some gumball machines and some big push brooms that must have been on sale. The Saturday afternoon traffic was still kind of slow. Most people must have been at the meat plant working overtime or at the football game at the high school or sitting at home like French with their dog on their sofas with their cold cans of beer and remote controls and warm hands nestled between the ridge of their pants and heavy autumnal bellies.

My brother pulled his blue stocking cap down once more and stepped through the open glass door. I followed. I had never known my brother to steal anything real before, not anything expensive, I mean. Sure, we used to steal candy from this store by our house back in Duluth, but that was nickel-and-dime candy that could fit in your palm and then would disappear right down the front of your shirt sleeve or into your sock. Heck, both of us were prone to stealing cash out of good ol' French's wallet or my mother's purse, even him taking Val's brassiere and that silver lighter weren't any things of any real value, but this moron was going to steal a knife, a knife worth something, right from under the clerk's nose, and no matter how bad either of us wanted the damn thing, I just didn't think he had the guts or mind to do it right.

The clerk behind the big silver register was a bald-headed man named Pete. People used to come in and say, "Morning, Pete." Then he'd nod. He didn't ever say their names back. He didn't ever say hello. This clerk Pete only had one working arm. His left hand was all twisted up and maimed, shiny and white and pink all over and covered in scars. The damn maimed hand looked like a bird's withered old claw. Maybe that ungodly hand made Pete just generally unfriendly. All I knew was Pete sure hated me and my brother. We had been in there once before to buy mercuric acid. If you mix that stuff with some tin foil and put it all inside a plastic soda bottle, you can make a bomb. Ol' Pill taught me that one. We used it to

blow that fat kid's, Dan Goosehert's, barn-shaped mailbox completely off its post. You should of seen that thing fly. Bloom!!!! Then
it was gone. Pieces of plastic everywhere. Man, that one still
cracks me up.

Anyway, ol' Pill walked inside the hardware store with his
hands dug deep into his pockets. He was wearing his gray hooded
sweatshirt and some jeans. He walked down the last aisle, not
making any kind of eye contact with Pete. Me, I stopped by the
front to pretend to be looking at a big rack of plumbing equipment,
septic tank cleaner, and pipes and hoses; I could feel Pete's hot
one-armed stare burning through the back of my neck, the fire of
damnation burning right in his loaded sockets. I kind of squealed
and turned, watching my brother circle down the aisle and walk
back up to the big glass counter in front by the register. The store
was almost completely empty. There were two big-gutted cowboys
in the automotive aisle, giggling and snickering as I passed by, staring at their black-and-white snake-skin boots.

"Then she tied me up in a goddamn chair," this cowboy with a
real clean white face and yellow hat whispered. "Tied me up a like
a goddamn animal. Look at this." He pulled his wide gray collar
away from his neck to reveal a thick dark red hickey.

"That sure is a crazy woman you got."

"Sure is."

My eyes widened as I stared at them from behind a display of
flat-head screwdrivers. I guess that was why I liked the hardware
store. That place was a brutal place. A place of honesty. A place of
nails and saws and spikes and sharp metal things that could draw
all the blood from your body. There was stuff you could use to
make explosives. Things to channel electricity. Things to dig huge
gaping holes. There were big square sheets of glass. Grout. Plaster.
Things of concrete eternity. Shotgun shells. Engine oil. Synthetic
lubricants. There were men there missing eyes and arms and
thumbs. There were men there who talked in swears and only
swears. There were things there that made you know the glory of
man rested in his mighty opposable thumb and hands. The hard-

ware store was a young bastard's dream of heaven, without a doubt.

My brother edged up to the glass counter and stared down at the beautiful red knife inside. It sat beneath that glass, glowing and shimmering, its tools honed and sharpened for use. You could do anything you wanted with a knife like that. With a knife like that, you could maybe carve your name in a tree or something. Maybe you could cut something right in half with that kind of knife. The possibilities seemed near endless. My brother's heated breath fogged up the glass where his nose nearly touched it. One-Armed Pete stood over him, empty black eyes glaring, his good arm was crossed in front of his blue sweat-stained shirt.

"Think I can see that knife there?" Pill kind of mumbled, staring up with his scabby eyes at that lousy one-armed man. His hands were pumping out sweat. His whole body was sweating. He held his breath, staring at Pete's huge silver steer-shaped belt buckle. "Just for a second?"

Pete finally nodded, sliding open the case door; his big white hand gripped the knife and planted it in Pill's near trembling hands. His pale blue eyes lit up as the knife touched his skin, stealing light from the florescent lamps overhead. My brother clutched the prize tightly, flicking open its folding saw and detachable toothpick. This was the greatest knife in the world. This was the greatest knife ever. I couldn't really breathe. I stood down the first aisle, peeking around the corner, feeling my own hands trembling at my sides. This was never going to work. My brother still had no idea what he was going to do. Pete would catch us both and cut off both our damn good-looking hands. My brother tugged down his cap, still holding the knife.

"How much is it again?" he kind of grunted. He felt like his tongue was heavy and swollen. His mouth felt like it was filled with lard. His forehead was dripping with sweat. He wanted to take the knife and run. He wanted to close his eyes and run like hell.

"That knife there is thirty-six dollars," Pete said. "Same as it

was last week and the one before that. Hand it back now." He
opened his big white palm for Pill to return it. My brother kind of
panicked and looked over his shoulder at me. His eyes flashed
with fury and hope.

He needed to do something. His hand was trembling. He held
the knife in his sweaty palm, staring down at its shiny metal
blades.

"Alright now son, hand it back."

He looked back over his shoulder at me again. His face was all
white. He was panicked. Ol' Pete leaned closer, his big gray
shadow growing cooler as he stared into my brother's sweaty face.
I kept waiting for Pill to flick that knife open and just cut that one-
armed bastard right apart, just cut his belly open like a fish and let
all that man's evil black blood roll out of his rounded gut, but my
brother, Pill, he didn't do a thing. He kind of just sighed and
handed the knife right back.

Damn our luck.

My brother turned and slunk out of the hardware store. I followed, shaking my head.

"Whatcha give it back for?" I asked, still kind of trembling my
own self.

"Shut your trap," he muttered. He turned and stared back at
the store.

He was just standing there, his face looking all serious. His
cheeks were just beginning to get tiny black whiskers, loose and
wild; he stared out into the street holding in his breath like he was
about to cry. There was something behind his eyes that was
stormy-blue and gray, like when a thick black cloud suddenly rolls
on in, swiping and moving across the sky. His eyes got real thin as
he clenched his fists at his side. He looked me right in the eye, not
saying a word.

He turned and faced the display of brown push brooms that
were there on sale.

I could almost hear that black-headed match snap to life right
within my brother's unkept head.

Snapppppp!!!!!!!!!

He flicked open his shiny silver lighter, struck the flint, and lit those brooms right on fire. Their shiny bristles lit up like grass, sizzling and shrinking until they were all on fire, cracking and rumbling orange and yellow in the shiny silver garbage can they were standing in.

"What the hell?!!" I could hear One-Armed Pete holler from inside as the fire began to roar, eating up the broom heads and handles. My brother took off, skidding down the sidewalk and out into the street. In the only sign of comraderie I could show, I kicked over one of those lawn mowers and ran, too. My brother's gray sweatshirt bustled behind him. I saw the back of his gym shoes, right-left-right-left as he moved, his blue stocking cap wavering behind his head. He was a lot faster than me. Hell, he was older and taller, too. My breath hurt in my chest as I ran, trying not to let out a cry.

"Hey!!!" I heard someone yell from behind. "Hey you little bastards!!!!" Maybe it was One-Armed Pete hollering. Maybe it was someone else. I didn't know. I wasn't about to turn and look. My breath was barely coming and my belly was hurting and my lungs felt like they were on fire and I guess I felt like bawling right there. My brother turned down an alley and grabbed me by my sweatshirt. We dodged down another alley and over a wire fence and ran toward home, covered in bare silver sweat. We didn't say a goddamn word, even when we made it to the big yellow field that led back toward the trailer park. Pill stopped running, huffing hard; he hunched over and stopped, dropping his hands to his knees to breathe. His face was all caked in sweat and his lips were full of spit. His face was all red. He wiped his mouth and stood up, coughing a little. I did the same, making a big ball of spit in my throat and let it fly. I looked at his face again. His eyes were nearly running with tears, too. His face was still red even after he was breathing normally. He was still sweating.

We walked across a field, crossing down to the main road, nothing settled in my mind much except how scared my older brother had looked after he had done it, and that made me feel even worse. He was scared all right. Maybe because he had never lit anything like that on fire before, I mean, not right in the day, lighting something public like that while people were just standing inside watching. Even when he burnt that dumb kid's porch down, it was all deserted and no one was really around. Heck, lighting a fire right in the middle of town in the middle of a sleepy day, that was a regular arson I guess you might have to say. I looked at his face again. It was still pale and white. Maybe he was still spooked because he knew some people had seen us there, maybe because he had realized how stupid it had all been to begin with, but his sore face was pale white as a ghost and he didn't stop running until he was on the dirt road and the silver splendor of the trailer park was back in sight.

"That was great," I tried to mumble.

He didn't offer any sort of reply. His face was all gray and white. Pill pulled his blue stocking cap down and looked back over his shoulder to see if anyone was running after us. He suddenly looked a lot older to me. His face was all thin and hard. His eyes looked like they were black and hurt.

"Don't talk about it now," he grunted. "Don't mention it again or I swear to God I'll cut you open."

I nodded. His face was still gray. He had gotten back at those bastards and he didn't seem happy at all. He had made them feel what he had been carrying around in his gut this whole time and he seemed worse off than he had before. I shrugged my shoulders and walked beside him and spit again. Nothing made any damn sense to me anymore.

Then it all got a whole lot worse.

Before we could cross the one last field to the basin of dry grey gravel and motor homes, a big white squad car barrelled down on us and skidded to a stop just a few feet from where we walked along the side of the road.

There's nothing you can say at a moment like that that accurately describes what a damn fool you really are. The best thing I can think of is when your mother walks in on you on the toilet and you're maybe reading a dirty magazine that just happens to belong to your older brother but still gets you into trouble just the same.

The squad car's sirens were all flashing and screeching, the engine hollering with steam, poor Pill let out a yelp and began to run again, traversing down into the drainage ditch along the side of the road, but this deputy was too quick and hopped out of his car, passed me, and caught hold of the back of Pill's shirt. The big, red-faced copper knocked my brother to the ground and held him there, then pointed to me.

"Stay where you are, you little bastard."

My face felt all hot after he had said it. Maybe I was scared as hell. The law hadn't ever really come down on us like this before. Not even when Pill lit that hedge on fire. They had just sat us both down in front of our mother and French and talked about responsibility and the like, but no one, no policeman, had ever knocked my brother down and called me a little bastard before. This copper was some sort of goddamn savage.

My brother wrestled around in a thick pile of dirt and leaves, flailing his thin arms. He kicked the copper in the belly, knocking him back a little, then tried to pull himself to his feet to run again, but the deputy turned and cracked him with the back of his hand, smacking my brother's nose. Crack!! My brother didn't utter a goddamn cry, he just held his nose and kept kicking; these two men, my brother and the deputy, both kind of snarled and had the same dumb look in their black eyes—anger, not just anger, but frustration, frustration that didn't have anything to do with each other or the goddamn fire, I bet. My brother and the deputy were the same. They had both been cheated out of something they thought they had deserved. They both thought they could get away with lying, cheating, and stealing, but the trouble was their poor crimes had already lit them up with a dull kind of black anger that they might not ever been able to let loose. They both had the look of doomed men, fighting and swearing there. Doomed. That's what my brother looked like lying there on his back like a dirty worm. Doomed.

The deputy finally slapped a pair of thick silver handcuffs on my brother's wrist and yanked Pill to his feet by the back of his shirt. My brother's nose began to bleed a little, pushing out blood from one of his nostrils. He looked pathetic. He looked beaten as a dog. The deputy yanked that beautiful silver lighter out of Pill's shirt pocket and shoved us both into the backseat of the squad car, then slammed the doors shut. The deputy fell back into his driver's seat, coughing a little. I kind of hoped he would just cough up his awful black heart and die, but he didn't; he sucked some snot down his throat and turned around to face us.

"You little bastards have got a lot of explaining to do."

"Go to Hell!!!" my brother shouted, but it didn't sound brave at all, it sounded almost like a cry, like he was ready to buckle into a whole ransom of tears. The blood on his nose didn't help him look any tougher, either. He looked like a fighter that had lost the bout. He looked like he had been knocked out cold and then found some fight after the bell had already rung. Me, I didn't say a word, I was thinking. I thought I could blame my dumb brother for most of it, except the part where I knocked the lawn mower over and ran, and even then I was deliberating whether this copper would believe it was all just a strange sort of accident or not.

The deputy switched off his siren and asked us where we lived and Pill mumbled it out and then he drove us toward the trailer park slow as hell, maybe trying to rattle us, I guess. He unrolled his window and lit a smoke as drove. He let the gray smoke kind of funnel around his mouth and drift up, real cool and relaxed, like he was somehow in some movie, starring him of course. This deputy I didn't like at all. He pulled into the trailer park, right between our motorhome and Mrs. Garnier's, the lady who lived behind us, and by then we knew he knew everything and we were done for.

He turned around in the front seat and stared at us, shaking his head with cold black eyes.

"So you little bastards think you can just go and light my town on fire, huh?"

We were done for all right.

"We didn't light nothing," Pill mumbled. "We didn't light nothing on fire." My brother kind of mumbled it to himself. He was out of it all right. Maybe it had nothing to do with the damn fire, maybe he was just so sick of being disbelieved and caught and treated like a goddamn fool, of being called a goddamn liar and trouble-maker, that his eyes kind of welled up with tears and his face got all hot and red as he closed his eyes and turned toward the car window.

Pride. That's what it was. We had lit the can of brooms on fire, the deputy knew we had done it, but my brother couldn't let it go, he couldn't let anyone put down his name, whether the claim was true or not, whether he had the goddamn evidence in his hand. That's the real problem of lying. You never do know when you're telling the truth or not because you're always worried that every-one can tell you're lying, and when they do, you're pissed that they'd think you'd do such an awful thing in the first place. The problem is you get indignant about some pride you probably shouldn't even have. Ol' Pill would suffer his whole life because of that. He was a goddamn fool that way.

Deputy Lubbock pulled another smoke from his pocket.

"I got three different folks that said you did it. And this nice lighter here which all of them can identify."

"Screw off," my brother grunted.

There was no hope. No hope, no hope for either of us. I thought about coming clean and spilling it all in one horrified mumble of muted cries, but I knew it wouldn't do any good. Maybe the law would think I was only an innocent tag-along, but my mother, my mother would see my hand in this, too, and punish us both for sure. I could feel the red-hot length of French's belt against my hide. I could feel my mother's hot tears wallowing in my ears. Then my lips began to tremble. Then my throat felt heavy and sore. I closed my eyes and opened up my red mouth and let it all out in one horrible bubble of snot and tears.

"He did it," I mumbled. "My brother did it. He said he'd cut me up if I told. Honest. He said he was gonna cut me if I told. Please don't tell our folks. Please. He won't ever light nothing on fire again. I swear. I swear. Please don't tell our folks."

Pill shook his head in disgust.

He stared at me without saying a word and I knew right then I was now a hated man for sure. Maybe the whole idea of stealing anything had been his to begin with, but I had gone along with him because I wanted the knife just as bad as he did and now I had just buckled and turned. I had wanted him to light that fire just as bad as he had and maybe worse. I had wanted to see that whole store burn, but I'd been too much of a coward to do it myself.

I had turned on my own poor brother.

I felt like crying all right. Not because of being in all that trouble, really, but thinking that I had let ol' Pill down that bad. My own brother of flesh and blood hated me more than he hated the whole town now. And worse of all, I deserved it. I was a snitch, I was a tattle-tale. I was a snot-nosed blabber-mouth. My eyes began to feel hot and sticky as some tears ran down my round face.

"Now ain't the time to cry, son," the ol' deputy mumbled to me over his shoulder. "No time to cry when you go around committing crimes like a grown man."

He took a long drag after that and I hoped again he would choke. He opened the car door and led us out and on up to our front porch. He knocked on the screen door just once with a big white fist.

"Police. Open on up!!" he hollered.

French answered the door in a pair of brown pants and a dirty tee-shirt. He shook his head as he caught sight of the both of us, my brother with the bloody nose and handcuffs, me crying like a baby; my God, after all of my mother's warnings and French's nodding and frowning along with her for support, they both had been right. We were no good. We were headed straight for the penn. The deputy flicked his cigarette out into the gray darkness.

"Looks like your boys here got themselves into some right-good trouble."

My mother appeared at the door, staring over French's shoulder. Her eyes went wild as she stared at my face.

"What happened? What did you do now?!!" she shouted.

"We didn't do a damn thing!" Pill blurted out.

Deputy Bullock let out a snicker. "Hey-hey, these boys here lit a fire down in the hardware store in town. I caught 'em with the evidence, red-handed."

"A fire?!!" my mother shouted. "A fire?!!" She stepped from behind French and smacked me hard, making the side of my face feel ripe. That's something you don't ever want to feel, getting smacked in the face by your own mother in front of the law and all.

"Pete down there said he won't press any charges, though I tried to convince him otherwise, as long as these boys don't come near the store and repay what they owe."

"Owe? What do ya mean owe?!!" my brother shouted.

"That fire you lit wrecked some merchandise good. In the neighborhood of three hundred dollars or so."

"Three hundred dollars!!! We didn't even light the damn fire!!!" My brother's face was all red. He was still fighting with his lousy pride.

"You best give these boys a whupping to learn them the difference between right and wrong or next I might be forced to teach 'em myself."

Deputy Lubbock jammed his key into the silver handcuffs and turned Pill free, shoving him a little.

"We will, Officer." French nodded, gripping Pill by his ear.

"I want my lighter back," Pill grunted through some tears. He stared hard right into that bastard's eyes and didn't look away.

"That's official evidence now, son." The deputy smiled. "I'd keep any lighters or matches out of this boy's reach."

My mother and French nodded.

The deputy hopped back in his squad car and tore away, kicking up gravel and dust, ready to bring down any other felonious eleven-year-old and his older brother with the swift and deft hand he called justice. Deft as a trickle of spit. That was what burned me so damn much. My mother and French shoved us inside and gave us each a whipping before we could explain anything about the knife or the deputy or the hardware store. French held me by my arm and whacked me with his belt hard on my behind without me saying another goddamn word. Then he did the same to Pill, who just stood still and didn't cry like me, gritting his teeth a little as the belt hit his behind with a thick smack. The worst part was the look on ol' French's face, stern and serious, but sad and disappointed as hell. He winced with every swing, looking like he was about ready to start crying, too. He held me by my shoulder and stared into me and my brother's face, strapping the belt back around his waist.

"This is it, boys, this is the last fire you start, understand?" I nodded, clearing the tears out of my head. Pill just stood completely still, his eyes were all hard and black and mean. He just kept staring right back in French's face, hating him as much as his tiny black heart would allow and his empty pupils would show.

"You're both gonna end up in prison or the morgue pulling shit like that, you hear?"

Me, I nodded again, trying to ignore my sore bottom-side. Pill just kept staring, maybe not hearing a single word. My mother was in the bathroom, crying like a real damn fountain, maybe mumbling the rosary through her sobs, probably praying for both our worthless souls.

Then French sent me and my brother to our dull lousy room all so fast I didn't even have any other chance to say a single word.

Prison or the morgue. Our damn room didn't seem any different. Any way it went, we were still both trapped. We were still both locked in alone with our gruesome thoughts and angry red hearts. My brother laid in the top bunk, not uttering a sound, his face red as hell. I laid there, too, beneath him, knowing how mad he was, not at my mother or French, or the deputy or the clerk, Pete, or even the whole crummy town we both always kind of counted on blaming, but me. Me. My brother was sore as hell at me and it had all happened before I could think what I was really trying to do or say. I had turned on my only brother and it hadn't done me any good at all. My face felt red and empty. My teeth felt hard in my head. I laid in my bed staring up, and reached out my hand to where my brother's weight made his dull blue bunk sag. There was nothing there but the cold plastic skin of an old blue bed-liner. There was nothing there of my own blood or desperate heart. I could hear him breathing. I could hear him hating me through his soft white sheets. Then maybe I started crying, holding my face in the pillow so he wouldn't hear. Then maybe I tried so hard to think of something funny to say and nearly said it, but then the words were all gone and I just laid there, mumbling contrite sounds all alone to myself, like a prayer.

# the pig pen

The Pig Pen was hell. One shiny grocery store that swelled full of meat and bread and milk and all other kinds of groceries and sundries and stupid people mostly. My brother, Pill-Bug, took a goddamn lousy job as stockboy at the only supermarket in town to pay off the three hundred dollars' worth of damage they said he caused by lighting the hardware store on fire. They made him a stockboy because he didn't have any real qualifications to do anything else and they sure as hell weren't going to let him by the cash register or anything important like that. My dumb brother spent all of his time arranging things on shelves, stealing food products, and smoking in the back of the store with the other loser stockboys, talking about how the check-out girls' breasts looked stunning beneath those pleated white shirts. None of the management really knew his name there yet, so everyone just called him "new kid" or "stockboy," the latter, I preferred, because it sounded like the most pitiful kind of super hero you might ever imagine.

In walked Mr. Klupshas. Grocery manager. Lunatic.

He came right down the aisle, past the rows and rows of soup cans and canned fruit and canned vegetables and canned hash and canned hams, he flew past the gravy mix and powdered drinks without a word, without a goddamn word. He grabbed the lowly stockboy, my brother, by the front of his bleached white shirt, crackling with starch, and shoved him hard against a metal shelf.

"What the hell do you think you're doing contradicting me in front of a customer?"

Mr. Klupshas's shiny white forehead beaded one huge blue bubble of sweat before it broke and ran down his neck. The huge gray rings of perspiration beneath his armpits were nearly legendary. The sweat-rings seemed to grow and throb with his rage, like the soft underbelly of a puffer fish. The lowly stockboy's face swelled red with panic, he flailed about a little, knocking over a few display cans of Mighty-Boy soup. But Klupshas didn't give a damn. Klupshas was a big man, with thick broad shoulders; he had served in the Marines; somewhere on his big gray bicep he had had his own name tattooed, "Frank," emblazoned right there over an anchor in his own flesh; don't ask me why he had his own name tattooed, I don't think anybody really knew. His head was square, his hair was nearly white-blond and cut cropped next to his rough pink skin. There was a fat pink scar that ran in a square around the top of his head. There was a stainless steel plate buried beneath that. They said he used to be able to pick transmissions from ham radio or local broadcasts and the sounds would reverberate in his teeth like a telegraph. His single black eyebrow formed a large fleshy ledge like a heaving neanderthal.

"If I say something to a customer, it's gospel, you understand? If I give them a price, you don't go and second-guess me. If I say we're out of something, we're out, do you get it?"

Klupshas checked the lowly stockboy again, knocking him against the metal shelf. Some stupid, big-eyed old lady shopper stood there slack-jawed, slowly dropping some pork and beans into her cart.

"Don't ever contradict me again, you got it, or the next time you can clean your locker out and head on home!"

His round pink head looked ready to pop and burst open with thousands of meaningless lists, orders, stock of all sorts, meats, cheeses, fruit-stand economics, his eyes were filled to the brim with anger and black heat. Maybe the only thing keeping it all in was that metal plate.

"Vegetables!!!" he shouted. "I need a man to clean up the vegetables out back!! Hendershaw, grab a broom!!"

He pointed to another stockboy, who kind of let out a whimper and disappeared down the aisle in a hurry.

"I could snap your neck," Klupshas muttered. "I could snap your puny neck with one red hand."

He shoved my brother once more and disappeared behind the wooden door demarcated "Manager" in faded red letters.

The lousy stockboy went back to sorting soup cans, moving their cylindrical forms flush to one another. His poor hands were still shaking. He hadn't said a goddamn word to any customer. He hadn't contradicted a damn soul. He had only punched in a few minutes ago. That guy was crazy. He was a goddamn maniac all right. My brother remembered old Uncle Burt; he had gone off nervous, locking himself up in his house because he said he had trapped Jesus in his front closet and the end of the world was nigh. The stockboy took a deep breath. This was not worth $3.50 an hour. At this rate, he'd never pay that money back. But no one else in town would hire him. There was nowhere else he could work. He moved some lentil beside a can of chicken noodle, still shaking a little. Blam. Oh, Lord. He dropped a can. A fat red and white and silver can hit the shiny white tile floor and died, a few droplets of chicken broth leaked out like wasted innards. He shook his head, then bent over, untucked the corner of his shirt and wiped up the goo, then tucked his shirt back in his pants. He put the dented can back up on the shelf as Klupshas marched through the wooden door and down the aisle.

"What the hell is that?!! What the hell is that?"

His big gray fist hammered out the repeated phrase, pointing at the wounded can. The pitiful stockboy shrugged his shoulders, staring up into the shiny white fluorescent lights, his heart pounding like a fist full of glue in his gut.

"Is that a dented can?"

My brother closed his eyes.

"Peterson?!!! Peterson!!!" the manager hollered. A thin stockboy appeared from around the aisle, sweating like mad, the whole acne-covered back of his neck glistened with newly bubbled perspiration as he approached, trying not to let out a whimper.

"Sir?"

"Peterson, is that a dented soup can?"

Peterson's eyes squinted a little as he fought to breathe.

"Is that a dented can, I asked?!!"

"I dunno, sir, I guess so."

Klupshas nodded, grinding his teeth. He stared at my brother, the lowly stockboy.

"Peterson, who is scheduled to be the pig today?"

"That would be me, sir."

"Peterson, I want you to finish the stock here and continue down to the bread aisle. This stockboy here has volunteered to be the pig."

Peterson nearly let out a whimper of delight. His thin white shoulders relaxed as he began to beam. "Thank you, sir. Thank you."

The lowly stockboy squinted a little. He had no idea what Hell was about to unfold upon him.

The pig was a huge pink and white pig-suit that covered your entire body, dented pig-head and all. The pig was the crappiest job to have in the whole lousy supermarket. Besides having to dress up like a goddamn moron in that costume and endure the ridicule of shoppers and fellow workers alike, mostly the resonant snort-snort-snorting of passersby, the pig suit had been poorly designed without proper ventilation, like an old metal box they used to keep goddamn war prisoners in; it was like a damn pink felt coffin, it was hermetically sealed and stunk of other stockboys' pubescent hormone-laden sweat. One poor stockboy passed out in there once and had his head run over by the front end of a station wagon, but the suit was so damn durable that the kid only suffered minor asphyxiation. Working at the lousy Pig Pen was bad enough. It meant you couldn't get a good after-school job at the pizza joint or hardware store or on a ranch. Being the pig at the Pig Pen, standing in front of the store handing out valuable in-store coupons or advertisements for specials on coldcuts and fruit meant you were the lowest of the particularly low.

This kid Peterson lowered the big pink pig-head over my brother's own, finishing the job. The stink, the undeniable stench of thousands of thirteen-year-old boys wafted up in his nose, worse than a millennium of gym locker rooms or jock straps. The stench nearly knocked him out. My brother stared out the tiny pig eyes at his own, pink-mitt-covered hands. Pathetic.

"Remember to remind people about today's specials. You can pat the little kids on the head if you want, but don't get too close to the old people. The suit kinda scares them."

My brother let out a groan. This kid, Peterson, must have been an old pro, all right. He led my brother, the lowly stockboy, now lowly pig-boy, down the far aisle and to the front of the store. Peterson's eyes got real dim and sad.

"You poor bastard," he kind of whimpered and backed away, flashes of the insufferable pig-agony must have burned through his head. Pill the pig-boy shrugged his shoulders. He walked outside. He turned and faced the parking lot. A mother and her two rug-rats in tow approached, arguing and hollering at each other.

"Hello?" my brother grumbled in a low voice. "Welcome to the Pig Pen," he shouted in monotone. "Do you wanna hear about the specials?" He held out some nifty coupons with his pink mitts.

The mother and greasy-faced kids barrelled past, ignoring him completely. My brother shook his great pig-head.

"Do you want some coupons?!" he shouted again, as an old lady in a bright green scarf and beige coat approached. The old lady let out a cry and wheeled past him, looking back in terror. Her thin gray eyes were burning with fear.

The pig-boy had begun to sweat. Not a normal kind of sweat. A sweat you couldn't just wipe away, because your own goddamn hands were pink pig-hands, because your goddamn skin was really buried beneath the pig insides of pink felt. His greasy face began to boil in there, creeping down his scabby eyebrows into his eyes.

"Hello?" he grunted as another young mother and her round-headed boy came closer. He extended his paw full of coupons as the lady blew past.

"Take the goddamn coupons," he hissed to himself. "Just take the goddamn coupons."

The lady and her kid disappeared into the grocery store, unaware. Some eight-year-old kids pulled up to the pig-boy on their dirty gray dirt-bikes, grinning and smiling. There were three or four of them; they circled around the pig-boy, riding around him, sneering.

"Snort-snort-snort!!" they all hollered, pushing the ends of their noses up, making horrible pig-faces, their whines and snorts rising in the air like a pink cloud of pure hate.

"Pig-boy!! Pig-boy!!!" They all laughed.

The pig-boy felt a single hot drop of sweat burn into his eye. He turned, gritting his teeth, and knocked one of the little bastards off his bike. This kid with red hair and freckles tumbled to the ground, falling on his butt. The little red-headed whipper-snapper stared up from the pavement, entirely stunned.

"Hey," the kid kind of mumbled. "You ain't supposed to do that."

One of the little bastards with a blue baseball hat pulled on the pig-boy's pink curly pig-tail. My brother spun around and gripped the kid by his throat, pulling him to the cold black ground. The pig-boy shook the kid by his shoulders, shoving him against the parking lot's mean surface, trying to brain him.

"Never touch the pig!!!" the pig-boy yelled. "Never touch the goddamn pig!!!"

He let the kid go, snarling all over the poor bastard. The pig-boy watched as the little rug-rat hopped back on his bike and him and his little buddies tore away, looking over their shoulders like they had somehow seen something that might leave a deep pink scar in their awful little hearts.

The pig-boy dumped all the valuable in-store coupons in the trash and walked around to the back of store, where crates and crates of food and perishables were loaded and unloaded every day. He took a seat on the loading dock and propped the big pink pig-mask up to his forehead, dug down the front of his suit into his human attire, and pulled out a pack of cool smokin' Marlboros. Then he plucked a single square out, and lit it, nearly singeing his pink pig-mitts. His cigarette smoke wafted up around his pink head as he stared down at his soft black-and-pink pig-feet. Pitiful.

"That's an awful sight," someone grumbled. The pig-boy snapped to his feet, nearly swallowing his cigarette, the pink pig-head came crashing down over his face as he dropped his square at his feet. He stared out his tiny pink eyes and coughed up a lung full of smoke.

"Mr. Klupshas would have a field day catching you smoking back here in that pig-suit."

He lifted up the pig-head and frowned.

Oh, Lulla.

He coughed again.

Lulla Getty. Sixteen, tall with green eyes and dark curly red hair that wound down around her shoulders, just above that thin white blouse with tiny elegant sweat marks beneath the arms. Mean as hell. Check-out girl, queen of all the high school sluts. No one really talked to her at school. No one offered to carry her books. But somehow there was always some lousy big-faced bastard like Rudy LaDell waiting to drive her home. Someone to see her home all right. This beautiful girl seemed like the loneliest, meanest creature in town. He remembered another stockboy had told him that one of the guys on the football team had spat inside Lulla Getty. Spat up inside her. All the dumb meat-eating jocks kind of giggled the whole story out right at school. That just didn't seem right. If this poor girl was nice enough to let a boy, you know, make it with her, well, the whole thing just didn't seem right.

Oh, Lulla's face was freckled and kind of struck him right away. Her eyes were dark and green but not real pretty, the way she kind of scowled at you. He wondered if what they said was really true. He had heard that she'd do it with just about anyone for ten bucks. Ten bucks, that was all. My god, he felt his sweat gathering all in his palms.

There was an unlit cigarette in Lulla's hand that she placed between two red lips, lips too red for a wholesome check-out girl like Martie Davis or Lucy Caldewick. The pig-boy lit up another smoke, fumbling beneath his pink suit for his matches. His pink hand kind of trembled as she stepped closer, closing her eyes, nearly shoving her unlit cigarette right in his face. He lit her cigarette, nearly burning off the whole damn cylinder, then backed away. He stared hard right at her.

They didn't speak. Sure, they had the same Sunday School class together but he could never do more than just stare at her all Sunday afternoon and dream of all the thousand tiny red undulating shimmers her hair made when it moved.

Hell.

The pig-boy sucked hard on his cigarette, coughing a little beneath the heavy pig-head. He could see the girl's soft white brassiere pushing against her blouse. There was a sound that that made in his head, like a baby taking a breath. Shhhhhhhhhhhhhh.

Lulla leaned against the brick wall like it hurt her to breathe. She bit at her thumbnail, letting the smoke waver around her big head of red hair.

The pig-boy kept staring. He could feel the sweat gathering along his palms beneath his pink pig-mitts. He smoked as furiously as possible, draining the square down to the filter as fast as he could. He made quick bursts of smoke like an amateur, unable to stop looking at the space where her freckled neck began, rising up from between her blouse. He could see one particular freckle that was shaped perfectly round. Like a perfect bead of water. He felt himself dumbfounded.

"Do you have a staring problem?" Lulla grumbled, squinting down her mean nose at him.

The pig-boy shook his head.

"Then quit looking at me."

He nodded and dropped the smoke under his pink-and-black-toed pig-foot, crushing it out. He backed away, tripping over his pink felt feet, returning to the parking lot.

The pig-boy stood in front of the store, beneath the hot-must of the pink pig suit, dazed. He could still see that one freckle in his head. He could still hear that sound, shhhhhhhhhh, as he stared up into the darkness and the parking lot lights flickered on overhead.

•  •  •

The tiny white package swung right past his lips.

"Take this to Ms. Dubuque. Tell her it's free of charge." Klupshas, lunatic, grocery store manager, shoved a tiny white paper bag in my older brother's face. He squinted a little, then stared at Mr. Klupshas's cold black eyes.

"Do you need to be told twice? Move, stockboy, move!!"

The stockboy skittered away, holding the bag in his sweaty fingers. He stared at the white bag then looked around the store. He had no idea what the hell he was holding or what he was supposed to do. He looked at the white bag again, hoping to discern some message, some pattern, some clue from its soft white folds or crease. Nothing. There was nothing in the size, shape, or color that gave the lowly stockboy any hint.

"Move!!!" he heard Klupshas holler from some other aisle. He could hear sweat and steam gathering in the madman's throat. The lowly stockboy shook his head and turned, barrelling past the rows and rows of shiny silver cans of soup, holding the white bag at his side. He could feel Klupshas's heavy grasp right around his throat. He needed to find someone who knew what the hell was going on. Someone who understood the way this cold white-tiled lunatic ward of fresh meat and ripe food really worked.

There was goddamn Peterson. Poor teenage acne case and lousy stockboy extrordinaire.

There was Peterson sorting through a rack of fresh produce. His face was thin and white and covered in tiny red sores of acne and sweat. His white shirt collar was upturned on one side. His eyes were dim and glassy from his task. He couldn't have been more than sixteen. Sixteen and his biggest goddamn concern was the number of Jonathan apples in old bin three. This whole goddamn town was the same. Dead. All of these lousy meat-eating bastards were already dead. There was no soft lust along his pallid skin. There was no hope in his dumb, seedy eyes.

The lowly stockboy stared at Peterson's grim face.

"Who the hell's Ms. Dubuque and what the hell am I supposed to do with this lousy bag?" Pill asked, still staring at Peterson's lifeless white face. There was a sudden twinge, like a sweet volt of lightning, like a red-clambering tremor of shock or fright. Peterson's black eyes snapped from his face as he straightened up, dropping his thin mouth open with a sweaty-toothed sigh.

"Ms. Dubuque?"

"Yeah, I'm supposed to bring this bag to her, free of charge and all."

"Sure," Peterson frowned, running his bare finger over the bare skin of an apple, staring dimly at the space around my brother's lopsided head. Charmed. My brother was breathing the charmed air of saints and kings. "Of course, they'd let you bring it. They wouldn't ask me again. Course not. They wouldn't want to go through that again."

"What the hell are you talking about?"

"There's no more beautiful woman than Ms. Dubuque in this town. Not even Mrs. Calhoun before she fell off that plow horse. No, Ms. Dubuque was raised like a real princess out in that big house. She was Miss Minnesota by the age of eighteen. Modelled in lingerie catalogs, starred in all the industrial films Minnesota made about dental hygiene, she had it all, then . . . "

"Then what? What?"

"Then they found out she had pleurisy."

"Pleurisy? What the hell's that?"

"I dunno, but now she can't leave her bed. Even to go to Sunday service. The most beautiful woman in this goddamned town can't leave her own house. Drove all the men in town mad. She must have had every man waiting to be her suitor. Ol' Klupshas was sure one of them. But that was all before the pleurisy. Nobody wanted to hitch up with a sick woman. Nobody wanted a woman they'd have to care for just to watch to die."

Peterson's face was all red.

"But they all still loved her anyway, I guess. A way not everyone can understand. There's some things you love from afar. There's some things you love from afar more than the cold things that fall all around you, I guess. Poor Ms. Dubuque. Now she just lays in her bed and sleeps all day."

"How the hell do you know all this?" ol' Pill asked.

There was a soft glassy blur over Peterson's dim eyes as he let out a whisper and said:

"Because I was the one that used to bring the groceries to her house. I was the one who saw the truth."

There were tiny silken fairies and a fat dove circling Peterson's head.

"Then . . . " Peterson muttered.

"Then?" my brother followed.

"Then I fell. Desire. I fell into her carpet full of sweet unholy desire."

Ol' Pill-Bug shook his head and backed away. He held the bag at his side, watching without a word as a puddle of sweat seemed to turn golden along Peterson's brow.

"Sure, sure, man. Where does this lady live?"

Peterson closed his mouth and placed his hand over his chest. "The directions are burned in my heart. They're as true as a hardened stab wound."

My older brother just nodded and shook his head, listening to the directions but not hearing a word. He put on his old gray coat and took the bag and followed the main road out of town and past the plant and down by the creek to an old white house that rose right out of the woods like a place in a dream. There it was. A dream trying to grow right on earth. There was a big black metal fence that was sunken in on one side, a kind of fairy-tale castle that had all fallen sick, turning rusty and gray where the white wood trim needed to be painted and scraped. There was thick green moss and vines that grew right out of the ground and led around the dirt and cobble path and ran right up to the house, growing brown and tough along the hinges of the door. This place was sure not right. The trees had begun to wilt and fade with the dark change of autumn in the air. All the trees were bare and worn like old gray fingers growing from a grave. No, this place wasn't right at all. Ol' Pill-Bug could feel it in his gut. This place was sure haunted with some kinds of devils or spooks.

He knocked on the big white wood door once then backed away.

The door creaked and shuddered as an old gray-faced man stepped from the darkness, groaning a little like he was made of the same kind of rotting wood as the rest of the lousy house.

"Yes . . . " the old man hissed. His eyes were dull and gray. He smiled, showing his bare pink gums and one single working eyetooth. He wore a black suit and white shirt like an old butler, hunched over from the weight of his duties and the decay of the house.

"I'm here to drop off something for Ms. Dubuque."

"Do you have her medicine?" the old man wheezed.

My brother shook his head, then unrolled the bag.

There were two perfect peaches nestled in the pouch, gently nudging each other with their soft furry skin.

"Fruit," Pill mumbled. "I brought her some fruit. That's all I got."

The old man nodded and opened the door, waiving ol' Pill inside. The whole place was dark and dim. There were huge gray paintings that had been covered by dirty drop-rags. There were statues of gold that were covered in film and dust. There was nothing but death and filth in the air. Pill scratched his chin and gripped the bag tighter. He could feel the place moving along his skin. He could feel all the dying and death breathing its breath against the back of his neck. He shivered a little, staring at a huge marble staircase that rose to a floor above.

"Her room is up there," the old man wheezed. "I cannot take the stairs."

My older brother shrugged his shoulders and started up the stairs. There was nothing but darkness and gloom all around, sinking down into his skin, shaking at his poor bones. He could feel all his sweat drying up in his head as he climbed to the top and turned, staring at a pair of huge brown wood doors. He knocked once, holding his breath inside.

There was no reply.

He knocked again, then nudged the doors apart with his foot. He could smell a blush of fresh flowers and perfume. He could feel heat, pure undeniable heat welter from behind the door in sweet, gentle breaths. He pushed the door open and stepped inside.

The color nearly fell out of his eyes.

There was a heaven in a pink bed blossoming all around him.

He felt his teeth chattering in his head.

This lady was nearly naked in her own bed.

His hands felt clammy and weak at his side. He couldn't breathe. He could not swallow. He could feel his own sweat turn hot on along the back of his neck. He could feel all his skin grow warm like he had been kissed.

This pink parlor was heaven.

This poor pale lady laid in her own soft pink heart-shaped bed, complete with floral canopy. This lady's skin was nearly blue. Not blue, but lighter, whiter, pale like an insect, like a dream, nearly translucent and gray. Her bare blue toes wiggled, showing her red-painted toenails, propped up on a thousand soft round pink pillows. Her lips were painted pink, pink like cheap candy you might fit in your pocket to steal. This beautiful lady wore shiny pink makeup. This lady wore makeup just to sit in bed.

The lowly stockboy felt like he might swoon.

Her thin blue-white legs stretched out infinitely across her bed. He could see where her dull white skin ran up and around her cold blue thighs to the white and pink nightgown that flapped around her middle. There was her long brown hair that curled around her shoulders, there was her soft pink and white mouth that moved gently open and closed as she breathed. Her eyes were covered by a small black satin mask. Her hands rested across her belly as if she had been lain dead. There were flowers all around her. There were thousands of songbirds calling from somewhere in the room. The stockboy held his sweat as he stepped across her carpet, gripping the white bag in his hand. His face felt too weak to speak. Every part of his body was imagining what it would be like to touch, to caress, to hold such a woman. To kiss her neck, to smell her hair, he felt himself sinking into her carpet, melting like soft cake.

They would kiss like old lovers, hold each other close and never let go. Or grip each other's bodies like animals and devour one another with their lust. He could feel that poor carpet nearly rising to his ears. He could feel himself sinking so deep. He could not break his stare. He could not look away. He was under her sweet unassuming spell, sinking further in his own lusty thoughts still.

He could see her blue veins running beneath her skin. He could feel her skin moving beside his.

This pale woman never left her bed. There was no need. Anything she wanted was brought and left at her tiny white feet or placed on a pillow for her to eat. The stockboy felt like his fingers were no longer his own. He felt like his hands and feet now belonged to this lady, this cold, blue-skinned woman, who pulled him closer, closer, closer with her shallow breath and eyeless stare. He stood at the foot of the bed, smiling like a moron, grinning at the way her skin shone through her white negligee. He could see her narrow hips and thin pink lips. He could see through every one of her pores.

"Did you come with my fruit?"

Her lips didn't move as she spoke each word. Her voice was lilting and metallic and cold.

He nodded, then stared at the black satin mask.

"Uh, yes."

"Then set it down on the bed."

He didn't move. Maybe he couldn't. That poor fool just stared at her bare toes until she sat up and lifted the black satin mask from her eyes. The stockboy felt his poor heart jump from its store. He breathed in hard, staring at her pale blue eyes. He grew dizzy fast as they glimmered like cheap jewels in her pale blue sockets, turning with silver and light.

"Do you have the fruit or not?" she asked.

He nodded again. He could feel each part of his face being drawn to her. His nose, his eyes, his ears, his lips, his teeth, his tongue, his hair, all of it began to move from his face as he held the white bag at his side.

"Then place it on the bed."

He nodded then took one step forward and placed the bag on a round pink pillow.

"How much do I owe you?" she asked.

He could barely breathe. He felt his lips flutter as he tried to remember what it was ol' Klupshas had said.

"Ten? Is ten enough to cover the cost?"

He nodded dumbly as she leaned across her bed and slipped a single ten-dollar bill from under a pink pillow and held it in her pale blue hand. The lady leaned forward a little, indicating that he may approach. My poor brother, Pill, nearly wilted, taking the bill from her fingers, there was a moment, there was a moment when her touch sent cold tremors along his flesh and through his heart.

He slipped the money in the front pocket of his shirt and turned. He held the one blessed hand away from his body to keep it pure.

This heaven was something in his skin. Something he could hold in his hand. This heaven was something he could now afford. This feeling was something he could now have.

He kicked a silver can down the road and spat.

The dark blue night had just begun to settle in. The dark blue sky began to sink in through his poor flesh. My dumb brother pulled the ten-dollar bill from his front pocket and gripped it in his greasy palm. He stared at the design in its green marks for his plan.

Ten dollars.

Ten dollars to make one night in heaven.

Ten dollars to make him a man.

# the glass eye

**M**y life moved like a bad dream.

All the awful things I noticed seemed to happen without any damn reason. All the worst things I could imagine began to slither right around me.

Me and my own older brother still weren't speaking. His voice had seemed to kind of dry right up. He seemed hoarse and tired even when he sneered me a sore warning.

"Don't touch any of my goddamn things," was all he would grunt. Then he'd look me square in the face like he wanted to hit me hard, but he didn't, he just gritted his teeth and turned away and left me feeling low as dirt. He had every right. I had turned him in to save my own skin. I had turned my back on my own brother to escape getting into trouble. No matter how many times I tried to apologize, he just sneered and drifted away, shaking his head to himself. I had hurt him worse than I thought I could hurt anyone. He was my only brother, my only brother, and now I had no one in that crummy ol' town. I barely got to see him anymore, anyway. He worked nearly every day after school at the Pig Pen, trying to pay back the damage he had done to the hardware store. The rest of my older brother's checks went straight to my mother's hands, locked away tight for book fees or school supplies. But still there was the pile of nudie magazines that kept steadily and silently growing, filling a whole shelf in Pill's dresser and then spilling out of the closet under his dirty clothes. My mother didn't ever go in our room, except to return the garments she had just taken to the laundromat to get cleaned, but even then, she would just dart in and lay the clothes down on my bottom bunk, probably keeping her eyes closed as tight as she could, trying not to see the lot of sin that was blooming under her own roof. That damn trailer was small and cramped and she sure knew it, so she never pried into the tiny bunker of privacy me and my brother had been given as our room. No one talked about the fire at the hardware store either. No one mentioned it even in some threat. But it finally occurred to me that if Pill had just gotten a job in the first place, he could have bought that knife, instead of lighting those brooms and starting all the trouble that led to the damn silence between us, but I don't think he ever really caught on to that. He was still quietly stealing cigarettes and candy and nudie books and then I began to notice a huge greasy-green wad of cash he would shove into his pockets every time he left our room. Nothing in him changed but the warnings he gave me.

"Stay away from my porno mags," was all he would grunt as he walked away. That was me and my older brother. That was all we had to say.

The only other person I'd even bother talking to, Lottie, had been forbidden to congregate near me, on account of my wicked influence. By then she had been grounded a few weeks for stealing that beautiful glass eye and then everyone in town had heard of the fire at the hardware store and no one in class would even speak to me, let alone shoot marbles or spit or share a smoke. Lottie's wicked old man even had her moved out of the seat next to me in our class, replaced by a Lisa Havinshamp, who didn't have any pig-tails or stories to tell and was ugly and cross-eyed and quiet as hell and stunk of an old dull gray fetid odor like a elderly corpse's mothballs. So then I decided to go visit the Chief and buy some cigarettes and bother him for some kind of lonesome fear or spare light of hope.

Me, I stepped right up to the counter with a big smile, holding some stolen money from my mother's purse in my greasy palm. I watched carefully as the Chief turned, taking a swig from his awful silver flask. The whole place was silent like a tomb. The whole filling station looked cold and empty and drab. There was a thin gray dust all in the air and the floor looked like it hadn't been swept in some time. There were hardened dry insects stuck to the glass, married to the dirt and the grime, and rows and rows of cobwebs that glimmered from the flickering lights overhead. The Chief looked bad. There was some dark red blood shining along his teeth. Dark and red and still shiny. His eyes were deep and black and hung with fleshy gray bags. He was teetering a little in his seat, staring off into space with a grim, empty-toothed frown. An old gray fly circled his head like a spell, flickering off his thickly wrinkled skin without the Chief making a move. The Chief looked like he had just died. The only sign I had that he was still alive was his heavy black chest that fell and rose, breathing in each labored breath.

"How are things, Chief?" I smiled, not looking him in his cold black eyes. He was staring right over my head, twitching his lips at something just out of sight.

"Fine," he grunted. He kept staring off, far and away, maybe seeing something past all this empty space to the unholy things that haunted him and hid like phantoms in his sleep. Then the Chief's eyes snapped awake, turning cold and deep red. He turned to me and nodded, not wiping the red blood from his chin.

"What is it you need?" His voice was thin and hollow. His eyes didn't move. His nose twitched a little and he cleared his throat. Then he wiped the blood from his hardened gray lips with the flat of his hand. He looked like he had just awakened from some dark dream.

"Pack of Marlboros." I frowned, staring at the knot of wrinkles which spread from the center of his forehead like a gnarled old tree. There had to be some kind of mystery, some kind of wisdom buried in that skin. The Chief let out a little grunt and dug behind the counter and placed the smokes on the flat white linoleum across from me. I reached for them, but the Chief swatted my hand away, and leaned over the counter close to my sweaty, round face.

"This things are a curse, boy. But you are too young and dumb to see."

I shrugged my shoulders, gritting my teeth in my mouth. He

was drunk as always and being just as ornery and mean. His hot, sweet breath slid over his lips across the counter to my nose. He smelled like he had been pickled, like his organs had been embalmed with some kind of sour rotten gasoline.

"Do you know what I think? I think I should not sell cigarettes to you anymore, boy. I think I should not add to your poor foolish life."

He laughed a little, then uncapped his silver flask and spilled some liquor into his mouth. It seemed like the only joy this bastard ever received was in bullshitting poor dumb kids like me and taking drinks. He took another swig, then capped the lid and placed it back beneath his greasy black shirt.

"Well, what do you think?" he said. His empty black eye curled in a little wink as he stared at me hard, looking over my face.

"Drinking's a curse, too, Chief," I mumbled without looking away.

"How do you know about being cursed, boy? How do you know such a damn thing?"

Me, I backed away and shrugged my shoulders. The stolen money felt dull and heavy in my palm, like it might slip and drop to the floor and I'd never be able to pick it up. The Chief leaned over the counter and gripped me by the collar of my old blue shirt.

"Being cursed is like carrying a wound. A scar right in your golden flesh. Something that will not go away. Something that eats at your own sorry blood. Every day, it is always there. Every night, it is always part of you. The curse is what makes you who you are. It is what makes you who you will be. It is something you can never run away from. It is something you cannot escape, even with a good drink." His old gray teeth had a kind of glimmer that seemed to gleam deep into my eyes. His face seemed huge and old and wooden like the side of an old maple tree trunk. He nodded to himself, then let go of my shirt.

"But like I just said. You are too young and stupid to know a damn thing."

He snickered to himself a little, then punched the register with a snarl. "One dollar eighty-nine."

I placed the wrinkled-up, greasy, knotted, sweat-covered two dollars on the counter and slid them across to his wide gray hand. He shook his head and unfolded the bills, then hit the Sale button and the register opened with a little ring.

He slid the cigarettes across the counter without another goddamn word. His black eyes glimmered with some light. Then he closed his eyes a little and stared back at the empty white space where he had just visited before, not making a sound, not moving his eyes or nose, but still twitching his lips.

A droplet of dark red blood ran from between his teeth.

Then another. Dotting the white counter. Drip. Drip. Drip.

Hell, I just slipped the cigarettes into my pocket and nearly ran out of the damn place, straightened my collar as I got out on the street. My palms were all greased with sweat. I left the damn smokes in my pocket and walked home without even lighting one, rubbing the perspiration from my forehead with my sleeve. The Chief was a crazy old sickly bastard all right. He was some sort of creep. Going around grabbing kids like that. My hands were still trembling. He had scared the hell right out of me. I began to wonder why it was I bothered to go there at all. I began to wonder why the hell it was I even bought goddamn cigarettes in the first awful place.

Me, I walked up the gravel road that led to the lots and lots of trailers and mobile homes, then crossed between Mrs. Garnier's and Mr. Deebs's, down one row to where Val's shiny silver trailer stood. I walked around the side and froze in my place, staring at a big white squad car parked along her sweet gray stretch of gravel like a nightmare made right in metal. No. Not my Val. She was too delicate. Too sweet. Nothing criminal should ever befall such a heavenly creature. Nothing ungentle should ever touch her face. But there the shiny star read "Sheriff" along the car's white door. My teeth grew still in my mouth. That squad car was a sure sign of doom. Nothing good could follow that forlorn white vehicle. Only anger and blood. Only prison and the morgue. No. Oh, lord. No. I shook my head and crept around to see what unholy thing had moved itself upon my own sweet Val, but then as I made my way around to the front of her trailer, there was the most awful sight I think I could ever think to see.

No. No, nothing like that could ever be true.

That bastard of a deputy was making it with my poor, sweet Val. Their lips were locked together in one long sweet embrace. He had some nice red and white and gold flowers in a vase, pressed between their tight bodies as they whispered and kissed. There was his goddamn white squad car parked right in front of her place. There was his hands on her hips. Her mouth moving on his unholy lips. I felt all the spit dry in my mouth. All the blood nearly fell out of my head. The sight was enough to make me sick for a week. I picked up a gravel stone and threw it hard against her porch and then turned around and spat into the dust. The cold black silence of them together glistened in my ears. The quiet little lack of sound their lips had made, pressing together, made me want to find an old desolate mailbox to burn. I ran to our trailer and pulled open our screen door, gritting my teeth, and made for my room.

Then all the dark fears in all my nightmares broke loose.

The cold-eyed sorrowful stare of my mother and French, silent at our kitchen table, stopped me where I stood. They looked like a pair of real parental statues, just trying to smile, sitting there. But then French's voice rung through the air like a sad little choir, rightly sealing my doom.

"Do you think we can talk to you for a minute, Dough?"

It appeared his mouth hadn't moved with any of his words. It was all like a lousy kind of dream.

"Huh?" I mumbled. There was my own sweet mother and French at our crummy yellow table. Their eyes looked sad and stolid and stern. French had on a long face behind his shiny black glasses, his lips were curled in a smile that even he didn't quite believe. My mother's tiny fingers and his big white hands were crossed between the two of them. My mother bowed and smiled a little smile like an old kind of saint. Then I heard the worst four words I think I'd ever want to hear.

"Your teacher called today."

This time I was sure their lips didn't move.

"Huh?" I took a seat at the table and stared at my mother's face. It was calm and sad and soft and sweet. Her eyes weren't all lit up with fire or anger. Her eyes looked ready to break apart into a heap of thin gentle tears. I suddenly tried to remember what I'd done in goddamn school that day. I tried to remember what it was that I'd done so I could try to formulate myself a sturdy lie in the short time before I snared myself in some kind of trap.

"Your teacher says you haven't been doing so well. She says she's afraid you might have some sort of learning disability."

"Huh?" I mumbled again. Disability? The words fluttered like a pair of sickly birds around my head. The only person I knew that had a disability was my fat third cousin Ronny who got all his toes cut off by a factory machine and got to collect a check each month just for being careless. Disability? I really didn't know any other kind.

"You've been getting straight Fs. You haven't passed one single test. She says all you do is draw pictures instead. She says all you do is sit in class and daydream or look out the window and sleep. She says you don't seem to be learning a single thing. She says she's afraid you might have dyslexia or some reading disorder."

"Huh?" I didn't care for a thing my mother happened to be saying. It all sounded like some sort of misplaced name for calling me stupid, which I didn't ever try to fight or hide from. Me being not so bright was something I didn't think I could change. Me sleeping in class and drawing on my tests was just some habit of my own particular nature, disability or not.

"She says there's other things, too."

"Huh? Other things?"

"She says part of the trouble isn't just your grades. She says you just don't seem to get along with any of the kids in your class. You don't talk or play with the other kids so well. And at lunch you just eat and lay your head down. She says it's like you don't have any friends in your class. She says it seems like you don't want to even try and fit in."

My mouth was gaping with disbelief. There was nothing I could think to say. My mother stared into my face, her eyes trembling with tiny silver tears. Maybe my eyes were trembling the same way. My mother stared me right in the face and then she could see the truth without me saying a goddamn word. Ms. Nelson was right. I didn't have a damn friend in that class or town or in the whole world. My own brother wouldn't even speak to me. My only friend had been moved out of her seat. There was no other sweaty, dirty-fingered bastard I cared to know. The rest of the kids in my class could all burn in Hell. They all were empty, dumb-eyed kids without hearts or brains or souls, all hollowed-out children who would smile and frown and grow into the quiet, well-behaved, deadened kind of Sunday choir people their own lousy parents had once been, without any imaginations or fears or hatred or dreams. They would all grow up and feed their own dumb kids in the same quiet ignorant town that didn't allow for anything different or true or sweet like an open-mouthed kiss or burning fire or single breath of hope.

"She says she wants to give you a kind of test to see if you got this disability or not."

"Huh? A test? When?"

"Two days from now. Friday. After school."

"Friday? After school? Can't I take it during class?"

"She says it'll be on all the things you oughta know. All the subjects. Even some listening skills."

My face was flushed bright red. A test. A goddamn test on Friday after school. There was not a thing I could think of that was so cruel and indifferent and downright mean. This Ms. Nelson was really no better than the rest. Long sweet legs or not, this lady didn't have enough heart to look me in my eyes and see, to stare into my dirty face and make out the ends of the dark black hatred that wallowed in my face and filled the empty skin on the inside of me.

"What are you thinking, pal?" French quietly asked, still holding my mother's hand.

"Huh." I stared up into their white faces, holding back my own tears. "I think I'll take that test and fail and then all of you can be glad as hell when you finally see how dumb I really am."

"Dough!" my mother cried, biting her lips. "We just want you to be happy!!"

"If you wanted me to be happy, we woulda never left home."

My mother hung her pretty little head low in guilt and shame.

"That's not the way you oughta talk to your mother, Dough." French frowned.

I gritted my teeth and stared him hard in his long white face. "Don't tell me what I can and can't say." He was not my old man and no blood of my own, whether he treated my mother sweet or not. He was someone I suddenly wanted to hate and blame for all the lousy things I'd ever done wrong in that lousy town.

French squinted a little, tightening his thin lips and keeping a real stern face.

"We're not trying to blame you, pal. We just want what's gonna be the best for you."

"This is what I say. Nobody gave a damn what the best was before we moved to this lousy place. Now I don't have any ol' friends and now I'm getting crummy marks. Tell me how that's supposed to be the best?"

My mother shook her head, filtered out a sob into her sleeve. French wiped his glasses off with the corner of his shirt and placed them back on his nose.

"Don't think we don't see you're hurting here, Dough. But there's nothing we can do to take it all back. You yourself haven't given it much of a chance, though, pal. Running around like a little maniac, stealing things and starting fires, how did you think you'd make any friends that way?"

My eyes were all runny with salt and tears. My hands were clenched gripping the end of the table. French's face was a blank white plain. His eyes were calm and sad and big and blue. More than anything I wanted to let out a growl and spit right in his goddamn eye. But something stopped me deep down in my gut. Something in me up and turned and made me worried that ol' stern-faced French might somehow be right. I kicked my chair away from the table and stood, staring into his eyes.

"Tell my teacher I'll take that goddamned test and pass it just so she can see how dumb all the people in this town really are."

French blinked and warmed a little smile. My mother coughed a little and stopped crying, gripping ol' French's hand like she was a rowboat and he was the land and she might somehow float away if she wasn't careful about keeping his touch. I marched into my room and laid down on my bed and buried my lousy face right in the thin blankets, hoping to give in and just suffocate. But my tears kept rolling out my eyes harder until my mother called me for dinner, then again, and when French told her to just give me some time alone, I finally just turned over and stared at my shadow along the wall and fell asleep.

My lousy ol' brother came home from work and got changed and turned on the goddamn bedroom light because it was too much trouble to let a doomed man suffer in goddamn peace.

"Turn off the damn light!!" I shouted, and then I remembered that was the first thing I think I had said to him in about a week, but I didn't give a damn because all my lousy tears had dried along my face and made the skin around my eyes swell and burn and it was hard to see. I buried my head under the pillow and tried to fall back asleep, but I could just hear my brother eating dinner by himself and French and my mother talking and watching TV and the dog howling to be taken out and that was when I was sure that dingy, cramped hellhole of a trailer was the worst place a man could ever live. Prison or the morgue. That's what ol' French had said. Living in a damn trailer for the rest of your days was even worse. At least if you're in prison or dead there's no lies to tell about it. You sure ain't fooling yourself, pretending you're free. Living in a goddamn town like Tenderloin where everyone thought and looked and acted all alike, all holier and sweeter and smarter than you, well, it was a punishment more indecent and cruel than any time spent in a prison cell or ungodly tomb. I gritted my teeth together to keep from shouting. I made my hands tiny white fists at my sides and kept my eyes shut until my brother climbed in the bunk and went to sleep. There was something I wanted to tell him. That he was the worst brother a kid could ever have. I wanted to just break it all up and give in cry and tell him I didn't have a friend in the world and ol' Val was making it with the deputy and I had to take a goddamn test just to prove I wasn't dumb and how I had made my mother cry and all of us were definitely cursed, and this town, this whole town, this whole year was the worst I had ever lived, but I just kept my eyes closed and held it in to myself and then stared at my hand above my face until I saw a tiny faint breath appear against my bedroom window glass.

A breath upon my windowpane.

A quiet whisper in the night.

I shot up in bed and slid open the glass. That crazy girl, Lottie, was there, holding her pink bike, dressed in her old white flannel nightgown and a big dirty gray hooded coat and her older brother's construction boots.

"Dough, are you still awake?"

I nearly burst out of my skin and climbed out the window so fast that I forgot I was wearing my own dirty pajamas with the hole in the crotch, so I pulled on one of my older brother's crooked blue sweatshirts and wrapped it around me good. I climbed on down and followed Lottie around to the back side of our trailer, then we both took a seat in the dirt, both of us smiling like mad. My god, seeing her dirty little face and hundred pig-tails and crummy pink bike made me want to break down right there and cry, but I just kept staring at her round little head and couldn't stop myself from smiling.

"Do know what?" Lottie whispered, still grinning. "I got big news. My older sister just had her baby. Just a couple of minutes ago."

Her face was all flushed and sweaty and red. It looked like she had pedalled non-stop from her house to mine, maybe not even singing or stopping the whole way to breathe. The silver glimmer and shine off the trailer's side burned behind her dirty hair like a holy light. Her face looked pure and sweet and happy and good. There was something in her greasy little smile that made me want to think there was such a thing as hope. Something that made me want to believe it all might be true. But then in a whisper that was gone, too.

"She had it right at home," she mumbled. "Right in her bed. But it didn't make it. It was born blue."

"Blue?"

"Born not breathing. Born dead. Her poor baby is dead," she mumbled.

"Dead . . . "

"My dad wouldn't take my sister to the hospital to have it 'cause she wouldn't tell him who the father was so she had it right on the bedroom floor."

Then I understood what the Chief had meant.

I was cursed. Not in a usual way, not like my dead old man or my brother, the lowly blooming criminal, but cursed in a way to watch all the poor fools I ever felt for burn apart and suffer around me sure as brimstone. Cursed just as my mother or French or Lottie or even the Chief. Cursed to stand there and watch and live and see the cold black hand of fate turn upon all the unlucky ones I ever held to my heart or soul. Cursed like every warm-blooded human being, I guess I mean.

"Her poor baby," Lottie whispered. Her eyes were all lit with tiny silver tears.

"Do you think your sister is all right?" I asked.

Lottie nodded. "The doctor says so anyways." Her eyes were gray and small in the dark. Her skin was so smooth and bright with lines of tears. She nodded to herself, squeezing my arm.

"Do you know," she whispered. "Do you know what my daddy said?" she asked in quiet sweet tones. He. He. The devil behind the windows. The man in the dark. He was their father. He was the empty-eyed old man, keen with knives and saws. The man who cut into dainty flesh. The man without a soul.

"He said that baby was better off being born dead," she mumbled. "Better off to die right then than to live and breathe in the dirt."

Her eyes shimmered with tears.

"He said that thing didn't even have a soul. He said it wasn't even a real breathing creature. He said if it had taken a breath and died then it would have been something, but like that, like that it was only skin and bones."

My teeth began to chatter in my head. Maybe Lottie's old man was right. Maybe that baby didn't have a soul. Maybe he was right, too. Maybe it was lucky never to breathe, never to see all the things it felt sorry for left to hurt, maybe it had only been skin and bones, but it had been a part of someone's soul. Her poor, poor sister. It had been a part of Lottie and a part of her sister just the same.

"Did your sister name it?" I asked, staring away.

"No name," Lottie mumbled. "That's what the doctor put on his report. No name, no father, not even a tombstone. They're gonna bury it out back behind the fields without a marker to maybe help the crops grow." Her eyes became wide and dark. "Maybe that's the only reason it came. To help those plants grow."

Her face was lit bright like a saint, her fingers gripped my hand and made me hurt to cry or turn, but I didn't, I just watched how her face seemed so sweet and round and kept growing in the dark sky.

"I oughta go on home." Lottie frowned. "My father's probably missing me as it is."

I nodded. There was so much I wanted to tell her, so many things I think I wanted to say. But nothing seemed like it could even be whispered. Nothing made any sense on my lips.

"Just thought you might wanna know," she said.

Her eyes ran dry with tears as she let go of my hand and hopped on her bike and pedaled back along the dirt road, skidding from shadow to shadow up along the path toward her home. I sat behind the trailer a while more. My palm was sweet and warm with sweat. My fingers felt tight and stiff. My fingers felt shiny like gold. I could still feel where the heat of her hand upon my hand had grown.

My body was shaking from the cold.

I pulled myself inside my window and suddenly felt like I was wasn't there alone. I climbed out of my bed and stared up at my brother's bunk. He was fast asleep, snoring like a saw mill, clutching his sheets like he was in the midst of some ardorous throes. I shook my head and looked around. Nothing. Everyone in our trailer was fast asleep. But there still was that feeling that someone was in that room right with me. A kind of warmth like a sweet breath or kiss, a kind of sign of hope or a golden flicker of a hidden dream, I could feel it all moving around my head, making me uneasy and uncomfortable as hell. I stared out the tiny window once more, looking for her breath.

The glass was dry and clean.

That poor girl was home by now, creeping through that old horrible house in the dark, trying to keep in her breath so she didn't make a sound, shuddering with every beat that echoed a little like her old man's steps, moving through the shadows and the night to find the comfort of her lonesome bed. I could see her bare white teeth and face and unwashed hair. Her eyes were wide and blue and gray and silent. Her lips quivered to make a scream. Terror. There was something so dismal that that girl feared. The dark in her own house. The thousands of whispers when night would set in. I could see her quiet and alone, hidden under the covers of her bed. Then I could smell her sweet, sugary breath like cold milk with cream but full of spit and fear. Then I pulled on my own drawers and shoes, put on my brother's stocking hat, then dug into the dark of my dresser for the cold perfect touch of the thing I most needed, placed it in my pocket, and climbed back outside with a hopeless kind of grunt.

The cold gravel moved right under my feet without a sound. I pulled that sweaty red hat down to my eyes and crept through the dark infernal night, walking along the deep ditches on the side of the road, ducking if the yellow cross-beams of a truck or car flew by. Then I was there, at the end of her lonely dirt road, hiding behind a thin, gray, barren tree. A dim yellow bulb flickered in her house. Right behind those big blue front window shades. I held in my breath, feeling the sweat grow along my back. I moved close to the dirt, skipping from dark shadow to dark space, holding my body against another tree, then a tiny wood shed that stood a few feet from her big white porch. The gold bulb flickered, dimming its light then turning bright again, casting thick black shadows over everything. Then there was a form, a form made in black, a shadow, a man's tall thin body moved behind the shade.

I stood there in the dark, fighting to breathe. The cold glass eye moved against my hand in the reaches of my dirty coat pocket. I held it in my grasp, gritting my teeth, watching as the dark man's shadow moved or grew, pacing behind the thick black curtain, barely visible by the flickering light.

Then I knew just what I had to do. I knew why I was standing out there in Lottie's front yard in the middle of the night.

I was there to save that poor girl's soul.

The darkness seemed to loom right over me. I felt sure as hell. I never felt more scared in my life. Not scared of what was about to happen, but scared because I knew it was sure something I had to do. I held that glass eye tight in my palm. I felt its cold round shape like one single drop of blood shared between me and her, a single moment between us trapped cold and solid in time, a single patch of hope and sight.

Then I let that glass eye go. It rolled off my fingers like a perfect pitch, hustling through the air without a single sound, moving through the black space in a perfect arc until it met the glass pane of that front window and then the whole dark world snapped awake. It was like a scream that suddenly broke right apart, fading into your ears all at once. All that glass shattered and crashed with a terrific BLOOM!!! all over their porch and I was running down the road as fast as I could and nearly home before I could check to see that no dark man was following in the blackness of night behind me. I pulled myself into my bed and locked the window tight, curling up under the blankets of my warm blue bed, sure as hell that in a moment I would see his thin black shape and feel his hand upon my throat and then, and then it would be just how French had said. The cold empty trap of prison or the grave.

I laid awake all night, trying to figure out a lie in case Lottie's father somehow found out it had all been me. Nothing I came up with in my mind made any sense at all, so I could only hope that I hadn't been seen. Then I laid there, watching as the sun began to peek through the thick gray clouds that seemed to gather right over me and my brother's bed, trying to ask myself exactly what I had done. But there was no easy answer I could give. I had no idea why I did what I did. That glass eye now seemed like it had always been there just so I could do one lousy thing: creep through the dark and break that cold front window out in the lonely middle of the night. It didn't make a damn bit of sense to me. But it was something I had felt, something I was sure of from a part of me that usually only felt a kind of anger or hate, something for some reason I knew I had to do. It was something I hadn't had any real conscious thoughts about. Then it all seemed to be like a distant kind of dream I always had; somehow I had always known exactly how it would all end without ever needing to fall asleep.

Thursday came and I wandered through it like a maze.

Poor, poor Lottie wasn't even in class. I wondered all morning what had happened to her. Maybe I had dreamed the whole thing. Maybe that glass had broke and the light poured in and her wicked old man just disappeared and she was free now somehow and maybe she just ran away. I could still feel the way her hand had cupped beside mine, her sweaty skin burning with fear and hope right next to me in the dark. A kind of thing like that will stay in your heart and head for a lifetime, I swear. It was like she was still sitting next to me all day, and when I'd look to stare at her dumb gray smile, she'd just disappear. The whole school day left me feeling desperate as hell, so I decided I might stop by Our Lady of Perpetual Martyrs church for some help.

There was really nowhere else to turn. I was in need of a real sweet miracle, and the way I had always heard it, those things only happen in church.

The place was dark and still and empty.

There was ol' Mrs. Pheeple, the blue-haired lady who played the big pipe organ at Sunday mass, humming to herself up in the balcony, paging through her sheet music for evening tarry service, and some dusty-looking priest I didn't recognize sitting in the very first pew, mumbling something sweet and shady up to God. There was nothing but that ol' priest's whispers and the light sighs of the organ keys being set into place, and the smell of golden burning incense and the white and blue light that cut through the stained glass in deep opaque shapes, and the clouds of dust that rose all above my head from the high glass lamps and steeple above, nothing but quiet and silence and the remarks of all these holy ghosts making their desperate prayers, so I knelt in the last row and decided to do just the same.

There was sweet Jesus nailed up on his cross.

His hands and arms outstretched in a beatific hug.

I closed my eyes and made myself up a proper prayer.

I prayed my sweet Jesus would see I was sincere and look into my poor unkept heart and make a change there that would save my soul and keep me from a life filled with fire and trouble. I knew he was the one to ask. If he could change water into wine and heal the dead and blind and sick, surely, surely the hopeless soul of an eleven-year-old couldn't be too much to grant. Let me pass the test. Let me pass the test. Make me smart just for tomorrow. Let me pass that test.

I opened my eyes and breathed in the holy dusty air.

I waited for some holy fire to burn above my head.

There was nothing. My armpits boiled with sweat. I felt my stomach turn. Nothing, no change, no weight lifted off my soul. I gripped the edge of the pew and stared up into his sore white face.

*No.* His long white face seemed to frown. This was something I had to do myself. This was something I was supposed to do by myself all along. I nodded and in my dull red heart, I understood. My sweet Jesus was right. Nothing good or sweet was ever handed out or just given to a plain fool. This was something I'd have to do all alone.

I knelt in the aisle and winked at him just once with a smile. This Jesus was about always right.

I crossed the dirt road home and up to our front steps. Things could be okay. But it was up to me to save myself. I had to pull myself out of my own mess. I sure as hell had no idea how I was going to do a crazy stunt like that. I marched up the steps, trying to think. The screen door was open and right away I could hear my mother crying to herself somewhere inside. I opened the door and held my breath and stiffened a little as I saw her sitting on the floor, sobbing beside an old small brown cardboard box. I knew right away what was inside. All my father's old rotten things. My mother looked up and forced a smile, then wiped some tears from her face, and then looked away.

"I'm sorry, baby," she said through a breath full of snot and tears. "I don't know what gets into me. I was just cleaning and I saw the box and then I just opened it up and . . . "

My mother bowed her head and finished off her sentence with some more tears. Then she took a deep breath and straightened herself up a little and lifted a tiny old photo out of the box.

"Look what I found."

I let out a sigh and stood beside her, gritting my teeth. There was nothing in that box I wanted to see. My old man was dead and gone. I was still feeling the curse of his hellacious life moving on my own. There was no photograph I cared to see that would somehow make me understand a goddamn thing about all those insidious dark dreams I had dreamed. My mother smiled, patting me on my greasy mop-head. There in her hand was a picture of me and my old man, standing beside his old yellow rig. The Hornet. That's what he had called his truck. There was no faster rig on his line. The Hornet 509. He used to park that big ugly yellow truck cab out in front of our house back in Duluth and all the lousy neighborhood kids would come on by and try to climb around on its huge tires and beg my old man to give them each a chance to blow its horn. That truck's horn was like a lightning bolt, man, that was like a call from God. Sitting up in that cab on my old man's lap, wearing his greasy blue Yankees cap, gripping the big black wheel and tugging the horn that gave a sound like a shotgun shell or mighty dam breaking, staring out over that dashboard and straight ahead to the road that seemed to stretch out for millions and millions of miles, looking straight into the future and somewhere past it all, somewhere far away but still close up ahead, well, that was about the sweetest moment I think I had ever had.

I gave my mom a good hug around her waist.

"It'll be okay, Mom. It'll be okay."

My mother's sweet blue eyes were all sagging with tears. She placed the photograph back under some of my old man's dirty clothes and bowed her head again. Then something in that dark brown box caught my eye. Something that wasn't right. I moved an old blue pair of jeans aside and shook my head, staring into the box without saying a word, without making a goddamn sound.

No. It couldn't be real. It couldn't be true.

My mother looked up and stared at my face with a frown.

"What's the matter, baby? What's wrong?"

My heart was beating full of my blood. My whole body felt like it was filled with ice. I couldn't afford a breath. I couldn't afford a whisper or sigh.

The green glass eye.

There in the bottom of that old dark box was that goddamn shiny green glass eye.

My mother gave a little smile and lifted that thing out of its place, cupping that unholy glass orb in the palm of her hand.

"Oh, this? This was your dad's. It used to belong to an old uncle of his. They were real close. Your daddy got it after his poor uncle was hung."

My face was bright red and still. I couldn't talk. I couldn't speak. I knew absolutely no words to say.

"But . . ."

"What? What is it, babe?"

My lips were fluttering beside my mouth. My teeth were shaking in my head. There shining in my mother's hand was a thing that had somehow outlived my father's death. A strange token that had moved beyond the grave. I suddenly forgot how his voice had sounded. I had forgotten all the lines on his face. It was like staring down into the depths of some dark well, so cold and hopeless and empty, and then instead of seeing your own face at the bottom, there was your old man's just floating there alone and out of place.

This was impossible. This didn't make any sense. I had thrown that eye through Lottie's front window. I had seen it break her glass.

"Nothing. Nothing makes any sense," I whispered, feeling my hands shaking at my side. I turned away a little as my mother squinted and then placed the glass eye back in the box.

"I know how you feel, Dough. There are a lot of things I don't think I'll ever understand about your daddy dying. But I guess it's those things you and I just have to try to make do with. All we can do is try to remember him and accept what we don't quite get."

No. No. No. This was surely some goddamn sign.

Her lips crowned the side of my cheek then she turned and disappeared into the bathroom. I could hear her begin to cry all over again. That green glass eye sparkled along the bottom of the box, shining and calling and speaking to me, and then, right then, right there I made a plan. I took that glass eye out of the box and made a plan to escape all the things that tied me to my minor un-kept life. All my things would not end up in a cardboard box. I was not about to send myself off to my father's same grave. I ran into my room and dug under my bed for all the stolen porno mags and cool smokin' unfiltered cigarettes I had taken from my older brother or the gas stations or convenient stores all around town, and I dumped some of them in my older brother's closet on top of his collection of pornography and oily clothes. Then the rest I heaved into the trash. I snapped every cigarette at its middle, then dumped them all in a big black plastic bag and emptied it all in the Dumpster a few lots away. I stood there outside the big green metal box, eyeing all my mess, staring down in the shiny rot and the glossy mold and the poor, poor dew of all the things I'd done when people like French and my mother and Jesus and my teach-ers told me not to. Now you might say that that green glass eye of my old man's was only some sort of coincidence, and so every-thing I did that followed was some sort of confused mistake, and you know what, I might be inclined to agree, but a change made in the heart doesn't always rely on what you think is the truth, more than likely it's something you just really want or need to believe. So I looked down there at all the lousy lies I had laid and unholy ways I had spent my time, smoking stolen squares and reading nudie magazines, and then I felt like nothing in me had really changed at all. So I dug down in there in the trash and saved one shiny nudie magazine and one broken cigarette in case I had been fooled again and later found out all that talk about redemption and hope and purgatory was just wishful thinking and I had been wrong. Those I kept in my bottom drawer, with my collection of goddamn vinyl wallets from Aunt Marie and a shark's tooth and a scapular and some shotgun shells and that green glass eye, which, in the strange workings of my unlucky life, might have all somehow served me good.

Then, after dinner, I read through all my books and studied as hard as I could for my goddamn exam. Nothing felt like it would settle in the hollow parts of my head, but I kept on reading and studying until it got dark and my mother whispered me off to bed and gave me a kiss goodnight and turned off the light and shut the door and I thought about that cold green eye just sitting in the bottom of that drawer. Now the dark had settled in and I felt like I couldn't sleep and there was nothing else to see in the blackness of my room but the truth.

That night I laid awake worried and scared, feeling the dull weight of my father's hands laid on my skin. I trembled under my sheets, trying to fall asleep, trying to take comfort in anything, anything I could think, but all I could feel was my old man's living fingers moving along my spine. There along my own poor flesh was surely the mark of his skin. But there was nothing there that showed a curse. There was no sign of any unholy blood or hex or bad luck. Then I felt something warm in my head. Then I felt it down in my heart. There was no proof that my old man's life had ever been bad. There had been no sign that he had been ever unlucky, except in the dumb things my brother had told me or the dreams I had dreamt in my own poor poor mind. All the things that had gone bad were because of me. Me and my older brother had taken all that dumb foolishness all in our rotten little hands and had dug ourselves deep in our own awful grave of dirt. There was nothing in our skins that made us doomed. There was nothing there that laid us down any dark path. All the things that had ever burned had fallen from our own dubious hearts. All the lies and pain and hate and rage had been ours. Our own to face and wrestle and finally set free.

I listened to my brother's breath as he fought to sleep.

His throat sounded sore and dry. His chest sounded full of weight. I climbed out of my bed and stood beside his bunk and stared at him as he slept. His face looked old and tired and sad. He looked worn and beat and saintly, like my own old man. His eyes seemed to roll with heavy dark dreams. His chest rose and sank as he mumbled in his sleep. There in that dark blue moment right before dawn I was sure in my heart that the both of us were certain to be okay. The truth was there in his gentle, unmoving face. Outside I could hear a moonlit cry somewhere in the night and I took it as some sort of sign. Right in the dark, I stood there beside his bed and folded my own dirty hands and made a prayer and mumbled it to myself until it was light and I was sure the both of us had been genuinely saved.

Tomorrow was Friday and the day of my test.

Tomorrow would come and nothing would ever be the same.

# hell's fire has arrived

The bed above mine burned while I was asleep.

Cold unholy morning light broke right through the nasal rhythm of my congested snores and the slippery folds of my own clenched teeth as thin gray smoke blossomed from the bunk above me.

I pulled myself out of bed and stared up as my older brother lit another unfiltered smoke. He was lying on his back. He was staring at a tiny silver spot somewhere above his head. There was something that burned there like a dream, but not that far away, something just a little closer, sitting in the space just out of his reach. His old tired eyes looked tiny and thin. His one eyebrow had begun to finally grow back. A thin black line of hair had sprouted through the thick red scab that ran from the base of his hair to the point right above his nose. A thin spurt of smoke poured over his lips as he took a long meaningful drag, shutting his eyes to keep whatever had woken him up trapped inside. His chest rose as he let all the smoke out through his nose, keeping the cigarette clenched between his thin gray lips. He caught sight of me staring at him out of the corner of his eye and then offered a thin silvery smile that seemed to glimmer with the mystery in his eyes.

"Go on back to sleep," he mumbled. "It ain't even dawn."

"I can't sleep," I whispered. I leaned against the frame, still staring into his face.

"Why's that?"

"Today's my test. I think I'm gonna fail."

"You ain't gonna fail. You're probably the brightest kid in that goddamn class. This whole damn town is stupid as hell."

I shook my head. "I dunno. I still think I'm gonna fail. Maybe I can just run away. Hide out in some boxcar for a while."

"Sure you could, but it won't change a damn thing."

"What do ya mean?"

"Can't change the way you are. You just always happen to worry about all the damn little stupid things."

He let out some more smoke through his mouth then turned on his side and stared right at me. The cigarette stuck to his lips as his face became very stern and serious and true.

"If you still think there's really such things as ghosts and the Devil and all that following you, well, you're a goddamn fool."

He turned back on his side and ashed the cigarette on the blue blanket beside his head. I stared at him for a while longer, then crawled back into bed. There were still a few hours left before I had to get up, so I pulled the covers up over my head and kept my eyes shut and finally fell back asleep.

RRRrrrrrring the goddamn alarm went off and I flew out of bed and made my way into the bathroom and washed my face and got all dressed and by the time I sat down to eat some breakfast, he was already gone. There was no big white cereal bowl in his place. No stains of gray milk or crumbs left where he would sit. I stared out over my half-empty glass of milk and felt that empty space all around my head.

"Mom, where's Pill?" I asked.

"He said he had to get to school early. Had to study for a test."

I nodded to myself and finished my cereal and glass of milk and got my things ready and stepped out the door for the worst day of school in my life. My mother stopped me at the door and kissed me on the top of my head.

"Make us proud, Dough," and then I realized that was her own sweet way of telling me I sure better not buckle in and fail. I marched through the gravel and the dust and the dirt, all alone by myself, watching as my lonesome single shadow crossed the flat gray space of the empty muddy road. I made it to school and took my seat and just sat there dreaming of what a horror that test would be. Lottie wasn't in school again and that worried me even more. Then before the bell rang, I heard from Mary Beth Clishim that Lottie and her sister had left town to go live with an aunt in Aubrey. I didn't know what to think. Maybe I was too worried about that test. I guess I felt good that they had both gotten away. There sure didn't seem to be any hope for me now, though. I don't think I ate a thing there during that lunch. My whole stomch was tied in knots the whole day. Then, finally, the last bell rang and when all the kids had left for home, my teacher, Ms. Nelson, patted me on the shoulder and then handed me the test. The test was five pages, thin and gray and black and white, there was a map of the world stitched somewhere in mimeograph on some facing page, empty multiplication tables, and a vocabulary test. There were missing blanks and true or false and multiple choice and every damn nightmare answer to every question I think I'd ever been asked.

I closed my eyes and felt like lying my head down on my desk and just letting myself fall into a deep soundless sleep.

But instead I just took a breath and put the pencil to the page and began to scribble whatever things wandered into my head. Then nearly two hours had gone by and I finally I just got up out of my seat and put the test down on Ms. Nelson's desk and stared at the way she tried to make a little white smile.

"Do you want me to look it over now or wait until after the weekend?"

Heck, I knew what this lady was trying to do. She had already thought I had failed that damn test and was asking me if I wanted a few days of time to breathe before my mother and ol' French and the whole rest of the world came right down on dumb ol' me.

"No. No, I wanna know now."

Ms. Nelson nodded a little over a frown, then took out her thick red pen and began marking up the goddamn test. She started with the geography part. Mark. Mark. Mark. Double-mark. Then the vocabulary part. Mark. Mark. Mark. The damn white paper looked like it had suddenly been infected by some horrible kind of red-blotch disease. I could feel the same color running all over my own skin. Ms. Nelson just kept marking away until she got to the math part. Then her pen just stopped. The red tip moved beside each answer, ready to strike, but it just sat still in the little air above the page. Then Ms. Nelson had on a big smile, grinning like a damn fool.

"You got all the math problems correct." She winked. Then she moved back through some fill-in-the blanks and the red pen began to dip and strike, nearly marking every answer I had made. Then the multiple choice and true or false were all the same. Mark. Mark. Mark. The damn thing made me sick. I shook my head, leaning against Ms. Nelson's desk, trying hard not to spit in her pretty blue eyes. Then she finished and flattened out the test and capped her beautiful red pen and turned to me and offered me the warmest smile I had seen.

"What?" I kind of grunted, looking away.

"It looks like I was right. You seem to have problems with your reading. Your math score was one hundred percent. But all the other questions were dependent on your ability to read. I think that's why you're doing so bad. I think you have a reading disability."

I shrugged my shoulders and felt like bursting into goddamn tears. Ms. Nelson put her soft white hand on my hand and gave it a little squeeze.

"No, no, this is good, Dough. Now we can get you some help. Now we'll get you some help and then you'll learn to read right and get straight As without even trying."

My eyes still felt hot with tears.

"Here." She wrote something in red pen across the top of the test and then let go of my hand.

"Tell your parents I'll talk to them this weekend, okay?"

I nodded. I looked at the test.

"Do you know what that says?" she asked, pointing to her red handwriting across the top of the page. The words kind of wavered right in my eyes. I tried to pull them all apart, but it didn't seem to make any damn sense to me.

"It says:

"'Dear Mr. and Mrs. Lunt,

"'Dough is going to do fine.' "

I marched on home with that goddamn test glued right to my hand. There in indelible red ink was my perfectly round handwritten fate.

The curve of her words were sweet as a kiss.

I walked right past my trailer and down the two lots and over to Val's shiny silver trailer to share the good news and then stopped still in my tracks when I saw her thin silver screen door hanging from one dull, broken hinge. The place was still and silent. There was no sweet singing coming from inside. There was no delicate whisper or soft sighs melting through the air like doves circling in a halo. I crossed up her gray steps and pressed my face to the lopsided door and then whispered her sweet name.

"Val?"

Her long white legs did not appear. There was no sweet smell of her cigarettes or the click of her cheap high heels against the tile or carpet floor. Her front door was wide open. There was no one moving inside. There was her soft red sofa. There was her black-and-red Oriental screen. But her blue lamp was broken on the floor. Two of her shiny cheap metal kitchen chairs were upturned on their sides.

"Val?" I called again.

No reply again. I stepped on inside, trying not to breathe. My heart was pounding in my ears. There were sure some signs of violence all around me. The broken vase and the chairs looked like the dead, just lying there in their places. The door thrown off its hinges swung back and forth a little. The nice blue shades were all drawn and it was all dark and empty and still. There was one of Val's long black stockings left thin and alone along the middle of the floor. It looked like a molted snake skin, all menacing and cold lying by itself there. Then I spotted the other stocking a few feet away, balled up in the hallway. Thin and transparent and looking as lost as hell.

"Val?" I called again.

There was nothing. None of her sweet white skin or glimmer of her precious voice. No sultry whisper or sound of her bare feet or sigh. My whole heart felt empty. My hands were shaking at my side. There was the sound of water dripping from her sink. Drip, drip, drip. Each droplet met the metal sink in a hard, mean-spirited little sound making the whole trailer seem old and empty. Drip, drip, drip. I couldn't hold my breath any longer. Then I could hear the creak of bare feet against the tile floor.

There was her long thin shadow moving down the hall.

"Val?"

Her lips didn't utter a sound.

My poor sweet Val stepped into the light. Her long thin body moved from the shade of the dark. My mouth trembled as I stared into her softened face.

This wasn't true. This wasn't her.

"Oh, my Dough. Don't look at my face," she whispered.

My lips turned still and dry. All my blood turned cold in my veins. This could not be her. This was not my Val.

"Please don't stare at me, baby. Don't stare at my face."

There were two huge black lumps beneath each of her eyes. Cold and dark and black and gray and burdening like weights. Then her soft pink lips had been split. Dead and red and gray and opened. Then there was a shiny red mark on one of her cheeks made by someone's teeth, dug deep into her soft skin, a bite mark, heavy and dark and running beneath one of her swollen eyes. Two indentations of teeth. She was wearing a heavy black sweater and loose blue jeans. None of her bare skin was showing. Nothing sweet of hers shone free.

"What . . . what hap-pened . . . "

"That man," her swollen red lips whispered. "That awful man came by again last night and did this to me."

No. My teeth rattled in my head. No. This wasn't true.

"The deputy?" I muttered, clenching my fists at my side. I could see his empty grey face. I could hear his empty throat and his voice and all his lies.

"No, no. Of course not. Mort would never do such a thing. It was that man, Henry, that cowboy with . . . "

The man with the sandy-colored Stetson hat. The cowboy with the bone-handled knife.

"They caught him right away. They got him right last night."

"What are those?"

There by her feet were two black suitcases, closed and tight and old and worn. They looked full and heavy and ready to go.

"I'm going away. I'm taking a trip. I need to . . . get away from all these things."

"But what about Pill and us? What about me?"

Val muttered something to herself in a whisper, then kissed my forehead with her bruised lips.

"You'll always be with me in my heart. You'll always be with me."

"But we need you, Val. We don't want you to leave."

"I know, I know, but I have to. I have to get away now or I'll never leave." Her darkened eyes were twinkling with tears. Her lips split apart to mutter something else.

"But we love you . . . " I cried.

"I know. I love you, too . . . " Val crinkled up into a worn face full of tears. "I . . . " She covered her eyes and turned, disappearing into her bathroom.

There it was, clear as a skull wound. My poor sweet Val was moving. My poor sweet Val was already gone. I looked around her soft, delicate place once more and saw her nice red sofa and black screen and those lacy stockings lying there by themselves, looking as dark as bruises, and then I felt myself turn ill so I ran right out to our trailer and straight to my room and laid down right in my bed, feeling all the tears burn along my face.

"How was your test, honey?" my mother called from the other room.

I lifted my sweaty face from the slippery pillow and let out a cry.

"I find out next week . . . "

I could hear my mother whispering and stepping down the hall toward me and my brother's room, then she was stopped by French's soft voice.

"Give the man a little time alone to just sit and think."

I could hear my mother's breath right outside the door. I could nearly smell her sweet hair salon stink. Then she stopped and gave in and turned away, closing our thin wood door the full way. I could still hear her whispering to ol' French out there, maybe starting to cry, but then I just buried my head under my pillow, laying there, hoping I might die so I could just end all this grief in one single blow.

About an hour later my mother came in.

The dark shadowed most of her face. The rest was bright and white and pretty. Her skin smelled of dried flowers, the kind your own mother might press between the pages of an old dictionary, kind of sweet and old and dusty. It made me feel hollow in my chest.

"Dough, honey, are you okay?"

"I'm fine."

"Val said you came by and were pretty upset."

"I said I'm fine." She patted me on my head.

"Do you want to talk about it at all?"

"No. I don't wanna talk about it ever again."

"Okay, darling. Okay. Dinner's ready if you wanna come out. French and I aren't going anywhere tonight. We'll be right out there if you want to talk, okay?"

I nodded just once then turned back on my side. I imagined all the lousy things happening in my life in one long dark night. My old man dying. Us leaving our home. Moving here. Getting in trouble in school for things I never did. The Chief looking into me. El Rey's fence getting knocked down. Getting caught for starting that fire. Lottie's old man. Her sister's baby dying. That glass eye. Taking that awful test. Having to look at poor poor Val like that. I could see it all, moving like the moon across a dark blue sky, stretched through empty clouds and stars, slowly setting, setting downwards to the golden dawn. I sat up and looked out my window and I realized the worst part of it all was how lonely I felt now without my older brother, Pill, there to help me walk through it, to whisper some dirty old joke or punch me on the arm to let me know I wasn't that alone.

I looked out my window and stared at how the night was setting in. My older brother would be coming home from work soon. He'd be walking right across the road all alone, maybe grunting to himself, smoking a cigarette, hating the way all those damn silver trailers looked, stacked so tight beside one another, the exact same way I hated it everyday I came home. It made me all worried suddenly. It made me suddenly scared. It was all running out on me. All these things were slipping right past.

I had something I had to tell my brother. I had to tell him about Val. I had to tell him some apology that couldn't wait.

I pulled myself out of my bed and stepped into the hall, then put on my older brother's sweatshirt and made for the front screen door. There was my mother and French curled up beside one another on the old rusty sofa, leaning into one another, holding each other tight. They looked good and sweet sitting there together. They looked the way a pair of folks should.

"Whatcha doing there, pal?" French smiled, tapping the silver top of a can of beer. I gave a little smile as I found the dog's old brown leash.

"I'm gonna go take Shilo for a walk and wait outside for my brother to come home."

He stared at me and nodded just once.

"That's sounds awful nice of you."

He winked at me, then turned his head back around to watch the game. My mother smiled at me, resting her cheek against his big square shoulder. I stepped outside, tying the dog to its leash. The dark was cool and blue and turning black in the sky. It was still kind of warm outside. I looked back quick and saw their two heads resting beside one another, then I smiled to myself. Seeing my mother and ol' French like that seemed like a good sign. It seemed like everything might be okay.

I laid down on my back and stared up at the dark blue sky, holding that big ugly dog close, watching the dirty gray road for a lonely thin shadow that would come shrugging from out of the blackness and into the pools of bright yellow cast by the dingy silver trailers' lights and then in that moment, seeing my older brother there, I would be sure that everything was going to be fine.

I laid there a long time, running my fingers under Shilo's neck, scratching its soft white fur, searching for chiggers or fleas or ticks. Its skin was smooth and soft and nearly pink and clean. That dog just laid there beside me, breathing against my face, staring at me warmly with its one working eye. We laid there together breathing on each other for a long time.

It was late as hell by now.

It made me worry that my older brother wasn't ever coming home.

They sat in the backseat of Lulla Getty's old man's car.

Making out.

This girl Lulla and my older brother were sweet and heated as all hell, going at it like they had just gone to prom or something. Their lips moved so fast, there was spit all along their chins. Heck, they didn't care. Soft little sounds muffled from their lips, mmmph, mmph, smooch, smooch. Boy. The shape of Lulla's fuzzy green sweater was like some ungodly soft slope with a gravity all its own. There right below her neck, Lulla's top sweater button was undone. One button had slipped from its spot which showed her white freckled neck. Shhhhhhh, it whispered. Shhhhhhhhhhh. My brother was sinking right into some poor poor infinite delight. He felt his own clouded gray sweat moving all along his paws. He felt the soft vinyl sticking to his pasty-white skin.

Those dark red lips.

He felt them sinking into his dreams. Kiss-kiss. Kiss-kiss. He felt himself nearly blossoming into a whole damn parade of foolishness and dumb things to say. But he just kept kissing her, looking at the way she kept her eyes closed and breathed through her nose so earnestly.

Those dark red lips curved just above her round little chin.

They parted as she mouthed him another kiss.

"Don't make any noise," she whispered with a smile like a little kid. Mischief. This girl was sure some kind of sorely wanted trouble. This girl was a lost sinner, too. Her face was soft and round and very prim like a real young beauty queen. The skin around her neck looked shiny and freckled all fright. Shhhhh. Shhhhhhh. That skin looked like the place where every good dream began. The dark blue car was parked in front of her own folks' house. There were some golden lights and the flicker of the TV running from her parents' window. They were both asleep, dreaming their own dull sexy dreams. There were two big maple trees that hung just over the car, making it nice and dark and shady. There was the soft whisper and fade of the night breeze moving tiny leaves against the windshield. Soft, soft. The whole damn world smelled soft and sweet like this girl's perfume. This girl's dark red lips moved next to his, slow as a Sunday School prayer.

"Do you have it?" She smiled, leaning in close to my brother's face. His heart was beating hard in chest. Oh, lord, he felt he might die. He felt ready to break. His hands were all slickered with sweat. He dug into his front jeans pocket and pulled out that ungodly rolled-up ten dollar bill. That money somehow seemed kind of blessed. That money sure seemed like a tip straight from God or the Devil or both. He placed it in the sweet white hollow of her small soft hand and fought to breathe. Lulla's lips moved a little, flowering like a beautiful little bouquet, as she folded the money up and put it in back pocket of her tight blue jeans. Man, her jeans were looking tight.

"Do you have a . . . you know . . . a rubber?" she whispered, moving her nose beside his soft pink ear. He felt his whole dumb weak body go tense. His forehead seemed to be raining with sweat.

"No," he mumbled, already shaking with hope and fear. That poor sap. He had forgotten. He had one condom hidden in his bottom drawer for about the last thousand years, just sitting there hoping and waiting. This poor damn fool. Her sweet sweet breath moved right over his skin like pink sugar icing. Like sweet glaze on a cake. Lulla kissed the side of his neck. She planted a red lipstick mark right there like a prize. Hello, it seemed to whisper. This makeup mark is love.

"That's okay. My daddy made me go on the pill when I turned sixteen." Her eyes became thinner. "You worried about Rudy or anything?"

"Why?"

"Him being my boyfriend and all."

"Boyfriend?!!" Pill backed away a little, rubbing at his neck. "I thought you . . . ya know . . . "

"Just fucked? Sometimes I guess. That's the only time I see him. I just wondered if you were worried about it at all. I mean, that's the reason you wanna do it right? Make it with his girl and all, huh?"

"I didn't know you were his girl."

"Sure," she said. "I'm not really his girl anyway. It was just a little joke I was playing." She looked around then shrugged her shoulders once. "Guess you're ready, then?" she asked.

He coughed a little, sitting completely still. Finally he gave a little nod.

My god.

This girl's tiny white hands moved like scared little birds over his chest, then down, down, down to his thighs, running between his legs then up again, stopping where she could feel him trembling in his middle. His eyes were wide and full of fear. Fear of what? Maybe peeing in the backseat right there like Bill Feckenstein did the time he tried to do it the first time. Fear? Maybe he would do it all wrong. Yeah, like he might take a turn at the wrong place and end up in the wrong town. Maybe she might figure he was still a cherry and change her mind. Maybe once the drawers were off, she'd shake her head, "no way, not that," and leave him there all undone in her old man's car. Christ, christ, anything could happen here. He was lucky if he made it through without wetting his goddamn underdrawers.

"Don't be scared," this girl Lulla said. Boy. That red smile was brighter than the whole dumb night sky and all its shimmering stars. That smile was enough to make you think making it in the backseat of a car was just about the best place you could ever choose for such a thing.

This girl Lulla leaned back a little, then unbuttoned her dark green sweater, button by button, one by one, down, down, down.

Hmph.

This girl's pert breasts curtseyed a little as she unclasped her deep black brassiere in the front. Then there shone the palest most beautiful plain of flesh my brother thought he had ever seen. It was like heaven, all right. But made of skin. He could feel his bottom lip trembling somewhere on his head. Shhhhhhh, he heard everything whisper. This is only your dream. This girl Lulla wrapped her thin white arms around my brother's head, kissing his mouth softly. This was all some sort of dream come true. He kissed her softly, feeling her tiny tongue moving in his mouth. There balled up in her cheek was her pink bubble gum. He got worried about it sliding down his own throat. He got all nervous and lost control and just bit her lip.

"Ouch," she mumbled, pulling away. "Watch my mouth."

"Sorry." He tried to smile. This girl nodded, then moved in close all over again.

"Okay, do you wanna do it, then?"

This girl whispered those words in his ear, close enough so he could feel her breath and soft silver spit. Her voice was like a warm little bird song that skipped in his head.

Do you wanna do it then?

Do you wanna do it then?

Do you wanna do it . . . then?

My god, his poor hands were shaking at his sides. He could not believe his luck. He could see all her tiny red freckles, like little roadmarks all over her body, tiny little magical whispers left along her cool white skin. Breathe, you dummy, breathe. He managed to moved his dirty mitts up along her bare chest, cupping her warm breasts, he could feel the heat burning all along his spine, all through his body, making him feel sick and weak. He could just about die or fall apart. This beautiful girl was nearly a woman. He could smell it in her sweat. This girl smelled sweet as summer. This girl smelled like every glossy magazine nudie he had ever dreamed. He smelled her sweet hair and kissed her bare shoulder, moving his hands down her thin white back.

"Take off that shirt. Oh, and your pants." She giggled, kissing

his neck. He nodded nervously, then unbuttoned his white stockboy shirt. It was stained with sweat and dirt and grease. He had a
dirty white tee-shirt on beneath. His hands were shaking as he unzipped his jeans and pulled them down around his ankles. He
stared at her bare chest. Breathe, you sap, breathe. Lulla gave a little smile that lit up her round cheeks. He took a breath. Then his
underdrawers, he tugged them down in one quick move, leaving
his poor middle naked and exposed. This girl Lulla moved on top
of him quick, pulling down her jeans, then her black panties, moving her weight on top of him. Then he felt her wrap herself around
him, on top of him tight, then they were sure making it as she
began jerking her hips up and down, her bare skin against his. My
lord. He felt like he was about ready to die. He felt like he might
just cease to exist. All these thoughts, all these dreams finally
came true and he felt like it was all the end of some long night. He
shut his eyes and trembled as she held her body right next to his,
holding her lips next to his ear, mumbling something he couldn't
quiet hear like "Shhhhhhhh, don't make a sound," but the sound of
her hips and the leaves whipping against the glass was all he could
make out, then his breath was coming fast, fast, until he was sure
he couldn't breathe, then oh, lord, oh, lord, he felt like he was
going to pee, pee all over the backseat, then it was all over, all
over, all over and done and a mess on his middle and Lulla gave a
little giggle and "Okay, baby, it's okay, it's okay" was all he could
hear or feel. Then she wiped between her legs with the end of his
white work shirt sleeve and pulled up her tight blue jeans.

"That's it," she said, giving him a little wink. Her skin was shiny
around her neck and pink and white. This girl's fingers worked fast
to button up her top. But he didn't let her go. He held her shoulders,
still kissing her neck. He held her tight, pulling her close, burying
his face against her neck. This was something he couldn't let go.

"Wow." She giggled, snapping your gum. "You sure like doing
it, huh?"

My poor brother didn't move. He didn't think he could. He felt
something unbelievable and golden moving from her skin. Oh lord,
he felt like a real man all right.

"Wow," she mumbled out loud again. "It's okay. I ain't gonna leave you here with your drawers down or anything." He stared into her face and felt like he had been made dumb. He felt like he had lived his whole life against her skin. Well, my brother let go and pulled up his pants and kissed her lips again. This girl just shook her head, still smiling wide. She dug into her tight pants and pulled out a cigarette and lit it with the lighter from the car's dash. She pressed her pink gum against the side window, then took a long drag. He stared at her for a long time.

"So." She kind of smiled, twitching one of her eyebrows. There was sweat all along her neck. Tiny droplets beside her lips. Lulla just cleared her throat a little, ignoring the perspiration, then shrugged her shoulders. Then she exhaled some smoke and gave a little sigh. "So?"

"Do you wanna go out sometime?" he muttered in a voice that sounded meaner and colder than he had wanted it to. "I mean, we could go do something if you wanted. I'd pay, I guess."

"Sure." This girl nodded. "As long as you paid."

He smiled. His face was still hot as hell. There was a sweet smell in the air. Hot and musty and clouded along the glass. Sex. This was the smell of his dreams.

"Guess I better get on home," ol' Pill mumbled, grinning like a damn fool.

"Guess so." She winked.

They finished getting dressed, Pill pulling up his drawers over his mess, Lulla taking the gum off the glass and putting it back in her mouth. Then they climbed out of the car and stared at each other's hot white faces. Their skin shined the same way with each other's sweat. Their eyes were bright like they had just told each other some pretty dumb secret. They had. It was something they couldn't share aloud. Something both of them were too lonely and too stubborn to say. Their eyes flashed with fire, glowering with some truth they could still feel in their fingertips. There was something there all right. Staring at each other in the dark, too afraid to kiss, they both realized there in that big blue backseat, both of them had lost something of themselves. Something they held so dear. Something they could barely afford. Their thin little ailments of pride.

Those dark red lips split apart after a moment or so.

This girl was too proud to fold.

"Do you want your ten bucks back?" she said.

"Huh?" ol' Pill asked.

"The money? Do you want it back? I kinda feel crummy about all this. I mean I'm not a whore. No matter what you might think. I mean you could have the money back if you want."

"That's okay. I don't have anything to spend it on anyway."

"Hmph. You sure are a spooky guy."

"Guess I am."

They stared at each other again, falling into the silence that surrounded their heads. Then it broke like a droplet of dew. This girl moved forward and kissed him once then pulled away, shaking her head with a grin.

"I'll tell you again, you sure are the strangest boy I've ever done this with."

"No stranger than you."

"Sure," she said.

He stood exactly still as Lulla turned and skipped up her front walk to her big white wood porch, still tucking in her shirt.

"You kissed me!!!" he whispered to her through the dark, feeling ready to burst. This girl stopped on her last step and turned around and stared at him, then shook her head. The boy was just standing there, smiling to himself, staring back at her in the dark like a loony. This boy really was really some sort of crazy all right. He had to be about the craziest boy in town. "You kissed me," he mumbled again. Those dark red lips parted over Lulla's bright white smile. He could feel her smiling in his own heart and chest.

"It's the least a girl like me'll do," she whispered back.

This girl turned off the front light and disappeared inside. He stood in the dark a little while, watching the way her house seemed to glow. Then he turned, still grinning to himself. This girl's soft white smile led him straight on home.

He was nearly skipping down that lonesome ol' road when I

caught sight of him, a dull thin form, grinning like a real fool all alone to himself. I stood out of the thin brown grass and met him on the road. His face was still all red and hot and glowing. He patted me on the back and just kept grinning as we walked together toward home. Ol' Shilo hopped along by my side, rattling his metal tags like tiny chimes.

There in the distance were all the lights of the trailer park, a blue-yellow glow rising over the squarish mobile homes. The whole place looked kind of empty now. Now that she was gone. Now that she had left it, all those trailers somehow looked cold and dark and unfriendly and lonely as hell. I had been let down. I had been let down over and over again in this lousy town, but this was something else. This was like the end of your only good dream, the only thing you keep wishing for when you fall asleep. This was it. This was some kind of end. I needed to tell him. I needed to tell him so he'd let me know that everything was going to be okay. Because I sure didn't feel that way myself. I needed him to muss up my hair or hear him laugh a little mean desperate laugh. I needed to know he was still my friend. I turned to my brother and just blurted it all out in one gulp.

"Pill," I mumbled. "Val . . . Val . . . she's gone."

He stopped walking and stared in my face. "What?"

"She left today. She's gone. Moved out."

"But what the hell for?"

"Someone beat her up pretty bad. Someone broke down her goddamn screen door and tore up her whole place."

My older brother, Pill, became still. His face became dark and gray. All the glow that had been in his eyes suddenly faded and disappeared down into the dirt. He didn't punch my arm lightly. He didn't say a dirty joke or a goddamn word. He just turned and looked over his shoulder down the lonesome dark road.

There was a pair of yellow lights there that began to shine.

They moved right over our faces as they came closer.

It was a car. Swerving on the road. Coming closer. Coming close.

He was spinning.

He could barely hang on.

The deputy had been drinking. He held a bottle of sour mash uncapped in his lap. Drunk. Drunk over a girl. His eyes felt sore as hell. The steering wheel was loose in his hand. His squad car weaved right over the road. He could feel the same dull movement in his belly. Swerve. Turn. His sweet pea of dream was gone. He had found a sweet woman that had made him feel brand new. Better than brand new. A sweet woman that never put up a fuss when he left. A lady that knew her place in his awful philanderous heart.

Johnny Cash belted his tune out of the Delco radio like a full-on choir. "Love is a burning thing . . ."

He took a swig, nodding to himself. There was nothing else left in this goddamn town for him now. Nothing with any hope. There sure was no sign of remission for his sickly wife. And all those cheap wives all across town, overweight and sweet and stinking of household laundry detergent and their kids dirty sheets, all of those women with their cheap dime-store cologne and their underpaid husband's pawnshop rings, they were always worrying about getting caught and not going too far and the awful ungodly debauchery and guilt of it all, well, hell, they were really all just the same, sad, empty kind of hopeless blur he had seen all his life, flashing right past, fading quick, right out of his rearview mirror's sight and then back into the dark. The dark he had felt in his heart all along.

There was no hope for him anywhere. Nowhere to turn on a straight, one-lane road.

Then there up ahead. Two shapes, a little blurred.

He squinted hard, leaning forward, then smiled to himself. Those two little bastards. Those two little thieves. The deputy gripped the wheel tighter, slowing upon the two black shadows left all alone on the road.

Those pair of unholy yellow lights was right in our goddamn eyes. Two high-beam lights laid upon our eyes as the deputy cruised behind us, slowing to our speed. There was his shiny white goddamn car with the shiny red lights on top. There he was grinning like a lunatic behind that loose wheel.

"Hell." Ol' Pill frowned, spying over his shoulder a little. I turned and caught sight of the deputy's sweaty, greasy smile, and I was sure as the grave that I saw him give a cold little wink.

He pulled the squad car beside us and rolled his window right on down.

"What you boys doing out here by yourselves tonight?" the deputy said, nodding to himself, leaning back in his seat.

Me, I didn't say a goddamn word. I froze in my tracks. My older brother shrugged his shoulders a little, then elbowed me to keep on walking. But I couldn't move. Those lights out by there trailer park seemed so far. And we were out here all alone. Here was that bastard's goddamn white teeth. Somewhere beside his belt was his shiny silver gun. I could imagine that deputy putting a bullet in the both of us and kicking us down into the ditch. I swore I saw him wink again. There was no way I could make a single move after that.

"Stand where you are," the deputy mumbled. He took out his flashlight and shined it right in our eyes, still sitting there with his awful smile.

"I asked you boys what it was you were doing out here tonight?"

Ol' Shilo gave a little yelp. I held its brown leash by my side.

"I was coming home from work." Pill frowned, gritting his teeth. He looked that bastard ol' deputy straight in his empty black eyes then turned away. The deputy nodded once, still grinning like mad.

"And what about you, son?"

"Meeting my brother to go on home," I mumbled.

"Is that so?" The deputy shortened his smile. He let out a little kind of muffled laugh and shook his head.

Then it all got dark as hell.

Darker than any shadow I had felt before.

I felt all the night around me run cold.

"Do you boys take me for some kind of goddamn fool?"

There, right there with those words I could feel my teeth turn to dust in my mouth. It was like seeing yourself drifting toward some sort of dark empty ledge, then slipping closer and closer then falling right over. This was going to be some sort of unholy trouble all right. I could feel it all boiling in my blood. The deputy's eyes were all wild and bright, his lips were twitching a little as he threw the damn car into park. I could hear the engine drop out of first and slide into a cool, spinning neutral. Then the snap of the deputy's seat belt as it became undone.

My older brother, Pill, just stood there still gritting his teeth. Then it got quiet as a beat in your heart. Then all the lights around us went completely dim.

"Run!!" my brother shouted, and pulled me by my sleeve. He ran straight down off the side of the road and down into the dirty brown ditch, towing me the whole way. Our dumb dog, Shilo, barked once then followed, too, hopping down the side of the road, moving quick through the wet brown grass on its thick three legs. My heart was beating right in my ears. All I could feel was my brother's hand on my sleeve, pulling me ahead, pulling straight through all that dark. Our feet were moving fast, crossing over all the wet grass, the dog howled a little, still following behind us.

Those pair of headlights suddenly turned right on us.

"Jesus!!" Pill screamed, stopping just for a second to see that bastard of a deputy drive his car off the road and down, down, down into the muddy ditch. But the damn thing didn't get stuck. It rolled down nice and slow and through the mud and straight on to the field, with those goddamn headlights blaring right on us.

"Run for the barn!!!" my older brother shouted, still pulling on my sleeve. Then it hit me hard, like a full slap to my jaw, there right ahead was the goddamn Furnham barn, standing still and red and quiet and haunted as hell. Pill kept pulling me by my shirt and the dog was howling and moving right in our tracks, hopping along where we moved, trying to stay out of the deputy's lights. That damn barn was just ahead. Pill stopped and turned again, fighting for breath, just as the deputy's squad car sank into a patch of dirt. Its shiny silver wheels turned and turned, throwing mud all over and into the air. Behind that shiny windshield glass, we could both see the deputy's face all hot and red and full of hate. He pounded the steering wheel with his hand about three times, then kicked open the goddamn door. Then the deputy was on his goddamn feet.

My older brother felt around in the dark for the barn door latch. Me, I held the dog right by my side, watching as that bastard's drunken form moved right toward us. He was wobbling a little, losing his footing in the slippery mud, cursing to himself in grunts as he strode up to us.

"Don't move!!" the deputy hollered. "Don't make a goddamn move."

All that darkness fell around us. All the cold night air hung over our heads and I could still feel the hot-red heat moving off that deputy's shiny white teeth and lips. He stopped where he stood suddenly and reached down and drew his sidearm. I could see it glimmer in the dull yellow shine thrown by his squad car's headlights. The gun. The gun. My heart pumped blood straight to my head. I gripped the dog's leash tight as I could, hoping somehow that gesture would alone keep me safe, hiding in the dull black shadows cast by my older brother and the barn, making all the prayers I could think to say, watching as my brother swore to himself, running his fingers over the dull red wood for the latch.

"Let me be home in bed," I kept mumbling. "Let me be home in bed."

"Stay where you are, I said!!" the deputy shouted, still wobbling toward us through the dirt.

Then that bastard of a deputy pointed his gun toward the sky and squeezed off a round.

BLOOOMMM!!!!!

Then all the blood shot from my ears and I felt myself crying, crying like a hopeless fool, mumbling more stupid prayers to myself as that man's dim black form kept moving close.

"Here . . . " ol' Pill whispered. "Here!!"

He slid the barn door open and shoved me inside, giving our dumb three-legged dog a push. He pulled the door closed, then yanked me by my shirt, drawing us deeper inside the dark. It was quiet and steady and full of that awful decaying stench. Nothing made a sound but our breaths. Nothing moved by our shadows along the thick wood walls. I followed my brother deeper inside the barn, him still tugging me by the arm and then I made the awful mistake of stopping and looking up.

This place was Hell. Without a doubt. This place was darker than any goddamn dream, dark as the Devil's own unholy shadow, covering everything with death and gloom, touching our faces like his thick, red burlap cloak. There were all the tiny silver spires and spindles of spiderwebs criss-crossing overhead, glimmering with the light from the moon, making all kinds of shadows breathe and move like a thousand tiny eyes or lips whispering your name over and over again. This place was sure full of all the intricacies of a rural death. There was the sagging old horse still rotting and old, nesting with thousands of sleeping fatted flies. There were the heavy wood beams that creaked overhead burned in a single spot by old man Furnham's hanging rope. There were old cardboard boxes of clothes and dry goods and stores that would now never be used. All these sad, sad dreams that came to lie and rest in the same awful patch of red-painted wood and dirt. My older brother tugged me toward the center of the barn, looking around for somewhere to hide, and then I could feel it, his hand was trembling, cold and shaking, his hand upon my hand, he was shivering like there was something here in this barn that he had seen in all his worse dreams, too.

The Devil's own dark red shadow swept overhead, his thin serpentine head glistened with a empty smile as he roared and hissed and the deputy fired into the night air once again.

BLOOOM!!!!!

I looked up into my brother's face. He was completely quiet and still, staring up into the dark black space that seemed to move right over our heads. There it was. Right in his eyes. They were wide and empty and hopeless and black and full of some awful kind of fear. He had seen it, too. He understood. His hand was gripping my arm tight. I could feel him shaking, sweating all over, unable to keep his body still. He had seen the same thing. We had been having the same goddamn dream. Our old man's mortal road had led us here. This was the place where it would all end. The same stretch of lonesome road that disappeared into the dark. The same hollowed shadows and blackened forms. I could nearly see my old man's rig parked somewhere close. I could almost see him lying all alone, left for dead beside the road. Then I could feel the Devil moving around us in the dark, ready to strike, ready to steal both me and my brother's blood. This was it, then. The end of it all. The end of all our darkest hopeless dreams.

My brother pulled my shirt again and shoved me behind a stack of some old wooden crates. He pushed the big ugly white dog beside me and then squeezed into the rest of the space, holding his breath, nearly covering me with his own body, still gripping my arm tight.

Then the wide red barn door creaked open.

"This is it, you little bastards!! Come on out now!!"

The deputy squeezed off another round and then stepped inside the barn. BLOOM!!!!! I could feel his blackened shadow moving right over the skin on my face. I could feel his hot, liquored breath seeping right through the air. I could feel him grinning, gripping his gun by his side tight. He might just find us and holler at us and let us go. As long as there was still some light, we might still be fine. As long as we weren't left alone with him in the dark, we could make it out okay.

The deputy grunted a little to himself, then slid the big red door closed. All the light disappeared from our faces. All of us fell straight into the dark. The dog breathed heavily by my side. I could smell its awful sour breath on my skin. It breathed quickly but didn't make a sound. It held its ugly face against my shirt and stood still between me and my brother, making its wide thick shoulders tense as the deputy's footsteps moved closer, then closer again.

"Think this is all some game, huh, boys?" the deputy mumbled to himself. "All some kinda joke?"

His shiny black shoes moved over the dirt. Scrape. Scrape. Scrape.

"Make a damn fool out of me, huh? Make me chase you out of here in the dirt?"

His black shadow wobbled a little, following his drunken
steps. Scrape. Scrape. Scrape. Then he stopped.

"You don't know what I'm battlin' inside me!!! You don't know
what it is that's got me hurting!!!!!"

His voice boiled like blood in his throat. I could hear him
breathing hard, angry as hell, gripping that gun tighter and tighter,
until it all felt sore in my own chest.

"All of hell's come down on me today, boys . . . Looks like
you're about to get the worst end of it now for sure."

The deputy laughed to himself a little, stopping to catch his
balance. The dark space spun around him, shaking him loose. He
felt his eyes nearly spin out of his head. His shadow faltered, cutting across our skin.

"Where the hell am I?" he kind of whispered to himself. "Let
my goddamn mind go out on me."

The dark crashed right down on his head, nearly knocking him
to his knees. He wobbled about a little, fighting to keep on his feet,
dangling the gun by his side. He felt sick, sick as hell, ready to lose
it all. All the dumb hatred and anger spun on through his skull,
shaking him loose in his skin.

Then he felt like something was moving over his head.

Something up in the beams.

He looked up and lost his balance and faltered to his knees.

"JUNE!!" he screamed. "JUNE!!"

He felt ready to gag then stumbled forward a little, falling
against some crates. He fought for some breath, still shaking with
sickness and fear, gripping his gun tight. His knees were so heavy
and weak. His body hurt so bad. He wiped some drool from his
mouth and lifted his head. He fought his body to stand. Just stand.
His eyes rolled about in his head. He squinted around to see, still
nearly buckling at his knees.

Then he caught something out of the corner of his eye.

There, right there, three shadows flashed before him in the
dark. He squinted again, then nodded to himself.

"You . . . " he muttered, then cracked a smile like he had just
met with some fine old friends. "I found you here."

He stepped forward and into the dark.

All the blood in our bodies turned cold. All our hearts turned to dust and crumbled red with terror like dirt. My brother gripped my arm hard and tight. Our breath just disappeared.

"You little bastards . . . ," I heard the deputy whisper.

Then the leash went loose in my hand and all the words I had ever wanted to say my whole life poured right from my mouth sore like a knife.

"Kill, Shilo, kill!!"

Our big white dog leapt forward and struck, clamping his big red jaws around the deputy's thick pale neck. Some black blood flickered through the air and dotted the cold ground. My older brother had me by the sleeve of my shirt and out the goddamn barn door and into the damp gray field before I ever heard that cold solitary shot ring out.

BLOOM!!!!!!

Tears fell right out of my sore eyes. I knew right then we had to go back, go back in and get our poor, poor dog, save him from all the ghosts and wicked things trapped inside, but my brother held me by my shoulders and in my awful heart I knew it was all too late, too late, too late for a thing like hope to ever change, so I fell to my knees and down into the dirt and just let myself cry apart. My brother held my shoulders tight as we sat like that forever, cold and still and staring at that empty old barn, wishing we were all dead, me crying like mad as a siren broke through the dark, flashing with bright red lights.

The shots fired had alerted all the goddamn neighbors and within a few moments the old gray-haired Sheriff Dugan in his shiny white squad car arrived and parked his car beside the deputy's and hustled across the field in his blue field pants and Stetson hat and white pajama shirt, fighting to breathe.

"What happened? Where's the deputy?"

My brother just shook his head and didn't say a word and pointed to the goddamn barn.

"Okay, alright, boys, stay where you are," the sheriff huffed, and walked past me and my brother, and the old gray-faced man pulled out his big shiny Smith and Wesson gun and stepped up to the barn door and listened inside. Nothing was moving. It was already all done. The sheriff twitched his white mustache a little, then fought around for the barn door latch.

"Goddamn it, where's the latch?!" Then he found it with his thick white hands and gave it a pull. That damn barn door opened with a creak and I stood beside my brother and stared inside and then, right, then I knew it was all lost and gone.

Our poor ol' dog was dead.

Ol' Shilo laid on its side, trembling a little in a dark black pool of its own shiny blood, twitching its feet and wagging its goddamn tail like the dumb dog it was. Me, I ran up right past my brother and the goddamn sheriff and fell right where that poor dog lay. I ran my hand over its soft white side and saw the huge red bullet hole that had been dug in its warm thickly coated throat. My whole face was covered with goddamn tears but I didn't care, I didn't gave a goddamn who saw me like that. That was my only dumb dog and now it sure going to be dead.

"Don't move, boy," the sheriff shouted. "Don't move, okay?" I nodded and stayed still, holding my dog around its bloody neck, crying to myself and not caring in the least.

The sheriff stepped inside and flicked on his flashlight. The thick yellow light burned through the dark. All the blackness separated and vanished and disappeared. But there was nothing there. There was no one in there.

"Mort?!!" the sheriff called. "Mort?!!"

But there was no reply. Not a word or steely sigh or goddamn whisper. He was gone. Gone, gone from all our miserable sights.

"Mort, give me a holler if you're alright!! Mort?!!"

The sheriff stepped into the middle of the barn, shaking his head. His flashlight struck the dark red pool of the deputy's blood, which shimmered and shone, drying up in the dirt.

There was no body beside. No sign of that bastard's breath.

The deputy was gone.

I lifted my head and stared up into the weave of cobwebs and wooden beams. It was dark up there, and empty and quiet and still.

The sheriff's light flashed overhead. There was nothing there. Nothing there. That deputy was gone. Taken in that barn by the Devil's horns or claws or thick red cloak. There was nothing, not a trace of that man's skin or soul. Not a shadow, not a sound, not a whisper or cry to make me believe he was still alive. He was worse than dead.

"This just ain't right," the sheriff mumbled, flashing his light into all the corners of the barn. All the shadows moved and parted then fell back into place. But there was nothing. No trace or sign. He had been taken. Taken back into the darkness that had hung just over his shoulder for most of his life. "This ain't right at all. A man just doesn't up and disappear."

The dark place of that lawman's past had finally caught up.

I nodded to myself, not saying a word. I just held my dog around its neck as it kept fighting to breathe, twitching its big white hind legs. Its breath smelled like copper and was all warm along the sleeve of my shirt.

"It's okay, boy," I whispered. "It's okay."

Then our dog became still and tensed, tightening itself in my arms. Then it was too late. Then it really was gone. I was sobbing like a damn fool and my older brother, Pill, had his hand on my shoulder and the sheriff stopped looking around and led me and my brother out of the barn and we stood there outside while that old sheriff looked around again.

"Mort? Mort?" we could hear him whisper, but there was no sound in reply but me and my brother breathing hard and the quiet burning of all that hatred and confusion as we stared at the dark black shape of that awful barn. I sat there in the dirt with my knees pulled close to my chest and my older brother stood right there beside me, holding my shirt, glaring hard at the way the outline of that barn's wooden posts cut across the black sky. It was done. It was all done and trapped inside. I could very nearly hear what Pill was thinking, standing there, gripping my shoulder tight, the thin snap of the match against the black strip then the quick burst of flame, something to burn that whole night out of his mind, something to make sure that nightmare wouldn't remain in its place.

He was gone, too.

This night had taken all of his hope.

The sheriff stepped out of the barn and took us to his car and had the dispatcher call our folks and then they came to bring us home and me and Pill sat in the backseat of my mother's crappy blue car, unable to speak, unable to utter a goddamn word.

"What were you boys doing out there? What happened to the goddamn dog?" French asked. His face was all white like he had just seen a ghost. There were lines from the pillow along the side of his face and some dried up drool on his cheek. "What did you boys do out there?"

The lonesome road flashed under the headlights of our car as me and my brother stammered a little, trying to think of something to say. Something to explain it all.

But we didn't know. We just didn't really know.

"This is it," my mother cried, turning to face us in the backseat. Her sweet white face was replete with shiny blue eye-shadow or any form of makeup. Her eyes were wide and red and sore from her tears. "This is the last time I get called on by the police. Do you understand? You're both heading off for military school in Aubrey in the spring if things don't start to change."

But we didn't really hear what she said. It was all over now and I felt like I was already home and in my bed and fast asleep and just dreaming a whole new kind of dream, a dream you're not quite sure how it might end, but you know it'll be just as strange and spooky and complicated as the one you just had.

Me and my brother laid in our beds, still unable to speak.

I could hear him turning in his bed. I could hear him grinding his teeth. There was something he felt he had to do. Something to set everything right. He turned over then back again, fighting with his own awful thoughts. I laid still on my back, doing the same.

What had really happened? Heck, I didn't really know. There were things in that barn and out in the night and in my own heart that I was sure I'd never understand. Even after it all and my poor Shilo was buried in the soft gray dirt beside a nice green weeping willow tree right by the mill pond out by Mill Creek Road and after someone found the goddamn bottle of sour mash in the deputy's car and the Johnny Cash cassette and they all ruled it was some sort of awful heartbreak that heartless bastard sure must have felt, even after all that, there were things about that I couldn't put into their right place in my mind. Maybe that was the way. Nothing could have changed how it all ended for the deputy, I didn't think. He would have overslept at some nice sweet and lonely housewife's house just once and meet the end of some angry husband's butcher knife before too long, I was sure. But my poor dog. My poor dog. There were a million ways in my head that seemed like I could have saved it. Maybe none of them would have really worked. That dumb old dog wasn't born to do much more than fight and kill and end up in the dirt, but it had; it had borrowed a dull hollow place in my heart and left its ugly blood-mark on my sleeve and in every insufferable sleep I would have to endure after that in my bed alone. It was gone. That couldn't be changed. There was nothing for me to do but fight against all those weepy thoughts and the guilt and anger and shame and just try and make it all right in my head.

That night I laid in my bed, hoping to hear that dumb dog's breath in my ear or gag on its sweaty stink but it never came. I listened to hear my brother start to snore, but he was just as quiet as me, letting his thoughts roam outside of the trailer and out onto that dark black road, past the barn and the deputy's squad car, past all the town and fields and trees, out into the future and into some distant space that seemed just like tomorrow but farther away, the days that hadn't even arrived and wouldn't for some time, weeks and months and then years away, and then out into a place that finally seemed to far, so distant and untold and free that I lost track of what he might be thinking and had to just shut my eyes and hold my breath and give in and fall asleep.

Snappppppppp.

That night I had another dream. I dreamed my brother was sitting on the edge of my bed and was staring right at me.

Then he started talking to me right through my sleep.

There was a glorious red and orange fire burning right behind his head. His whole face was hallowed in flames like an awful kind of old saint. He frowned a little as he patted my shoulder and whispered a quiet little good-bye.

My brother was going away.

"Don't do it," I mumbled, not knowing why I said what I said because it was all blurred and heavy and his face looked more round and more sweet than it all should have been. "Don't burn it down. Don't go off and leave."

"This is all I can do. I gotta set things right. It's gotta burn. It's got to fall. And I need to leave. That way we'll both be free. We'll both be free."

"But it won't do any good."

"Sure it will."

"You can't just leave. What about me? And Mom? And ol' French? What will they say?" I said.

"They don't understand. I can't change the way I am."

"But they ain't that mad," I pleaded. "They ain't gonna really send us away."

"No, maybe not now, pal. But it don't really matter. It's only a matter of time before I foul up again and then that'll be it. Then I'll be dead or in a jail or worse off than that. And I couldn't stand for you to watch it all happen. I couldn't stand for it. Don't you worry, pal. I'll be okay. I swear. Everything will be okay." He patted me on the shoulder like he was twenty years older and disappeared back into the unlit night.

That dark dream shook through my bones.

I shot out of my bed as soon as I was awake and stared up at his empty bunk. I pulled on my jeans and shoes and ran out of the trailer, nearly knocking the lousy screen door from its gray, rusted hinges. The sky was still blue and black, it wasn't even dawn, maybe earlier, maybe three, three lonesome hours since midnight. There were still shiny silver stars up in the sky and the clouds hadn't gathered anywhere in view. I ran down the front steps and around the bend of the gravel drive and then out onto the long dirt road and then I could see it, sitting square against the horizon, a black shape, a lone dot, the Furnham's blackened barn and the ungodly plumes of thick, voluminous smoke rising gray from it like ghosts, and the shallow white-orange flames and the great red fire that burned brightly at the building's wooden posts.

Then I saw something else.

There like a cloud of smoke and dust, as bright as the fire but cold, a truth so cold and hollow that I could feel it in the ends of my toes.

He had been wrong. My brother had been wrong about it all.

Burning that barn wouldn't do any good. Not for me or my brother or any of the memories of the souls of the things trapped inside. All those things were already done. All those things were already dead. He couldn't free himself of all that ugly past like that. Now I knew. Now I could see it. I had tried hard to bury or break all the things I hated or feared, too. But seeing the fire like that now, I could tell it wasn't the way. We had both been wrong. But now he would never be free from it all. Not even by running away. All those feelings were trapped inside of him. All that fire was in his own veins. Burning that building wouldn't do anyone any good. It was already too late for all those things that had already been done. Poor ol' Pill could have changed. He could have made a try. But he didn't. He just lit that fire and ran away. He felt all that anger and confusion and just gave in to it all anyway. He hadn't learned a damn thing from that awful night. He hadn't learned anything from our miserable lives in that awful place.

The gravel was wet and cold against my bare white feet. I shut my eyes. I could feel them swelling up ready to cry. I could almost feel that fire moving along my face. I stood there for a long time, not moving or making a noise until I was sure that that barn had been burned completely to the ground.

The dark sky was still dark.

The taste of smoke hung in my throat.

The night was not over, but my brother was gone, long gone, never to be heard from again, left only in my mind as a name and a single shot of a photo no one had ever had the chance to take; a desperate gray-eyed boy, by himself on a dark silver bus, headed south, headed lost and all alone, fighting to forget all the things that hung in his awful dreams, where the tender reach of a fire would somehow always glow.